A Victim in Victoria

An Elspeth Duff Mystery

Ann Crew

Also by Ann Crew

The Elspeth Duff Series:
A Murder in Malta
A Scandal in Stresa
A Secret in Singapore, 2nd Edition
A Crisis in Cyprus
A Gamble in Gozo
A Deception in Denmark
A Blackmailer in Bermuda
A Presumption in Perthshire
An Ultimatum in Udaipur
A Legacy on Lewis
A Betrayal in Belgium
A Challenge in Chelsea

The Portia MacRoberts Series:
A Matter of Murder

To departed friends

List of Characters

Elspeth Duff, special security advisor to Lord Kennington, owner of the Kennington hotel chain

Eric, Lord Kennington, Elspeth's blustery employer

Pamela Crumm, his silent business partner and Elspeth's friend

Janet Church, manager of the Kennington Victoria hotel.

Sir Richard Munro, Elspeth's second husband, senior member the British Foreign and Commonwealth Office (FCO)

Jason Ravensworth, once of the Canadian Embassy in London, now head of the conference in Victoria

Charles (Charlie) Ballie Shaw, Elspeth's cousin, a journalist from a prominent British newspaper

Lady Elisabeth Baillie Shaw (Biddy), now married to **Max Douglas Forbes, QC,** Charlie's mother

Alistair Craig, Elspeth's ex-husband

Takanori Sakurai, head of the Japanese delegation, and his wife

Oh Seung, head of the South Korean delegation

Chao Kai and Chin Mei-su, joint heads of the Chinese

delegation

Fedor Petrovitch Dvorkin, Russian delegate

Katherine Croft, US delegate

Four Inuits, from three different nations—US (Alaska), Russia and Canada

Michelle and **Tommie**, protestors

Kim Bae, husband of Oh Seung, an official in the Korean government

Madame Svetlana Mihailova, Fedor Dvorkin's wife

Police Constable Claudia Mills (Dee) of the Royal Canadian Mounted Police (RCMP)

Detective Inspector Brewster Clough of the RCMP

Dr Halloway, hotel doctor

Detective Superintendent Henri Gilbert of the RCMP, Michelle's father

Ron Dillard, assistant manager of the hotel

Robert Kahn, Jason Ravensworth's partner

Detective Sergeant Bastien of the RCMP also known as the Wicked Witch of the West or W3

Greg Allen, Katherine Croft's aide, a shy young man

Detective Sergeant Flannigan of the RCMP

Phil Watkins, of the 'US State Department'

Faith Fitzhugh, Michelle's mother

Johnnie, Lord Tay, Elspeth's cousin and Biddy's brother, longtime friend of Richard Munro

Madelaine, his wife

Dougal Cameron, builder

Tobey, the border collie who lives in the barn at Tay Farm

Prologue

Sir Richard Munro looked across the dining room table at his wife, Elspeth Duff.

"I'm ready for a new assignment," she said. "When are you off to Vancouver?"

"I'm scheduled to speak in the middle of January. Hardly a time one would want to go to Canada, but because it is on the Pacific Ocean the weather there is milder than the rest of that country. Rain not snow. Doesn't the Kennington Organisation have a hotel in Vancouver?"

"No, but they do have one in Victoria. My geography in that area is vague. Are Victoria and Vancouver close to each other?"

"They aren't that far apart. I believe you have to take a ferry or fly between them because Victoria is located on Vancouver Island, which is to the west of Vancouver itself."

"Maybe I should have asked for an assignment at the Kennington Victoria. At least we would be somewhat close to each other."

"You could come and hear me speak. There will be a reception beforehand and it would be a great honour to have you there."

"You know how much I dread receptions but I love you and will bear up for one evening. At this time of year whatever could go wrong in Canada? Kennington hotels in the winter are sluggish in northern countries. Eric eschews ski resorts. He occasionally books in conferences in January and February to help the revenue schemes."

1

January 2009

I want to kill him. He deserves to die. I must work out a way. But I don't want to be caught. Should I push him under a car? No, I could be seen. Poison? Too detectable despite all the fiction to the contrary. Guns and knives are too messy. Perhaps the best way would be to have it seem as if someone else killed him. He is a known figure and has many enemies, open and hidden. If one of them could be found guilty, then I would be in the clear. But I must be very clever. We are due in Victoria next week for the conference. Protestors will be there, probably some hostile ones. An attack from the crowd? Could I hire someone to be in the mob? No, hiring someone could be traced. How can I do it so I won't be discovered?

Elspeth Duff woke with a jerk. She no longer could hear the caressing sound of the Cadillac limousine's engine; its absence disturbed her dozing. Twelve hours on the plane from London to Vancouver, even first class, and by limousine to the ferry to Victoria, had left her sleep deprived. East to west trips always did this to her.

"I thought you'll enjoy the ferry ride," the cheeky young and capless chauffeur with spiky hair and three rings in one ear was saying. "Everyone who comes to British Columbia finds it totally awesome. Besides you looked real uncomfortable back there. The break on the ferry will be good for you."

She stepped from the long, black car and followed the crowd up to the passenger deck. She chose a seat at the front of the boat and looked out over the mountains to the north and to the Pacific Ocean around her. Even to a jaded traveller such as she, the expanse of ocean and the snow-brushed grey landscape beyond was indeed awe-inspiring. As they left the ferry terminal, Elspeth saw the ocean spread out in front of her, and drew in her breath at its power, and despite its name, its destructive powers. Soon they entered a passage between the islands nearby and she even spotted a killer whale.

Four days and she would be back in London and its grim winter pallor but here she sensed an openness of the air and sea that filled her with overwhelming wonder. It made her shed the claustrophobia of the plane.

"Thank you for the break," she said to the driver, as they landed on Vancouver Island. "I need to be sharp when we get to Victoria."

"You picked a classy hotel," the chauffeur said. "It must cost a bundle."

Elspeth laughed. "More than several bundles. Luckily I'm not paying. I work for the hotel chain and am on assignment." Elspeth wondered why she gave him this information. Perhaps it was because she found Canadians so open.

"Cool," he said. "How did you get a job like that?"

"Pure luck," she said, which was only partially true. "But the work's not as easy as you would think. I travel a lot, which is stressful, particularly when you do as much as I do. You're better off staying in one place."

"You're English, aren't you?"

"Scottish. In the UK we make a difference." She had said this so many times. If she had spoken with a burr it might be different but from the very beginning her family and school had insisted she speak cultured English, now called Received Pronunciation, without a trace of the Highlands in her voice. She had no doubt that it was one reason Lord Kennington had hired her as his special security advisor and allowed her free rein at his string of international boutique hotels. She was one more tool used to see that his hotels worked seamlessly. No one paying the prices he demanded should ever experience even the slightest inconvenience or suggestion of danger during their stay.

Elspeth considered her assignment. Since the economic downturn, Eric Kennington had begrudgingly agreed to more conferences and business meetings than he had tolerated in the past. The forthcoming one hosted members of a group of Pacific Ocean countries with oversight of the ocean's whaling.

Times were changing and Lord Kennington had acknowledged the ebb and flow of the economy despite his distaste for the commercialisation of his rarefied hostelry. As always, Eric Kennington wanted Elspeth at the hotels as a buffer, a quiet presence in case there was any disturbance. There might be outside demonstrations considering the volatile nature of the topic of the conference but that was the purview of the police not the Kennington Organisation. Little could happen inside the hotel considering the high government positions of the delegates to the conference. A dull few days, she thought, that would offer little excitement, unlike the times in the past when she had become embroiled in murder, a crime she detested. No life should be taken wrongfully, no matter what the circumstances. She understood how terrifying the act of killing must be to the victim just before death and how devastating for the murderer when caught. She wondered if any murder was psychologically painless. Perhaps only if one was near death anyway; then murder might be a relief.

Elspeth stretched and yawned. She put her morbid thoughts away.

"How much farther?" she asked.

"Perhaps twenty minutes, maybe more with traffic," he replied. "Is there any rush?"

"No. They know I'm coming this afternoon but I didn't say exactly when. I feel better now. Thanks for the ferry ride."

"No problem," he said. "Unless you fly it's unavoidable. We'll be there in a flash."

He was as good as his word. He pulled up in front of the Kennington Victoria twenty-five minutes later, jumped from his seat and opened the wide back door for Elspeth.

A tall, open-faced woman with a broad smile and intelligent dark eyes was standing by the doorman and stepped forward as Elspeth folded herself out of the car.

"I'm Janet Church," the woman said. "Welcome to the Kennington Victoria. You've made good time from Vancouver considering the timetable of the ferry. Lord Kennington said to expect you about four."

*

I wonder why they picked this hotel. He would have come a day early but I suspect he couldn't afford it. Still he needs to pretend he is important. I must look around carefully to see what opportunity I can find here. Everything is so grand, so immaculate and so well staffed. I see other members of the conference have already arrived. I recognise some of them. He goes to greet many of them. Some of them seem to remember him. Does he have associates here who I can pin the murder on? I must watch carefully. I wish I had a stronger plan in place.

Who is that handsome woman who has just come in? I would like to have a suit like hers, understated but rich. But I don't walk the way she does so it wouldn't look good on me. Someone in authority is greeting her. I can tell by her voice that she is English. The English are so superior about their accents. More than other people. I don't like the English. He tries to emulate them. Next he will be saying he went to Oxford or Cambridge. Ha! He would be found out in a minute by anyone from there. I pity the world if he is ever selected for a higher position.

Now I must use all my imagination to kill him. His death will save his country and more importantly it will save me and my career. But I must not be caught.

*

As she led Elspeth back to her office, Janet Church, the manager of the Kennington Victoria, said, "I've put you on the same floor as some of the delegates. Our hotel is small by Kennington standards so I have had to spread those attending the conference on two floors. We don't try to rival the Empress, Victoria's signature hotel. They do everything on the grand scale but in the summer they have become so popular that I think some people would prefer a smaller hotel. But, of course, I am prejudiced."

"Lord Kennington is finicky. He wouldn't mind my saying so. In fact, he would be flattered. He considers that everything is in the small details and that most people don't notice them consciously but that they contribute to the overall experience of staying at a Kennington hotel, and may I add, paying his outrageous prices. I can tell already that your hotel has that quality that he insists on in all his hotels but also the uniqueness of being in British Columbia. I've never been to Victoria before but I already can feel its draw. I'm looking forward to my stay."

Elspeth had given this speech many times before in her nine plus years in Eric Kennington's employ. Each manager needed reassurance that Lord Kennington's personal representative was appreciative of the particular hotel manager's position and that Elspeth's presence was to enhance not detract from the manager's authority. Elspeth knew it was a tricky balance, one she had honed carefully.

They walked through the richly appointed lobby, which gave a nod to the culture of the Pacific northwest without blatantly encompassing it. Janet unlocked a hidden side panel and took Elspeth down a well-lit corridor.

Janet's office was typical. Like all Kennington managers' offices, it had the stamp of its current occupant. Janet's style reminded Elspeth of Charles Rennie Macintosh, elegant simplicity with a touch of understated decoration combining geometric design with organic sensibility. Yet like all the managers' offices, the equipment was up to date and one wall was lined with monitors, showing all the public parts of the hotels.

"They're gathering now. The Japanese came in this morning. We expect most of the others to filter in today.

Some of the Americans and Canadians are already here. The South Koreans arrive this afternoon and the Russians early this evening. The Chinese just arrived and have retreated to their rooms."

"How many are there altogether?" Elspeth asked.

"Six countries. Those I've named."

"How many people will be staying at the hotel?"

"A chief delegate for each country, although the Chinese have two. Then there are the spouses and secondary officials. Twenty-one altogether. You make twenty-two."

"That's quite a large number to keep an eye on. Does your staff know what my function is here?"

"No, at Lord Kennington's request. You'll be treated as a guest. I hope that suits you?"

"For the time being it will. I don't expect anything unusual to go on in the next three days but if something happens, I may call on you and your staff to assist me. The staff will have to know who I am at that point. I hope that's all right."

Janet nodded. "Of course. Let me show you to your room. It's a room not a suite, but I hope it's ample for your needs."

"I only get a suite when I am going to stay for a long time. I'm sure the room will be more than adequate, as if it could be anything else," Elspeth added with a smile.

Elspeth liked this tall Canadian woman instantly. She had the warmth and open manner of so many North Americans. Elspeth had lived in California for over twenty years but still found these traits refreshing. Her room was on the second floor overlooking a public garden and not the wharf. It had a small balcony, which in the cold weather was barren. The room was large, with a sitting area and a place where Elspeth could set up her laptop. As usual, the room was equipped with all her personal preferences, gleaned from the hotel database. Her clothes were hung in the walk-in closet and her shoes lined neatly below them. She had them sent from London by FedEx the day before she left, as was her usual routine when she needed a large change of wardrobe. Janet did not need to ask if she needed anything else.

The opening event of the conference was a drinks reception in the conference area in the floor below the lobby and entrance hall. Unlike larger conference hotels, no signs advertised the event. Two concierges, however, were on duty in the lobby to direct the conference attendees. The pair had already learned the names of the attendees and their wives, this being standard Kennington hotel policy. No guest stayed in the hotels namelessly to all the members of the staff in the public areas.

Elspeth dressed with the same care she always used. The reception was listed as black tie optional. As a lover of clothes, she hoped the Asian women would wear traditional dress. She selected a heavy silk dress and jacket of a blue colour that complimented her deep blue eyes. She had brought a small amount of jewellery with her, all of it understated but fine. She felt a certain comfort in these clothes as she had selected the material for them in Singapore and had it made for her by her French dressmaker in London.

She had been provided a list of all the attendees and knew that the name badges would not appear until the formal meetings began. She had a quick mind for faces and assumed she would have added names to faces before the conference began. Twenty-one people would present a challenge. She read over the list once again, struggling most with the Russian surnames, names and patronyms.

The reception had begun when Elspeth arrived. The waiters stood passively behind the buffet waiting for the crowd to gather. Elspeth surveyed the canapés and as always rued the fact that she needed to be discreet in her selection, or her clothes, so precisely bespoke, would cease to fit. She took a glass of white wine and stood at the edge of the room watching the guests enter. She wanted to see everyone but not stand out. Within twenty minutes most of the twenty-one guests were there. The US delegation was talking among themselves and obviously enjoying their drink. The others drifted in. Some went immediately to the buffet. Others ordered their drinks first. The Chinese arrived last. Elspeth was disappointed that the one woman in their delegation was dressed in a plain silk evening blouse and black trousers. The Japanese and Korean women more than made up the deficiency of traditional dress by the Chinese delegate. Their bright clothes cheered the room. The Russian woman had dressed in utilitarian cocktail frocks, probably bought off the rack at Gum or some other bland department store. Elspeth rued the fact that the Americans and Canadians were dressed more casually than the rest, although two men wore black ties, as did most of the other men.

Elspeth had identified about half the people in the room when a cheerful voice broke into her task.

"Lady Munro," a man said from behind her. "Is it really

you?"

Elspeth froze. She disliked the title she had acquired when she married Sir Richard Munro over two and a half years before and only used it at Foreign and Commonwealth Office functions in the company of her husband, a distinguished diplomat. Occasionally she shamelessly erred from her resolve to keep her own name, usually if it suited her need of the moment. Now was not one of those times. She turned to the man and saw a familiar face, Jason Ravensworth once from the Canadian Embassy in London.

"Hello Jason," she said. "Are you here officially?"

"Yes. Are you? I heard that you worked for the Kennington Organisation."

Elspeth put her finger to her lips, grinning, and then hissed "Ssh, I'm here quietly."

"My lips are sealed. Are you here to meet us?"

"I am. Will you introduce me, but please just as 'Elspeth Duff'?"

"OK, if you wish."

Jason knew most of the people in the room and introduced Elspeth as they went round the room. She greeted each person by name in order to cement each face and identity in her mind. She would be mingling with them over the next two and a half days but doubted she would have much personal interaction with them after tonight. Richard, her husband, would have done better than she could at small talk but then again he was seasoned in the art of diplomacy. Elspeth's function was not a social one and consequently she kept her conversations brief. She was tired from her trip, having risen twenty-eight hours before in London, and was looking forward to being finished for the day.

Jason was a pleasing companion. He held her possessively by the crook in her arm, put his hand over hers and looked into her eyes frequently enough to make her feel cared for. A handsome man of almost film star looks, he gave her middle-aged heart a 'wee patter', as they might have said in Perthshire, where she was born.

I'll use her as my decoy. How did Jason Ravensworth greet her? Lady M something. I wish I hadn't moved off so quickly and could have got it right. Something is strange about her. When we were introduced later, Jason used another name. She is definitely one I can target. There would be no greater satisfaction that putting down an English aristocrat while I achieve my main purpose. She won't put on those airs in prison. I don't think she noticed me particularly, which is perfect for me. But my real target came over and slipped his hand around my waist. I don't think anyone spotted him doing it. I hope not. I don't want him to become possessive. I want him dead. And I will have it pinned on Lady M. That's what I'll call her. She looks so smug, so sure of herself, so condescending. Now my purpose is two-fold. I shall enjoy this. But I have to think fast. First I must find which room she's in. I'll follow her when she leaves. Maybe she'll take Jason up to bed with her. I can tell she's married. She has a wedding ring and a very fine ruby and two diamonds on her left ring finger. From looking at her jewellery and dress I think her husband must be very rich. Will she cheat on him? I suddenly think all of this is going to be fun. But I must focus. The most important thing is to do the deed and not be caught. The perfect crime. How am I going to do it?

2

Janet Church looked over the conference room one more time. She wanted the setup to strike a balance between casualness and formality. Each delegation would have its section of the tables formed in a loose hexagon, one leg for each country, so that no hierarchy could be assumed. She had confirmed that everyone in the room spoke proficient English and therefore she had not arranged for translation services but recording devices had been set up to document the proceedings. The microphones were in place. Placards at each table identified the country of each delegation. Flags might be common at other hotels but they were not up to Kennington standards. She knew the exact number of each delegation and had the appropriate number of chairs set out at each table. She put several chairs and empty tables along the wall in case they were needed. She debated about where to put Elspeth Duff. Elspeth was handsome enough that she would not blend into the décor unnoticed. Janet had seen Elspeth the night before at the reception and knew her presence had been noted. The men would have seen her striking demeanour: the women her clothes and jewellery. Janet was aware that last night Elspeth's intelligent eyes had seen more than the delegate's evening clothes and at the time was probably assessing the dynamics in the room.

Janet was grateful Lord Kennington had sent someone out to help with this group. Whaling was a contentious topic in the northern Pacific and might arouse tensions. She hoped all would run smoothly. That was her job. In a last-minute decision, Janet put the chair for Elspeth to the left of the dais and at the edge of the room. The spot would identify Elspeth as an observer but not a delegate. Satisfied, Janet left the room.

*

Charlie Baillie Shaw woke at the insistence of his wake-up call in one of the smaller rooms at the top of the hotel. He had tossed until two o'clock in the morning British Columbia time, and felt he had just fallen asleep, when the ringing of the phone at his pillow would not be quelled. He rose with a curse.

Charlie was based in New York and had travelled west as late in the day as he could get a flight. He had arrived at the Kennington Victoria after dinner and sat in the bar until well after midnight.

His paper told him to keep down expenses as much as possible so he had paid for his own drinks. He was told to blend in as if he were a hotel guest and not a journalist. He knew the whaling conference had been kept under tight wraps from the press. By sheer chance Charlie had heard it mentioned in New York a month earlier when his friend Jason Ravensworth was visiting the United Nations, Charlie's normal journalistic beat. Jason had squirmed after he leaked the information. He made Charlie promise not to broadcast the conference to his colleagues at his own paper or anyone else. Charlie said he would stay silent only if he could have exclusive rights to any breaking story. Charlie was making a name as a respected journalist who shunned sensation and wrote seriously on environmental topics.

Jason had said he would agree to Charlie's terms because he said he feared exposure if he did not.

Charlie had not been invited to the reception the night before but Jason had said he would share the high points with Charlie in private. Jason had asked him to keep as low a profile as possible. Charlie's journalistic nose told him that more was brewing than a mundane recital of the issues surrounding whaling which had been re-hashed many times before in the press but he did not know why Jason was so tense. This tension had brought Charlie to Victoria. He had some difficulty persuading his editors that something was in the air. He knew his job was on the line if he failed to deliver a credible series of articles. Jason's nervousness over leaking the conference, however, had made Charlie feel he was on to a something beyond the mundane. He took a deep breath and rose exhaustedly.

Charlie dressed in a new shirt and conservative tie he had bought at Saks Fifth Avenue in New York. His paper would not pay for this finery. Charlie hoped he would have use for it again. His normal garb was more relaxed and certainly not so funereal.

His mother had told him about the Kennington hotels. He wondered how uncomfortable he would feel in the posh atmosphere that she had described despite his being one of the up-and-coming journalists for his conservative British paper.

He took the lift down to the breakfast room. He surveyed the room taking in the long buffet. What must have been members of the conference were bunched at one end of the room at tables that had been reserved for them. And then his eyes fell on Elspeth Duff, sitting at a table with

Jason Ravensworth. Jason's hand was resting gently next to hers. This was indeed unexpected. Charlie realised she worked for the Kennington Organisation, but never expected to find her in Victoria—and with his friend.

Jason looked up and saw him. Jason motioned for him to come and join them. Elspeth had her back to him and did not turn towards him.

On Charlie's approach Jason said, "Charlie. Good morning. Let me introduce you to . . . "

Elspeth looked up and started to smile what looked like a practiced smile and then jumped up and threw her arms around him.

"Do you know each other?" Jason said.

They both laughed. "Elspeth is my cousin," Charlie explained. "She and my mother are like sisters so I call her Aunt Elspeth. I've known her all my life."

"Charlie, I'm not going to ask what you are doing here. Part of my job is to chase journalists away, you know. Am I going to have to have you ejected?" Elspeth said.

He could not decide if Elspeth was being serious or not. Her deep cobalt blue eyes held his of the same colour, a Robertson family trait that had come down from Elspeth's grandfather through her mother and from Charlie's great grandfather.

She cocked an eyebrow. "I'm serious, Charlie. I'll overlook your profession for the moment but tread lightly."

The caution was real, he knew. He also knew enough about Elspeth's background to know she took her job seriously. His mother, Lady Elisabeth Baillie Shaw, called Biddy, and now married to Max Douglas-Forbes, QC, had once been involved at a case at one of the Kennington hotels and still talked about Elspeth's skill at keeping the press at bay. But Charlie speculated nothing could happen here to stir up the gutter press the way the killing of a curvaceous film star at the Kennington Stresa had several years before. Whaling might be a serious ecological issue but it hardly could incite anyone in the Kennington Victoria to murder.

They chatted amiably until the delegation rose and Jason with them.

"Are you joining us this morning?" Jason asked Elspeth.

"I'll be along in a minute," she said.

Elspeth visibly relaxed out of Jason's presence. "I'm on duty, Charlie, and may see very little of you for the next two days. Now tell me news from Scotland. I haven't been there for six months and miss your mother and the farm."

Charlie knew that Elspeth's last visit had been complicated, one that his mother only alluded to by saying it had been difficult. Charlie had kept his curiosity at bay because from his mother's tone of voice he knew that whatever had happened was a closely guarded secret. Elspeth was the most colourful member of the family beyond a doubt and her adventures were often perilous and much relayed through family circles.

Charlie loved Elspeth like an aunt. When he was small, he had visited Elspeth and her first husband, Alistair Craig, in Hollywood, where Alistair choreographed fight scenes for the movie industry. In doing so Charlie had roused feelings of mad jealousy in all his friends at school. He had gone on film sets and seen several mock fights directed by Alistair. Bam, pow, he thought, and smiled at his boyish recollections. Charlie wondered why Elspeth's first marriage had gone so badly. He asked his mother who had simply said that the marriage had run its course and there was no way back.

Charlie found Elspeth's new husband stiff but she seemed to love him. Fondness crept into her eyes whenever Richard's name would appear. Charlie sometime speculated on what went on when they closed their bedroom door. Max, his mother's new husband, was a bear of a man, whose affection was open; Richard's manner was closed but Elspeth seemed to hold him dear. Each to his own, Charlie thought.

Charlie was a journalist at heart. He hoped a serious thought piece might come out of the conference, one that would scoop his colleagues. Or possibly more would happen, something news breaking. Elspeth was attending the conference, which spiked Charlie's antennae. Knowing her position with the Kennington Organisation, he thought she might be paying more attention to the delegates 'safety' than the subtler issues on whaling. She also would hear what was going on, and might give him some unbiased information. How much he could cajole out of her? Since he had known her all his life, he knew her soft spots, he being one of them.

As they ate, they spoke of Scotland and his mother's farm on Loch Tay and of her elderly parents who lived by Loch Rannoch. Charlie was aware that in the hotel setting, she was more than a family member. She had a role and a presence he had not seen before and it suited her.

Finally Elspeth rose. "Charlie, let's meet after lunch. There is an hour's break and I want to hear more about you and New York. I must go now because I need to be at the conference downstairs. But after lunch I suspect many of them will want a lie-down because most have come from some distance. Why don't you come to my room at half past one?"

With these words she hurried off.

*

Now she is talking to another young man, a handsome one who I also think is very intense. I didn't hear their words but she hugged him and put her hand over his several times. She seems to attract young men. A seductress? Many hotels have middle-aged women who are on the prowl. And to think she wears her wedding rings so boldly. Maybe that attracts them. No strings attached. But she also was at the reception last night, so must have something to do with the conference. It doesn't matter what her position is just as long as I can implicate her in the murder. My plans are forming. I must act tonight. I don't have much time. When I passed them, I heard her invite the redheaded man up to her room. Charlie, that's what she called him. When she left she gave him a long hug, the second in ten minutes. His eyes glowed with affection. Who is he? I'll find out.

*

Leaving Charlie in the breakfast room to tackle another round at the famed Kennington hotel buffet, Elspeth straightened her suit jacket, which fit impeccably, and made her way downstairs. She knew little about whaling other than that Pacific rim nations disagreed on the killing of the giant mammals. She thought of the great beasts leaping from the sea, which she had seen many times during her residence in Southern California, and wondered how anyone would want to harm them. She supposed that profit was a strong motive for some, ancient tradition important for others.

Janet Church was standing at the door and helping the delegates find their seats. She pointed out the chair that she had set out for Elspeth but turned her attention to an American who asked where her delegation was. Elspeth made her way across the room but did not sit down. She did a quick reconnaissance. Confusion filled the room until everyone was seated. She recognised all the faces from the night before and saw several new ones.

She glanced down at the agenda that had been put on her chair. The morning session was to last for three hours with a break half way through. Her job was to watch the delegates and their activities in the room, not to listen to what they were saying. Their tones of voice were more important to her than their words.

Jason Ravensworth pounded a gavel and the murmur of voices stopped. As the head of the Canadian delegation, he welcomed them to Victoria and British Columbia. He explained that the morning session would be for each country to explain its objective for the conference. He conceded that by the end of the next day there might be no agreement but at least positions, both scientific and political, would be clear. He said he would take the information gathered and return to New York to give it to the United Nations and to the Clifton Trust, which was sponsoring the conference.

Elspeth watched the faces. She felt a collective sigh of relief that the purpose of the conference was not consensus. Four faces caught her attention. The head of the Japanese delegation, called Takanori Sakurai, had an unsmiling and arrogant expression. He looked suspiciously at the Americans to his left and Russians to his right and then smiled almost imperceptibly at the South Korean chief delegate, Oh Seung, an attractive woman who nodded but did not smile back. The Chinese delegation had two chief delegates, a man Chao Kai and a woman Chin Mei-su. They whispered to each other. Elspeth wondered why there were two chief delegates and if one was a party member and minder of the other.

The Russian chairs were empty. Elspeth had seen them at the reception and thought their absence unusual. The head of the delegation was Fedor Petrovitch Dvorkin, a distinguished tall man who reminded Elspeth of a Slavic version of her husband Richard. Elspeth had chatted with him the night before. His English was unaccented to Elspeth's British ear. He had expounded on the virtues of international dialogue. His wife Svetlana had stood dutifully at his side but looked bored. This morning Fedor had not yet appeared.

Elspeth glanced at the American delegation, also headed by a woman, named Katherine Croft, a stern no nonsense type in a severe navy business suit and crisp white blouse. She was old enough to make Elspeth think she had made her way belligerently through a man's world. She was chatting with a man sitting behind her who was clearly an Inuit. Elspeth did not see a name on the list that fit his cultural heritage. Perhaps he had taken an English name.

Jason stopped when the door opened and Fedor Dvorkin came in with two people behind him, both sharing the same weather-beaten facial characteristics as the Inuit with

Katherine Croft. He spoke quietly to Jason and apologised generally for his lateness without an explanation for its occurrence.

The delegates all shifted in their chairs as the Russians took their seats. Jason repeated the agenda of the morning session. The topic at hand was culling the herds. Soon Elspeth stopped listening, but was acutely aware of the body language that existed in the room. Takanori Sakurai, who spoke first, took a stern tone defending the Japanese position on sanctioned commercial whaling. His voice rose and became aggressive. The other delegates sat stonily. Only Oh Seung, the South Korean, watched Takanori and nodded occasionally. The four Inuits, from three different nations—Alaska in the US, Russia and Canada—followed Takanori's words closely but their stoic faces gave no indication if they agreed or not with what the Japanese was saying.

Finally Jason called a halt. "Your position is clear, Mr Takanori. We look forward to your scientific report later today."

Takanori Sakurai started to object but then bowed curtly to Jason's authority and sat down abruptly. Katherine Croft from the United States seemed to be the only one who wanted to take Takanori on. She stood, smoothed back a piece of hair that had come loose from her brushed back and lacquered hair and cleared her throat. As she began to attack the Japanese stance, she spoke as if she were a representative of the Green movement, denouncing the Japanese government sanctioning whaling. Her speech was long and finally concluded with a note of condescension to the Inuit sitting behind her. She ended with an acknowledgement of the Inuit tradition of whaling on a small scale for their dietary needs and not for profit. The four Inuits looked satisfied.

The time for the break came before the other delegates could speak, but the two opposing views expressed by the Japanese and Americans had created a feeling of static electricity in the air. Janet Church was overseeing the coffee and tea service. Elspeth watched the delegates relax and choose appreciatively from a selection of rich pastries and cakes, which had been set out outside the conference room doors. Katherine Croft went up to Takanori **Sakurai** and spoke to him with a smile. Elspeth could not hear what Katherine said but Takanori laughed as he would with a friend. Elspeth wondered if these two had known each other a long time and no longer considered their adverse stances as a deterrent to congenial personal relations.

Oh Seung stood nearby listening without expression. Fedor Dvorkin came up behind her and spoke into her ear. She jumped slightly and turned to him.

"Good morning, minister," she said politely but not warmly. She turned and went to the buffet. He followed.

"Have you tried these?" she said picking up a small buttery tart topped with fresh wild strawberries. Then she added with a more familiar tone. "It should satisfy your sweet tooth. They're good. This is my second."

"And you are accusing me of a sweet tooth, Oh Seung," he said with a chuckle. "I'm slimming after the holidays and will stick with coffee. It's an excellent blend but I know you prefer tea."

The two Chinese stood to one side and sipped bottles of water they had brought with them from their rooms. Elspeth watched them. Why did they isolate themselves? All the others were interacting as long-time associates and even friends.

Jason came up to Elspeth and put his hand on her arm. "So what do you think of our lot?" he asked.

"Interesting dynamics. Do you know them all?"

"Mainly by reputation. My job in Ottawa is wider; whaling is only one part of it."

"Who's paying for this? Surely the Canadian government doesn't have the funds for a Kennington hotel."

"A rich activist under the cover of the Clifton Trust. He knows the bias of each person here but keeps hoping if they continue talking they will find more common ground. I'm pleased we have representation from the Inuit community. They have a small part in whaling but their presence lends a certain perspective to the call for an all-out ban. I'm not an expert but hope to learn enough to present a report to our sponsor and, if he agrees, to the environmental committee at the UN. I need to satisfy him that the expense and time of the conference is being worthwhile. He chose the Kennington hotel as an enticement. Only the proletarian Chinese delegates seem to be holding back from all the frills. I don't know why. They aren't paying. Maybe they want to show that they are above high living. Which one do you suppose is the party member watchdog?"

"I think she is," Elspeth said, although she had no idea.

"I opt for him," Jason replied chuckling.

During the second half of the morning session, the views expressed were quieter. Oh Seung from Korea addressed the problem of illegal whaling by her fellow countrymen. Chao Kai reiterated his country's support of the total ban on whaling. A woman aide to Jason Ravensworth spoke about the Inuits in the northwestern parts of Canada and their reliance on whale meat for their diet. She argued that if the environmentalists were so keen on protecting the caribou, a staple of the Inuit diet, why were whales considered in a different light? All four Inuits nodded, their faces lively for the first time.

Fedor Dvorkin was the last to speak. He rose with great dignity and looked down his nose at all those assembled. Elspeth wondered that if there were a contest for arrogance who would win—Takanori Sakurai or Fedor Petrovitch. Despite Fedor's erudition, however, he added little new to what already had been said. He came down on the side of the greens.

Elspeth knew little or nothing about whaling but she knew about people. Despite the congeniality during the coffee hour, the positional lines were drawn. Elspeth could see no possibility of consensus and now understood why Jason had not required one. She had been watching people's reactions. The morning had been productive in cementing the identities of the attendees in Elspeth's mind but she still did not understand the interpersonal relations that infused the room. She had no idea how important these relationships would be later in the evening.

Elspeth waited until all the attendees were standing and straightening up their papers. She approached Jason Ravensworth.

"Discounting the Inuits, who seem to me to be a special interest group, I noticed that all the delegations have a third member except the Americans, who have four. Do you know why?"

He smiled. "Probably security."

"But my question still stands. As the person in charge of security for the hotels, I'm always aware of inconsistencies."

Jason had not answered her question. Elspeth was not certain if he had organised the conference yet he was the chair. She wanted to know more about the make-up and why these particular delegates had been chosen. Although this might not be important, it was the type of exercise Elspeth normally indulged in to keep herself alert when on security duty.

*

There she is talking to Jason again. They have quite a thing going. I can understand. He is so good looking and has not brought any wife. He's not married, maybe on the prowl. She seems so eager to comply. I can exploit it if I time my plans exactly. My skin tingles when I think of my revenge.

3

Charlie Baillie Shaw was waiting as the participants came out of the lift and headed towards the dining room. He had done a reconnaissance of the room earlier and saw that a section of tables with enough seats to include all the members of the meeting downstairs was empty. He also saw that the maître d' seated each person or group that came in so that no reserved signs were necessary. Charlie looked for Elspeth but she was not amongst the conference group. He suspected she had disappeared into the back areas of the hotel and was conferring with the powers that be. He wondered how much attention she could give him.

Charlie, because of his profession, was a snoop. He enjoyed this. He used his wits, crisp British accent and the good manners his mother had taught him to inveigle his way into groups where other journalists could not. His mother had insisted that he learn to speak without a Scottish accent. She could slip into the accent of Perthshire when needed but did not do so naturally. Their branch of the Robertson family was aristocracy and his mother never let him forget that. He had grown up on a farm on the banks of Loch Tay, filled with Scottish history, but was a gentleman and his mother had seen that he stay so. As a child he hated this stricture but when he went to Oxford and later to the Harvard School of Journalism, he was glad she had been so insistent. He was not teased, even when he wore his kilt. In fact his plummy accent and Highland dress was a real draw to the girls in the

28

States.

He approached the maître d' and told him, truthfully, that he was Elspeth's cousin and, untruthfully, was joining her for lunch. The maître d' looked at him questioningly and then led him to an empty table near the window overlooking the harbour but away from the delegates. Charlie and the maître d' were halfway to their destination when a cacophony broke out in front of the hotel. Two men, the concierge Charlie had seen at the desk in the lobby and a doorman, were trying to restrain at a small crowd of young people just outside the front door to the hotel shouting and carrying placards. The hotel staff members were losing their battle. The maître d' pulled out a mobile phone that had been invisible in his suit pocket and tapped in a code, obviously an alert.

The waiters who were not serving ran to the door to the dining room. Shortly afterwards Charlie saw Elspeth arrive. Unlike the others she appeared calm.

"Good people," she addressed the crowd, "come, let's talk."

The leader of the crowd, a young man with a 'Save the Whales' tee shirt, stopped and looked at Elspeth. Charlie had never seen her in action before. She radiated authority but spoke with understanding.

"Let me hear what you have to say," she said. "Then we can decide what to do to help you."

Charlie noticed that Elspeth's request had quieted the crowd.

"Come in to the hotel. I'll find a place where we can talk."

Elspeth fearlessly took the leader's arm and guided him through the door. His flock followed. So did Charlie. Elspeth led them all to a corner of the lobby farthest from the dining room and the main entrance. Charlie calculated the mob had less than fifteen members, about half male and half female. Most looked unwashed and smelled so as well. Charlie had seen enough protestors around the United Nations to recognise the type.

Once she had assembled them in a corner, Elspeth spoke politely. "Please tell me. What is it you want?" she asked.

Her courtesy seemed to calm the mob.

"We want to make a statement about the whales," the leader said.

Elspeth caught Charlie's eye. "Perhaps it would be best if you came back to our conference room and we could take this down. Let me introduce you to Charles Baillie Shaw. He is a respected journalist from a British paper. If you follow reporting on the whaling problem in the UK, you probably have read his work. He's willing to listen to what you have to say."

Charlie knew Elspeth was improvising. Charlie had not written about whaling before but the crowd would not know that.

The leader looked at an attractive blonde woman who seemed cleaner than the rest. She nodded back at him. Charlie wondered what this exchange meant. The leader seemed to lose his belligerency.

"People don't listen to us. I guess that's why we make so much noise." He smiled as he spoke.

Harmless, Charlie thought, but dedicated to the cause.

Elspeth rallied the crowd. "Come with me. I'll see if I

can get some sandwiches for all of you."

Janet Church appeared at Elspeth's side.

"I have them in hand," Elspeth whispered. "Bring sandwiches, hardy ones and some tins of soda, no better, fruit juice, something organic."

Charlie was impressed at his cousin's quick thinking. He followed Elspeth and the crowd back through the lobby and into a room that must usually be used for small conferences. A large table with chairs for fourteen stood unused in the centre of the room.

"Ms Church, have the staff bring in more chairs. Ladies and gentlemen, take seats. Lunch is on the way."

The group seemed nonplussed. Charlie doubted that they had been treated this way before.

"I apologise for the delay," Elspeth said. "We weren't expecting you."

The irony of her statement seemed to pass over their heads.

Charlie took a seat at the side of the room, allowing the protestors to gather round the table. Elspeth stood at the head of the room and spoke calmly. Charlie realised she was speaking in her American accent. He had heard from Elspeth's children that she spoke flawless standard American English but this was the first time he had ever heard her do so. He would not have known she was British. The strategy was a good one. Many Americans and, he suspected, Canadians considered cultured British voices to be condescending. Elspeth sounded like she was one of the protestors, passionate for their cause and wanting to help them.

Five minutes later the sandwiches and juice arrived. Greedy hands cleared the platters and accepted the glasses of organic pomegranate juice.

Elspeth took half of a sandwich and motioned to Charlie to do the same. He chose a roast beef one and was delighted that the meat was not processed but must have been cut from a standing rib. He bit in eagerly, hoping that he would now be able to skip ordering lunch at the extravagant Kennington hotel prices. He noticed that many of the protestors did not eschew meat, although vegetarian choices were provided. A waiter poured out some juice for him.

Janet Church reappeared and Elspeth whispered something inaudible in her ear. When the protestors' hunger seemed to have satisfied, Elspeth spoke again.

"Now, folks, what do you have to say that you want Mr Baillie Shaw to hear?"

Charlie straightened his back and pulled out his Blackberry. The leader ranted on about saving the whales and the cruelty of commercial whalers. Charlie's knowledge of the issue was superficial but he made up for his ignorance by showing his enthusiasm. Charlie pretended to take down notes. Elspeth let the diatribe go on for fifteen minutes before she called a halt. At no point did she acknowledge that a conference was underway in the hotel addressing in much more depth the items the leader of the protestors barely touched on. The leader seemed taken in by her sincerity without realising her evasion. How brilliant on her part, Charlie thought. No wonder she kept her job.

"Now I hope you'll excuse me," Elspeth said. "I have other work I must do. I'm sure Mr Baillie Shaw would like to hear more. I've ordered dessert for everyone. While you're enjoying it, you can arrange a time with Charlie to show him your local haunts and talk more. Charlie will show you out when you are ready. Don't rush."

Charlie shot Elspeth a killing look but she smiled back at him and mouthed, "I owe you one." With a boyish grin he acknowledged her skill at roping him in.

When dessert was finished, the blonde woman who had spoken to the leader at the beginning came up to Charlie.

"Hi, I'm Michelle. Meet us at Moe's," she said. "It's near the bus station. We're meeting there about nine this evening to talk about what to do tomorrow."

Charlie followed the crowd to the street. As he left them he heard the leader say, "Well, that was unexpected. I think we have been heard. And those were the best sandwiches I have ever eaten. Maybe we should make enough noise to get more tomorrow."

Charlie walked slowly back into the hotel. Elspeth was waiting for him in the lobby. "Dinner's on me," she said. "Don't worry, I'll put it on my expense account."

"Aunt Elspeth, what made you think of inviting them in?"

"An old strategy, I'm afraid. With young people, feed them and they'll calm down. I used to do that when you visited, and you, Peter and Lizzie got out of line."

"Will the hotel pay for everything?"

"To get rid of the disturbance, yes. Come up to my room, Charlie. We need to talk."

*

Elspeth took in a deep breath and considered what had happened. She had no idea how the protestors knew about the conference, which had been kept under the strictest wraps as far as she knew. Only a member of one of the delegations, a member of the hotel staff or the person paying for the conference could have leaked its existence. Elspeth began to wonder if Lord Kennington, her employer, had known trouble might erupt. Otherwise, why would he send Elspeth, one of his senior security staff who reported to him directly, to as banal a gathering as the morning session would seem to indicate, even if she had asked to come? She had already detected that all was not as it seemed on the surface. Why was the conference called in the first place? Jason Ravensworth had brushed her off when she had challenged him. Did he know what the real purpose of the meeting was? Elspeth suspected it was not just to hash over positions already expressed to the outside world.

Word of something about to happen had been leaked, at least to Charlie. He had said Jason Ravenscroft had let the news slip by accident but was this really intentional? Elspeth's suspicions had served her well many times and her intuition was buzzing loudly now.

With a discreet knock, Charlie announced himself. Elspeth greeted him at the door to her room. As always, his beguiling charm came with him.

"Charlie, why are you here?" she said bluntly once he had taken a seat. "Surely there must be more than meets the eye. The whaling question hardly seems world shattering.. Is environmental news so slow that your paper is willing to foot the bill for your room at a Kennington hotel to cover the story? Or do you know something that I should know? Did Jason say anything to you that sent you pounding to western Canada from New York?"

34

She watched Charlie to see if he were going to lie. She had seen him lie as a child. When he did, he made a fist. His fingers tightened.

"All right, Charlie, tell me the truth."

"I promised Jason to say nothing," he confessed.

"But the news will be breaking at the end of the conference?"

"It might."

Elspeth stiffened.

"Who else knows? Charlie, I need to know the truth. I don't care about your story but I do care about the people who are here at the hotel. Jason told me that this conference is privately sponsored. Do you know who is behind it? And why?"

"Aunt Elspeth, I . . . I'm sworn to secrecy."

"You're a journalist, Charlie. I understand why your profession hides behind confidential sources. You won't get the exclusives without them. But I need to protect the people here, and if anyone is in danger, I need to know. I set you up downstairs earlier and I think you know I owe you for that. Yet what you're implying now is that the routine discussion of whaling may not be the main issue. Charlie, confess. I'll keep everything you tell me confidential, unless the safety of the guests is compromised. In their interests, I'll have to act."

She did not add that the comfort and security of the guests was always her priority. "Service and Comfort" was the motto of the Kennington hotels and Lord Kennington never let any of his staff forget that.

Charlie looked abashed and then belligerent. Elspeth

knew all the signs from his childhood.

"Let's compromise," he said after a long pause.

"How?"

"I'll let you know when anything is about to happen. I can't before."

"Why?"

"You'll know when and if the event happens," he said stubbornly.

"So there is going to be an event."

He nodded slowly and said, "Maybe."

"A big enough one to bring you to the Kennington Victoria. I'll have to trust you, Charlie but you know my position. Do you know who is sponsoring the conference?"

"I can't tell you exactly. I think someone through the Clifton Trust, whatever that means."

Elspeth wished Charlie had not inherited her grandmother's stubborn streak. She had it herself.

"Do you know about this someone?"

"I can't tell you," he said again.

"Or won't, no matter how much I wheedle. Charlie, I don't want to put anyone in danger. You can understand that, I hope."

Elspeth regretted these words the minute she said them. She was treating him like a child.

"Yes, Aunt Elspeth," he said in a childish voice and looked impishly at her.

"Charlie, you always were a bit of a rogue even as a child. I'm going to be at the conference all afternoon. Let's meet for drinks at six and have dinner here in the hotel. That will leave you plenty of time to go on to our protestors' meeting."

Elspeth paced her room once Charlie left. What could it be that was brewing? Charlie left her with the distinct feeling that whatever it was, it had nothing to do with whaling but perhaps a lot to do with the participants at the conference. She got out her list from the morning session and went over it again. At half past two she made her way back down to the room in the lowest floor and took up her place at the side of the room.

*

She did not come to lunch but went with the crowd of young people instead. What is she doing? How can I turn this to my advantage? She seems to be allying herself with the mob of Greens outside. Does this somehow implicate him? That may be a stretch. Now I need to work out the fine points. I must strike this evening.

4

The afternoon dragged on. Several members of the delegations nodded off. The speeches were scientific and statistical. Elspeth did not try to follow them. Instead she watched, wondering what crisis might arise out of this benign group that was critical enough to have Jason Ravensworth leak something and lure Charlie to Victoria. Her attention caught the second aide to the American delegation who had just appeared. An odd duck, she thought. Both aides were men. One seemed docile. He whispered to Katherine Croft and handed her several papers from a portfolio he had on the table in front of him.

The other watched the proceedings intently but did not interact with Ms Croft. Elspeth focused on this man. She couldn't tell his height because he was sitting but his upper body was long, suggesting that he was tall. He was perhaps fifty years old, but his body, at least that part which Elspeth could see, was lean and fit. His hair was carefully combed to hide thinning at the top and he was dressed more casually than the others. Elspeth followed his eyes. They focused intently on each person as they spoke but held Chao Kai, the man from the Chinese delegation, in their view for longer than the others. Why this intense observation? And who was this man? Could he be from one of the US secret services? If so, why was he here sitting tensely and watching Chao especially? Did his presence have anything to do with Charlie's secret?

Elspeth checked her list again. Two aides to the US

delegation were listed: Greg Allen, the obvious flunky, and John C. Smith. John Smith? No one was called John Smith, not often anyway. John Smith bore watching. Elspeth thought other than herself he was the only person in the room who seemed more interested in the delegates than the words they spoke.

When the afternoon tea break came, Elspeth rose, rotated her shoulders and stretched her back, both stiff from sitting. She wandered over to the US delegation but John C. Smith had slipped out of the room. Elspeth spoke to Katherine Croft instead.

"I hope your stay is being pleasant," Elspeth said banally. "As you may have assumed, I work for the Kennington hotels. My job here is to see that all of you are comfortable and safe."

"A hotel security agent?" Katherine asked. Elspeth heard contempt in her voice.

"Something like that," Elspeth said, annoyed. "We always like to see that conferences such as this don't encounter any unpleasantness."

"So that's why you shunted the rowdies away at lunch."

Elspeth smiled. "I don't think they'll bother us again. But I am concerned about how they knew your group was here. Nothing has been publicised, has it?"

"No, at least not in the States. I don't know about the others. Save the whales isn't at the top of protestors' priority lists these days. Iraq, Afghanistan, and the new president are. Besides, I don't think what we are discussing is new. I wonder why I was sent at all. It was I who protested when given this assignment. It must be a nod to the rights of the

Inuits. You must have noticed that four of the people here are from the northern tribes."

"I thought so. Is that the purpose of the conference?"

"I have no idea," Katherine said. "My boss at the State Department said come, so I came. Blessedly it's only for two days. And the hotel's far better than most of the places we stay."

"Do you know who's paying?"

Katherine burst out laughing. "You bet your bottom it's the US government. I understand all this is being covered by a private grant from the Clifton Trust."

"Do you know who the Clifton Trust represents?" Elspeth asked.

But they were interrupted before Katherine Croft could tell her, if she even knew. Elspeth wanted to find out who the real sponsor was. Charlie must know but he had refused to tell her? Elspeth wished that Lord Kennington had not been so offhanded about her assignment. Perhaps because she had asked for it. She figured it was now close to midnight in London and she could not call and ask.

Elspeth moved out of the conference room and into the reception area. She hoped to speak to John C. Smith but he had disappeared. She found Jason Ravensworth talking to Fedor Dvorkin and joined them.

"Have you found the afternoon as boring as I have?" Fedor asked her.

Elspeth was puzzled by his remark. Throughout the afternoon he had appeared to doze but one foot crossed behind the other fidgeted the whole time. He may have been thinking of other things but he was not asleep.

"I'm neither a scientist nor an environmentalist,"

Elspeth replied. "Much of what was said went over my head." But people's body language had not.

"And just who are you?"

Elspeth thought carefully before she replied. "I work for the hotel," she said finally. "I'm here if you need anything from us. It's one of the services we offer to our guests when they are in a large group."

Fedor shrugged and then laughed. "Then you have to put up with us."

Elspeth smiled. "I've put up with a lot worse. You don't appear to be enjoying the conference."

"Repetitious. I don't know why I'm here. But I am enjoying your hotel."

For the second time in less than ten minutes a delegate had speculated on the necessity of their assignment in Victoria. What was going on?

Jason Ravenscroft broke in. "Will you join us for dinner later?"

"I'd promised my cousin to buy him dinner here in the hotel. May we meet afterwards?"

"So Charlie really is your cousin," Jason said. "I thought he was lying."

"Not at all. I've known him since he was born and his mother is perhaps my closest friend. At dinner I'm looking forward to catching up with his activities in New York. I haven't seen him for a long time, although his mother keeps me posted on his activities."

"Who is this Charlie?" Fedor asked.

"My cousin, Charles Baillie Shaw. He's also a guest here in the hotel. He and Jason know each other from New York, where Charlie works and Jason occasionally visits."

"Does your cousin work at the United Nations?"

Elspeth became circumspect. She did not want to reveal that Charlie was from the press. "No," she said. "He and Jason are friends."

Jason, who was standing opposite her, held her eyes for a moment and blinked in what she thought was approval. "Friends for a long time," he added. "Once he stole a girlfriend from me. I'm not sure I've forgiven him completely. She was gorgeous."

Elspeth said, "Oh? Do I need to tell his mother there is something going on here?"

"Sadly for both of us, we all moved on," Jason said. "I'll see you after dinner. In the bar at eight? Fedor, will you join us?"

"My wife wants to go out to a nightclub," Fedor said. "I indulge her whims when we are outside Russia. She finds Moscow a dull place, although under the new regime there is plenty of nightlife. So I will say no."

Elspeth left the two men and circulated. Oh Seung, the Korean delegate, was with the two Chinese, who stood stiffly in front of her. Elspeth could tell that Oh Seung was trying to generate some conversation but was getting nowhere. She would make a remark and one or the other of the Chinese delegates would respond politely but monosyllabically. Elspeth decided to help out.

"Good afternoon," she said, giving a slight nod. "I hope you all are enjoying our hotel."

"You work for hotel?" the woman who Elspeth knew

was Chin Mei-su said.

"I'm here to ensure you have everything you need," Elspeth said.

"We are happy here," Chao Kai said. "It is good that Chinese government is not paying. We are glad for benefactor who pay bill. We have many luxury in China now but not always like this hotel. Chin Mei-su and I appreciate it."

"I do," said Oh Seung. "I was amazed that this conference was called and was to meet here. A Kennington hotel! Do you think Lord Kennington will choose Seoul for one of his new hotels?"

"Do you know Lord Kennington?" Elspeth asked.

"When the invitation was sent for the conference, I googled the Kennington hotels. I was very impressed."

The Chinese man said nothing.

Moving on, Elspeth approached Takanori Sakurai. He was standing by himself and was on his mobile and speaking in rapid-fire Japanese. He seemed upset. Elspeth left him alone but wondered if the source of his distress were personal or professional.

Outside the reception room was a small enclosed terrace, grey and uninviting in the January wind. Several leaves whirled in a dance on the slate tile flooring. A small sign warned that the French doors were alarmed and should be used in an emergency only. No exit, she thought. She could have done with a breath of fresh air, even a wintry one.

The conference was due to recommence at four and run until six. Elspeth thought of two more hours with dread. On an impulse she took the lift to the back offices of the hotel and rang Charlie Baillie Shaw. She found him in his room.

"Charlie, I need your help. What are you doing right now?"

"Writing. I have a four-thirty deadline."

"Deadline? What possibly is there to write about here at the hotel? If you do mention the hotel, let me see what you've said. I can't have my cousin giving the Kennington Organisation adverse publicity."

"Don't worry. I'm wrapping up a story I started in New York. I'm just about finished. And I have no complaints about the hotel. What can I do for you?"

"I want you to help me track the spouses of the members of the conference. I can't monitor what's going on down here and keep an eye on them as well. There are three, a Korean man and two women, one Japanese and one Russian. I want you to go down to the lobby and see if they are anywhere in the public rooms of the hotel. I'll call the manager, Janet Church, and she'll help identify them for you."

"And if I see them, what do you want me to do?"

"I'm particularly interested in the Russian woman, Svetlana. Can you find out anything about her? I would use Richard's in similar circumstances but he is on a plane, I think. Or should be soon."

"And what am I to do if I discover more about her?"

"First find her and see what she is doing. Be discreet. I don't want to alarm her. If she's not about, see what the others are doing. They may all be out, but in this cold and with the attractions of the hotel, I doubt it. I'll be finished here at six. Come to my room then."

*

Charlie sent off his dispatch before thinking about Elspeth's request. He had not been entirely honest with her before. Jason Ravensworth had told him that there would be breaking news in Victoria but had clammed up after he had realised he had said something he should not have. Charlie had wanted to impress Elspeth. He also had inflated the importance of his lead from Jason to his editors, who trusted his instincts and were willing to pay him a large per diem for him to come to Victoria. Charlie was making up the difference, which was considerable. Perhaps, if he could convince Elspeth he was useful, he could get a discount on his room. His mother had told him how important Elspeth was to the workings of the Kennington hotels and that she reported directly to Lord Kennington.

Charlie was making a name for himself with his paper by playing his hunches. So far most of them had paid off. The prospects of a scoop were becoming better and better and with it might come a bonus. Because Charlie tended to follow a story whatever the cost, he often found himself short of funds, just as he did now. Sometimes he joked to himself that by the time he had made his mark, he would be a pauper.

Charlie straightened his clothes and made his way down in the lift to the main floor. Elspeth's request gave him an insight into the workings of the hotel and might be a benefit before the two days were out. A tall woman greeted him as the doors opened on the ground floor. She introduced herself as Janet Church, the manager.

"All three are here in the hotel," she said without further introduction. "Mr Kim Bae, from Korea, is in the exercise room. Madame Svetlana Mihailova is in the tearoom, indulging in one of our special teas. Mrs Takanori has not come down from her room all afternoon as far as I know. She ordered green tea and light refreshments to be sent up at half past three."

"You keep a tight watch on your guests," Charlie said.

"For their satisfaction and security," Janet said. "No guest is aware of all we do for them. It's part of the package. Elspeth said I will help you in any way possible."

"Could you get a table for me next to Madame Mihailova?" Charlie asked.

Janet walked with him to the tearoom and whispered in the maître d's ear. Charlie followed him to a table near the buffet next to one occupied by a woman of obvious Slavic origin who was enjoying a large plate of cakes, pastries and savouries. Charlie imagined her licking her fingers in delight, although she did not.

He went to the buffet and served himself carefully. The wide array of treats was tempting but Charlie was conscious that too many meals at the Kennington Victoria equalled a drain on his finances plus too many hours in the gym back in New York. He ordered the special Kennington Darjeeling tea but no cakes or savouries. At any rate Elspeth had offered him dinner.

He seated himself and smiled at Svetlana. She finished the bite of cream cake and smiled back.

"I always enjoy these teas when visiting a Kennington hotel," he lied. He wanted to see her reaction.

"This is my first time," she said with a thick Russian accent. "I hope it is not my last. My Fedor likes to treat me to good things. The government does not always allow much money when we travel outside Russia. You are Canadian?"

"Scottish," he said, "although I live in New York."

"I look forward to visiting New York. I have not been there. But I will go there soon. I hope," she added at the last.

"May I join you and tell you about New York?" he asked.

Her eyes, probably her best feature, lit up. "Please."

Charlie knew he had the ability to charm and now he did so. Svetlana became more and more excited, asking him the obvious questions about the Empire State Building, Ground Zero and the Statue of Liberty. Charlie made them seem more thrilling than he actually found them to be.

"When do you leave for New York?" he asked innocently.

"To . . . I'm not sure," she said. Svetlana seized up after uttering these words.

What was "to". . . ? Today, tomorrow, or something else? Why had she frozen?

"I must go," she said. She looked around hurriedly and rose without saying goodbye to Charlie. He watched her stout figure retreating with great haste.

So something is going on, he thought. Was this what Elspeth was looking for? He could report her words and actions but not any reason for them. But his reporter's sensitivity saw the beginning of a story.

Charlie went upstairs and changed into shorts and a tee shirt. He took the heavy cotton robe from the hanger in his bathroom and made his way down to the exercise room. The only occupant was a tall East Asian man, who had to be Kim Bae. He was on a treadmill, which Charlie noted was going at a slow speed and low incline. Charlie took his place next to him on a stair climber. Soon he began to sweat.

"I'm not as in good shape as I should be," Charlie said to Kim Bae.

The Korean took in a deep breath and said, "I also am not. I promised my wife that I will work out every day." His r's became l's. "This is a very good machine."

"This one is too. Better than the one in the gym in New York where I live."

Kim Bae did not react to the mention of New York. He went back to concentrating on his walking.

Charlie waited a few minutes before speaking again.

"Have you been to Canada before?"

"No. My wife travels but I usually stay home with my job. This time though we have a chance to stay in a Kennington hotel and have our rooms paid for. I know of the Kennington hotels. They are among best in world. So I agreed to come with my wife."

"When do you leave?"

"Unfortunately tomorrow night when my wife's work is done."

"Are you going back to Korea?"

"Yes. I like the hotel but I will be glad when our long return flight is over."

Kim Bae seemed relaxed about his plans. Charlie could not find anything interesting in what he said or how he said it. Svetlana was definitely a more intriguing subject. Charlie worked out for another twenty minutes and watched Kim Bae leave.

Charlie's third subject was Mrs Takanori Sakurai. Janet Church had said she was in her room and Charlie could think of no way to gain entry. He went back to his room, showered and dressed in his funereal suit and tie. It was now approaching six and Elspeth would be waiting for him.

5

Now the plan is in place. I need to be careful no one sees me. I have seen the cameras hidden in the ceilings in the hallways. I know I must hide my identity when I am in public places. It is good that I got the hat. I can use it as a disguise. That is the last perfect thing.

*

"Charlie, you say there is a breaking story but on the surface I can't see anything unusual. However, Fedor Dvorkin is so tense that he could run a spring-loaded clock. Svetlana talks of going to New York and then shuts up when you ask her when. Takanori Sakurai is obviously agitated. There is a silent man in the American delegation who doesn't listen to the speakers but watches everyone like a hawk and makes himself scarce during breaks. The chief US delegate seems completely disconcerted and doesn't know why she is here. What does it all mean? Jason must know but he's being evasive," Elspeth said.

"Our only option is to sit and wait for things to develop," Charlie responded, sensing how puzzled Elspeth seemed. "It's the part of my job I like least."

Elspeth changed the subject abruptly. "Do you know anything about Inuits and their culture? The four at the conference spoke eloquently during the last session, making a plea for understanding of the role whaling plays in their customs and livelihood. They convinced me but I'm not too sure they swayed any of the others. Their earnestness was palpable. In the end, however, I had this feeling that their plea had nothing to do with the reason we were gathered in the conference room."

"I know a little. They figure in the conservation movement in the north," he said, but felt she wasn't listening.

"Let's go down to the bar and circulate among the delegation. We may hear something that will make things clearer. Let's split up when we get there and then talk over dinner. I've had our table set away from the delegates so that we may talk privately."

As she spoke, Elspeth rose. Since he had become an adult, Charlie had always admired Elspeth's deportment. She walked with consummate grace, holding her head high, and moving in a way few British women did. It reminded him of upper-class Frenchwomen he had seen on the Champs Elysées or on the Riviera. She appeared to be in complete command of her body and it made her beautiful, although she had too strong a jaw and too chiselled a nose, both family traits. She complemented her bearing with expensive clothes chosen with immaculate classical taste. He thought of his mother, who so closely resembled Elspeth physically, but who had chosen to remain in Perthshire and the family farm. His mother was as down to earth as Elspeth was sophisticated. Charlie felt proud to be seen in Elspeth's company tonight but was glad his surviving parent was more approachable. Charlie found Elspeth a little frightening. She was quick to notice things and did not soon forget them. He supposed that these qualities made her good at her job. He did not want to cross her, however, because even as a child he could not fool her.

As they entered the bar, Elspeth pointed out Fedor Dvorkin. "Svetlana's husband," she whispered nodding in his direction. "Kim Bae's wife, Oh Seung, is talking to him. The Chinese delegates aren't here yet. Takanori Sakurai's wife is in the corner but he is outside in the lobby on his mobile. I'll tackle him. The woman getting her drink is Katherine Croft, the US delegate. Talk to her first, if you can. I've already arranged that your food and drink will appear on my tab so order what you like."

With those words she turned and headed for the lobby. Charlie watched her go over to the reception desk and say something that brought a smile to both of the staff working there. Elspeth then leaned on the counter waiting to approach Takanori Sakurai. He snapped his phone shut and started for the lift. Elspeth followed him, speaking to him quickly. He turned towards her and spoke. Even from where Charlie was standing he could hear that the words were angry, even if their meaning was inaudible. Elspeth flushed and set her jaw. The doors of the lift slid open and the Japanese stepped in. Elspeth was right beside him. The doors closed taking them both upwards. A few minutes later Elspeth came back down. Her cheeks were reddened but she walked with perceived calm towards Charlie, who was talking to Katherine Croft and finding her dull.

"Good evening, Ms Croft," Elspeth said as if nothing had just happened. Charlie was amazed by her composure, which undoubtedly was a trick of her trade. Soon Elspeth's colour died down and she left Charlie to go and speak to the Koreans who had joined Mrs Takanori.

Conversation died down, as it often does in a room filled

with people at a social gathering. Charlie excused himself from Katherine Croft's company and went to his cousin.

"Are you OK?" he asked.

"Never better." She replied and lifted her head.

When they reached the dining room, the Chinese delegation were already there. The maître d' showed Elspeth and Charlie to a table in a small niche and hurried back to the door to escort those who had followed Elspeth and Charlie to their respective tables a short distance away.

"I don't think Takanori Sakurai will come down. He was terribly angry when I left him. I tried to calm him down but didn't succeed. I see Mrs Takanori has joined Kim Bae. Oh Seung has probably gone to freshen up," Elspeth said. "There she is. I don't expect to see the Russians. They are off to catch the night life."

"So Svetlana hoped," Charlie said.

Charlie looked up and saw Jason Ravensworth come in. He had not been in the bar. On his arm was a tall blonde woman of about thirty, who was dressed in a low-cut evening tee shirt, tight jeans and very high heels. She was chatting with great animation and Jason was apparently closely in attendance.

"My goodness, she's changed. In the conference rooms she was definitely mousy. She's Jason's aide. Her name is Brittany Rogers," Elspeth said.

"Do you know all their names?" Charlie asked.

"It's part of my job. I learn them as quickly as I can. So do all the staff at the hotels. Lord Kennington insists. It's a skill I had to learn when I began at the Kennington Organisation."

The waiter came over and handed Charlie a menu.

"He already has my order," Elspeth said. "With the quality of the food at the hotels, I'd be a blimp if I didn't order slimming food beforehand. Don't worry about me. My food will be light but excellent."

"I'll have the same thing," Charlie said. "What is it?"

"Do you doubt me?" Elspeth said with a cocked eyebrow. "In the Pacific Northwest one should always have salmon. Actually, dinner will be a medley of four kinds of salmon interlaced on skewers with warmed salad. If you're still hungry, there's always dessert. Now tell me if you found anything interesting in your conversations in the bar."

"Very little. Most of the people were marvelling about the hotel and chatting about how unexpected the conference was. No one was complaining."

"And the people from the US? I notice only Katherine Croft and one of her aides are in the dining room. Their conversation seems to have lagged a bit. The Americans have two aides. The second one isn't here."

Charlie smiled. "Knowing the Americans' penchant for work, he is probably in his room on the web or responding to his emails."

"Maybe," Elspeth said enigmatically.

Charlie wondered what she meant. He watched her. She kept up a rapid survey of the room, seldom letting her eyes leave the members of the delegation, even when tackling her fish.

"What are you thinking?" Charlie asked.

"How few people are taking advantage of a dinner at a Kennington hotel. That's unusual in itself and even more strange considering that it's free. Have you been able to pick up anything more about who is sponsoring this conference? Janet Church tells me that arrangements were made by money transfer and everything was prepaid. If I were the sponsor, I'd be upset that my largesse wasn't more appreciated."

"Isn't the Clifton Trust paying the tab?" Charlie said.

Elspeth shook her head. "From what I can intuit, only nominally. Can you find out more from Jason? Or prowling around the internet? I've never heard of the Clifton Trust but that doesn't mean anything. But I like to know who they are and why so much money is being funnelled into the hotel to sponsor twenty-one guests. That's more money than you and I together make in a year, unless you are paid much more than I and I'm well remunerated."

"No problem," Charlie said. "When I get back from Moe's, I'll get on my computer. Do you have any advice for me with that mob tonight?"

"Frankly, I think they are benign. Any difficulties we have will come from inside the hotel, not outside. Enjoy yourself. I think you'll find the protesters refreshing after our stuffy atmosphere."

She reached out and put her hand over his in a touching gesture. He had not realised before how much he loved and admired her.

*

Elspeth watched Charlie leave the dining room and rose to keep her appointment with Jason Ravensworth. The

Chinese and the Canadian aide in the dining room seemed involved in deep conversation. Elspeth wondered what common topic of conversation had engaged them so ardently. Only Chao Kai seemed withdrawn. Chin Mei-su seemed to ignore him and had become animated. Elspeth changed her mind on the identity of the public security member. Chao was now the obvious choice. The Inuits had eaten together and had left as soon as they had finished their meal. Katherine Croft and her aide left the dining room at the same time as Elspeth. The Chinese and Mrs Takanori followed closely behind them but O Seung and Kim Bae remained behind, talking to each other.

Elspeth went to her room to freshen up before joining Jason Ravensworth in the bar. She sat in front of the mirror in her small dressing area and looked at her face. Would she seem attractive to any man other than her husband? Shallow lines had begun crossing her face but she consoled herself that they were smile lines and therefore acceptable. How soon would the finer lines of old age appear? Richard would not see them but she would. She grimaced at herself in the glass. Why this sudden need to appear young? She knew. She was feeling attracted to Jason Ravensworth and even her love and commitment to her husband could not put down the emotions Jason roused in her. For professional reasons she hoped she could hide her feelings; for personal reasons she was glad she still had them. Nothing need happen but each time Jason had put his hand on her arm, she had felt warmth spread through her body. She was sure no one had noticed but she had felt herself redden. Elspeth spent a good portion of her life away from Richard but never before had she thought of straying from her commitment to him. A passing thought perhaps but the possibility was there. She frowned at her reflection and wondered what had come over her. But it was almost five in the morning in Brussels, where Richard had a small flat, and it was hardly the time to call him and profess her love.

She freshened her makeup, stood and smoothed out her frock. She must not keep Jason waiting. Why? After all, it only was a casual meeting in the bar. She wanted to talk to him about her conversation with Charlie but she also secretly wanted to spend some time alone with him. How could she prolong their meeting? Silly old woman, she said to the image in the mirror.

At eight, she took the lift down to the public rooms, her emotions sternly in check.

Jason was at the bar and chatting to Katherine Croft. Brittany Rogers was hanging on his arm possessively. So much for getting Jason alone. Still Elspeth did need to talk to him privately and made her way with as much dignity as she could muster to where the group was standing.

"Elspeth," Jason called out. "What have you done with Charlie? I saw him scurrying out of here just a moment ago, his journalist's nose leading him. Do you have a story for him?"

Jason obviously was a little tipsy and Elspeth regretted this. He might not be capable of talking to her seriously about Charlie's perceived threat. With two women fawning over him, how could she distract him? She smiled as widely as she could.

"Charlie is off to see a blonde French Canadian woman called Michelle. I don't expect him back early," she said

Brittany rubbed her nose against Jason's ear. He brushed her away. "Brittany, have you got the papers ready for tomorrow?" he said almost harshly. She drew back, apparently startled at his tone. "Yez, boss," she said in a not-quite sober voice.

"Go check them again," he said. "I want everything in order for the morning."

Brittany drew herself up and walked unsteadily across the bar and out into the lobby.

Katherine Croft said, "I'm off too."

Elspeth let out a short sigh. "Jason, we need to talk but not here. Charlie has said some things to me that I need to clarify with you."

Jason grinned. "About his love life as his cousin/aunt, or about the members of the conference as a member of the Kennington Organisation?"

Charlie's love life might have been an excuse but Elspeth did not use it. "About several of the guests. Will you come back to the rear of the hotel and we can talk in the security office?"

"Why not come to my room? It'll be more comfortable there and we can order a nightcap from room service."

Elspeth would have preferred the back rooms, considering how she was feeling about Jason but she conceded to his suggestion. Lord Kennington had made sure that all the rooms were soundproofed and she felt she could talk without being overheard.

He rose from the bar stool and Elspeth took his arm. She did not need to; she wanted to. He squeezed her interlinked hand affectionately. Maybe the back room was a better suggestion.

They walked companionably to the lift and found themselves alone on the ride up to the second floor.

"I always kiss beautiful ladies in elevators," he said and was true to his promise.

Elspeth blushed deeply, not at his act, but at her reaction to it. She could feel the kiss all the way down her body, although it was only chastely given. She withdrew her arm from his and said, "Jason, we need to talk seriously. I know it's been a long day for us all but certain things can't wait."

"Such as?"

After alighting from the lift, Elspeth looked up and down the hallway and saw they were alone. "Such as why we all are here. I can no longer avoid the implication that this conference is a front for something bigger. Charlie wouldn't be here if the only story was an extension of what happened downstairs this morning and afternoon. His journalist's nose, as you call it, is sniffing around because you led him to believe there was more than meets the eye."

They had reached Jason's room and he inserted the key card. The green light came on.

"Ladies first," he said.

Elspeth stepped into the room, which was in darkness. The last thing she remembered was a cloth with a sweet antiseptic-like smell being placed roughly over her face. Her last thought was—chloroform.

6

Charlie found Moe's only after asking three people where it was. The bar was in a basement and the sign small as to be almost indiscernible to the uninitiated. The loud music emerging from the door each time it was opened proclaimed the place to be the haunt of the young. At thirty-two Charlie no longer kept up with the music trend of the moment. He never had enjoyed punk rock or whatever the teens called it nowadays and wondered how he was going to talk over the vibrations of the amplifier. He was here to feign interest in a small group of protestors. Charlie knew his serious paper would never publish their angst but Elspeth had coerced him at least to hear what they had to say.

He went down the wintery stone stairs and erred on the side of caution by hanging on to the handrail. He pulled open the door and walked into an atmosphere that ensured deafness almost instantly. The blonde girl from the group that had invaded the Kennington Victoria spotted him and waved frantically at him. Was her name? Michelle? Charlie made his way through the crowd loitering about the tables. Michelle rose and gave him a hug. Charlie had been in North America for eight years but he still was not comfortable with this type of informal closeness from strangers.

Since the noise forbade any oral communication, Charlie ordered a beer on tap by using sign language. The waiter brought it and put it on a sodden chit. Michelle attempted to give names to her buddies but Charlie could not hear. He took a large swallow of his draft, although he did not want anything to drink. One of the girls at the table was obviously drunk and tried to get up on the table to dance. In doing so she knocked over Charlie's glass. The amber liquid spread across the table and Charlie only jumped up in time to avoid having the brew soak his lap. Everyone laughed and Michelle signalled to the waiter. Charlie shook his head. He did not want any more.

"Does anyone want to talk?" he yelled out.

"Christ, not now," the leader of the group responded. Charlie read his lips more than he could hear the words.

Michelle rose and whispered in his ear. Charlie thought she was asking if he wanted to go elsewhere.

"Yes," Charlie shouted, hoping he was answering correctly.

Michelle dragged her duffel coat from the back of her chair. Charlie had not yet removed his woollen trench coat or scarf, and so could easily follow Michelle out of the door and into the silence.

"Do you come here often?" Charlie shouted and then said more softly, "I'm terribly sorry, I think I've been slightly deafened."

"Tommie likes it," Michelle said.

"Is he the leader of the group?"

"Sort of. We're not really a group. Most of us are just out for the fun of it during winter break. I only met Tommie three days ago. He's a friend of one of my roommates at university."

"What do you know about Tommie?" Charlie asked.

"Not much. He's at the University of Washington and

his mother lives here in BC. He poses as a radical but I don't think he is devoted to anything but making a lot of noise. He'll go wherever he thinks he can produce a row."

"How did he find out about the whaling conference?" Charlie asked, as they reached the top of the stairs and began to walk along the street.

She put one arm through his and interlaced their hands together. She leaned slightly into him.

"He said he snoops around on the internet, you know, to see where he can make the most disruption of local events. He does it not from any particular point of view, although this time we were supposed to shout "Save the Whales". He had no idea if that was what the conference was about but it was a good rallying cry. Tommie's fun, and handsome. My roommate, you know, has a real crush on him, although she's at the University of British Columbia and he's at Washington."

"Is he American?"

"You know I don't know. I think he may be at least half. His father works for Boeing in Everett, Washington, although, you know, his mother lives here in Victoria. They may be divorced, you know. Tommie hates his father and big business."

The use of "you knows" made Charlie think she was getting nervous at his questions. He softened his tone.

"Do you normally get involved in protests? I've always had to stay neutral because I'm a journalist but I've been to several large protests in New York. The police can be brutal there. You're lucky Ms Duff let you off with Kennington hotel sandwiches."

"They were fantastic," Michelle said. "Is the food

always so good there?"

"Better."

"Are you staying there?"

"On an expense account," he said partly lying. He did not add that his finances were being stretched because of Jason's lead. If what Jason said was true, the story would be a big one

"It looked like you knew this, what was it, Ms Duff. She kept looking at you. I thought she was giving you signals."

The tables have turned, Charlie thought. Now she's questioning me but I won't bite.

"I'm here for a good story. Do you think Tommie can give me one?"

"I doubt it. He's just a bag of air. I wouldn't trust anything he said."

They proceeded on. Charlie enjoyed the feeling of her arm wrapped in his and the casual bumping of her body against his as they walked together. He could smell a clear scent in her hair and thought of the herbs his mother dried at the farm on Loch Tay. They talked a bit about Victoria and the skyline at night, about the clear night sky and if it would rain or sleet in the morning. Charlie told her about Scotland and his childhood there. She told him about hers on Vancouver Island.

"Do you want to go back and talk to Tommie?" she finally asked.

"Not tonight," he said. "Quite frankly, you've led me to believe that there's no story there."

"Do you want to go somewhere warm and quiet? Somewhere where you won't have your drink spilled and we can talk more?"

"I'd love that."

They found a quiet bar and talked for two more hours. Finally she said her father would be would be waiting at the door if she wasn't in by midnight. "How's that for being home for the holidays? I'm twenty but you'd think I was fourteen."

Charlie called her a taxi and made his way back to the hotel on foot. He had drunk little but he felt he was floating. He had not met a girl like Michelle for a long time.

The doorman at the hotel stiffened as he saw Charlie.

"Mr Baillie Shaw, please come to the manager's office. She will explain when you get there."

Janet Church was waiting for him. Her face was drawn and her eyes were filled with fatigue. She cleared her throat.

"There's been an incident involving your cousin," she said.

"Is Elspeth all right?"

"Not exactly. Let me take you upstairs. The police are there now."

7

Elspeth's first impressions were of a room filled with light, a ladder in her tights and a stabbing pain in her foot, which she noticed was twisted at an odd angle. She closed her eyes and waited, hoping she was dreaming, but the pain did not go away. She opened her eyes again and saw that she was lying at the outside corner of the entryway into a hotel room and that someone was lying on the bed farther in the room. She could see all the overhead lights and several lamps were on. She propped herself up on her elbow and looked about the room. The body on the bed did not move nor make any sound. The room, however, was in disarray. Cushions were thrown off the sofa, the chair at the desk was on its side, and a lamp, unlit, was lying broken on the floor. Papers were everywhere.

Elspeth tried to sit up but her foot cried out. She clenched her teeth and forced her body into a more upright position. She blew out her breath in pain. She groped for her mobile phone in her pocket and then remembered that she did not have a pocket in her evening jacket. Where was her shoulder bag? She couldn't see it. She tried to stand but her stomach turned. She blew out her breath again and grimaced. Slowly she pulled herself along to one of the sofa's side tables, which had a hotel phone on it. She took the receiver off and tapped 7-7-7. "Help, come quickly," she said and then fainted.

When she came to, she was in the bed in her own room.

A young woman with pulled back dark hair, whom she did not recognise, was sitting on the sofa. Elspeth moaned. The pain in her foot throbbed. An unseen force had removed her shoes, a pillow placed under her head, and a light blanket thrown over her.

The woman rose and came over to Elspeth.

"Are you awake?"

"My foot hurts," Elspeth said, since her state of consciousness was clearing. "Please get someone to look at it. The hotel has a doctor on call. And who are you?"

"Police Constable Mills."

"Police constable? Why?"

"Let me call the doctor."

"No, let me. I'm an employee of the hotel chain."

"And I'm here to make sure you don't make outside calls." The woman's tone was polite but at the same time hostile.

"What's happening?" Elspeth asked.

"I can't answer that."

"I saw a person on the bed in the other room. Was it Jason Ravensworth? Has something happened to him? Is he all right?"

"You'll have to talk to the detective inspector."

Despite the pain in her foot and muzzy head, Elspeth immediately rose to do her duty. "Here in the hotels we prefer the police work go through our security department. Guests here should not be subject to police interrogation without explicit direction from our security staff. I am from our corporate offices in London, and am responsible to see that no guest is disturbed."

"I'll call the detective inspector and let him know what

you said," the woman replied dryly.

"No, call Janet Church, the manager. I must talk to her at once."

The woman frowned but seemed to respond to Elspeth's tone of authority.

"Use the house phone. Dial 7-7-7." Elspeth said. "That's the number the security staff use to contact any person in authority at the hotels in an emergency. "Do it. Tell Ms Church that I must speak to her now. And, for goodness sake, ask her to send a doctor to tend to my foot."

Elspeth did not remember the time between the constable's call and the arrival of Janet Church. She must have fainted from pain. Janet was holding her hand and saying her name.

"Elspeth, can you hear me?"

"Yes, I can but my foot hurts desperately. Will you call the doctor?"

"I already have."

"Tell me what's going on."

"We found you in Jason Ravensworth's room. Unfortunately, although you were injured, he is dead. I called the police. They've come quietly, up the service elevator, but I'm afraid it's murder."

"Murder? How?"

Janet swallowed hard. "He was stabbed," she said. Her voice croaked and she paled. She cleared her throat and began again. "Security passed on to me that a woman's voice was calling for help in Mr Ravensworth's room. I came myself and found you and . . . and his body."

"How did you know he was dead?"

Janet swallowed and clung on the arm of her chair with tense fingers. "A skewer had been thrust up his nose. His eyes were wide open in terror."

"I see," Elspeth said. She remembered each time she had seen violent death. Nothing inured one to it. "I'm sorry you were the one who had to find him. How long ago was that? I don't remember anything from the time I made the call until I woke up a few minutes ago."

"About half an hour ago. I rang Security in London. They said to bring the police in quietly and leave the rest to you once you came to."

"Yes, That's best but what about Police Constable Mills?"

"The detective inspector, whose name is Brewster Clough, thinks you may be involved. He wants you kept out of the investigation."

"Oh, Janet, I'm so sorry. This must all seem new to you and discovering Jason Ravensworth's body must have been sickening. Death is never pretty and this kind of death is devastating. Can you get Detective Inspector Clough to come here?"

Janet rose to do so when a soft knock came on the door. A balding man with a wrinkled and kindly face came in without waiting to be asked.

"Dr Halloway," he said by way of explanation. "I'm sorry for the delay. Now what seems to be the trouble?"

His hands were gentle but no softness of touch could stop the pangs that shot up Elspeth's leg. He drew a syringe from his bag and said, "This will make you a bit sleepy. I need to get you to the hospital. It's not far. We need an x-ray."

"But I can't," Elspeth said. "I'm on duty here and in any case the police may have objections."

"I'll get the detective inspector," Janet said. "Doctor, I won't be a minute."

She left the room before Elspeth could object.

"What's the matter with me?" Elspeth asked.

"Have you ever had difficulty with an Achilles' tendon before?"

"About a year and a half ago in Scotland, but it's healed. Oh, I'm sorry for the pun."

He chuckled. "You may have injured it again but I can't discount a broken bone. To the hospital it is."

"Doctor, I can't."

"You must. I'll speak to Janet. I'm sure she can find someone to cover for you until we get you better. I'll see that Brewster releases you from here."

Apparently the doctor was on first name terms with both the hotel manager and police. Victoria was a smaller city than Elspeth had at first imagined.

The jab he promised sent Elspeth back into a semi-delirious state. She later had vague recollections of the ambulance and the emergency room. People seemed to be bustling efficiently around her but she could make no sense of their words. Finally she heard a voice of authority.

"You're lucky, Ms Duff," the voice said. "Your only problem is a few broken bones in your foot. The pain came from one of the bones rubbing a nerve. We have fixed you up with a foot cast, which should solve the problem. You'll be on crutches for a while but no serious harm has been done. We're going to keep you here overnight, but, if you are feeling well enough in the morning, you should be free to go."

"Take me back to the hotel now," Elspeth said, knowing doctors had absolute authority in hospitals. Her demand sounded as weak as her spirit.

The emergency room doctor, who looked about the same age as her son, shook his head. "We'll see in the morning."

"Is anyone here from the hotel?" Elspeth asked.

"Ms Church called about fifteen minutes ago. She said to tell you all was in hand and that you should rest."

Inside Elspeth writhed. Janet Church should not have to be orchestrating the details of the investigation of Jason Ravensworth's death. Elspeth could think of nothing to do from her drugged state. Eric Kennington would not be pleased.

They transferred Elspeth to a trolley and strapped her in. She saw the lights in the hallway and on the lift but little else. When they reached the room where she was to stay for the night, she turned her head and was surprised to see a uniformed policewoman at the door.

"Is this necessary?" she asked, mustering as much indignation as the drugs in her would allow.

"Detective Inspector Clough said it was a precaution. I'll be outside and won't disturb you. I hope you will be feeling better soon," the police woman said.

Unlike the attitude of PC Mills, the young woman was polite. Elspeth suspected that she was new to the force and that sitting all night outside a hospital room was boring duty. Wickedly, Elspeth thought that she could try to escape. But she soon fell back into a narcotic haze.

*

Charlie Baillie Shaw stared at Janet Church.

"The police? Is she all right?" he asked again.

"As far as we know, she was attacked, possibly drugged and has been injured. She is in the hospital now with a badly damaged foot."

"Attacked? But how?"

"She called from one of the guest rooms to say there was trouble. When I got there, she was unconscious. We took her to her room and the hotel doctor ordered her to go to the hospital."

Charlie shook his head. "You're not telling me the whole truth," he said. "What's happening? Why the police?"

Charlie watched Janet Church formulate her reply. He could tell that she was dealing with something more monumental than Elspeth's attack and foot injury.

"I will have to trust your discretion, Mr Baillie Shaw. I know you are a reporter, which normally we discourage in the hotel, but I hope your familial ties will make you keep what I have to say confidential. Your cousin was injured but another guest was killed. The circumstances suggest that he was murdered. The police are here because of this."

"Which guest?" Charlie shouted.

Janet looked distraught. "I can't tell you. You must understand. The privacy of guests has to be respected."

Charlie growled. "I know. But where is Elspeth? She's my cousin and surely I'm allowed to see her."

"They've taken her to the hospital to treat her foot." Janet gave the address. "I just talked to the doctors there and they are keeping her overnight. She's been sedated."

"I'll go anyway," Charlie said. And then with a smile added, "My mother would never forgive me if I didn't. In the meantime, have you contacted her husband? He should know."

"I . . . no, I assumed that the security office at the Kennington Organisation in London would."

"Let me," Charlie said. "It's the least I can do. Has Pamela Crumm rung you?"

"Ms Crumm?"

Charlie could tell that the name commanded Janet's respect. After all, Pamela held as much sway in the Kennington Organisation as Eric Kennington despite the fact that her name never appeared to the public.

"She's very close to my family. She'll want to know all the details," Charlie said.

"Of course," Janet said stiffly. Charlie had wondered if Pamela's name really carried that much power with the Kennington hotel managers. He saw that it did.

The doorman found Charlie a taxi despite the late hour. He had decided to see Elspeth before calling Richard. When he arrived at the hospital, he was informed that visiting hours were long past and would not resume until the following afternoon.

Charlie thought hard. The night receptionist went back to her computer. She seemed to be inputting some data and soon was absorbed in her work. Charlie left by the front door. He saw the sign for the emergency room and an idea came to him. He made his way across the car park and walked toward the entrance where the ambulances arrived. Two came blaring in and Charlie joined the tangle of paramedics and orderlies dealing with two bloodied men on stretchers. Charlie took the end of one of the stretchers and was inside the emergency room without anyone seeming to notice he was wearing a trench coat. He slipped behind a door, where he found a stack of green scrubs and caps obviously meant for the emergency room staff when their clothes were soiled. He slipped off his coat, jacket, shirt and tie and pulled a green tunic over his head and fitted the paper cap on his head. He walked out and into the main corridors of the hospital. He might be challenged, which would be unfortunate. He was not sure he could talk his way out of his deception.

His next difficulty was to find Elspeth's room. He took the back stairs to the second floor and came out near a nursing station.

"I'm Doctor Shaw," he said and hoped he sounded authentic. "I'm looking for an Elspeth Duff. Which room is she in?"

The nurse ruffled through papers on a clipboard and said, "In the pink ward, room two seventeen."

Charlie nodded and walked off. The nurse, who was young and a bit rotund, giggled. "The other way, Dr Shaw."

"I've been on duty a long time," he said by way of explanation.

He went in the direction on which the nurse pointed. Then he saw the pink striping on the floor and followed it purposefully. Down the corridor, a policewoman sitting in a chair, her head down upon her chest. She gave a small grunt and went back to sleep. Charlie opened the door to Elspeth's room as silently as he could. The policewoman did not stir. Sedentary night duty in a quiet hospital defied vigilance.

Elspeth turned in her bed and let out a sharp yelp of pain.

"Doctor, I need to get back to the hotel," she said. Her voice was groggy.

Charlie put his finger to his lips and moved into the dim light over her bed.

"Charlie!" she said in a loud whisper. "How did you get in here?"

"Doctor Shaw at your services," he said, feeling impish.

"But my police guard?"

"She's enjoying her nap, even if she looks a bit uncomfortable in her chair."

"Charlie, you have to get me back to the hotel. I can't leave things to Janet Church. She has too many other things to cope with."

"I've managed to sneak in here," he said, "but sneaking you out is going to be a bit harder, particularly with that cast and with Sleeping Beauty outside."

"I see your point but there must be a way. Damn, I wish I weren't so drugged. I can't think straight. Think for me if you can. You're clever."

"We can't climb out the window. We're on the second floor and besides I don't think you could manage. If only I could get a wheelchair and get it in and out without the policewoman seeing me."

"There's one in the corner," Elspeth said. "They brought it in earlier and never came to fetch it. Will that help?"

"We can try. Are you game?"

"Anything to get me out. Can you be very quiet?"

"If we go very slowly. You'll have to hold the door open and help guide the chair so that it makes no noise. I think we can do it."

"How far is the lift?"

"Too far and besides we'll have to go past the nursing station. Do you have any crutches?"

Elspeth pointed to a pair leaning against the wall near her bed. "In case I need to go to the loo."

"Let me take those out first. There's a staircase just down the hallway. I'll hide them in there."

"And if she wakes up?" Elspeth asked.

"I'll tell her they're needed for another patient. But she seems quite lost to consciousness. I think we can pull this off. If not, I'll think of something else."

The policewoman, however, was fully alert when Charlie opened the door. He shoved the crutches back in the room, hoping they would not fall. Luck favoured him.

"Constable, it is constable? I see you're awake now" he said. "I need to get Ms Duff down to get an x-ray. Can you help me get her into the wheelchair? The nurses are short staffed this evening and help would be appreciated."

"Who are you?" the sleepy young woman said unprofessionally.

"From X-ray," he said.

"You don't have a badge," she said.

She's sharper than I had hoped for, Charlie thought. He decided to play on her guilt at falling asleep.

"Night duty is tough. My badge? We've just had a multiple accident in the ER. My badge must have fallen off." He pointed to two holes on the breast of his smock where badges must have gone. "Can you help me?"

She rose, flushing slightly, and came into Elspeth's room. Charlie saw that Elspeth was feigning sleep.

"She's fairly well knocked out. They've put her on massive doses of painkillers. We'll have to lift her from her bed. Dead weight," he added for good measure.

"It's not part of my responsibility," the policewoman said. "I'm just supposed to stay outside her room and see that she doesn't escape."

"Escape? Why would she do that?"

"She's a suspect," the policewoman said.

Charlie did not have to pretend surprise. "Suspect? But how?"

"At the station they said she she's suspected of murdering a guest at the Kennington hotel. She seems a nice enough woman. You wonder why she'd do that."

Charlie recovered his composure and said, "Who was murdered?"

"A guy by the name of Jason Ravensworth but I shouldn't be telling you this. Not that it would matter to you."

It did matter; it mattered a great deal. Jason was a friend, Elspeth a member of a family. Charlie could see no reason in the world why Elspeth would want to murder Jason. Charlie tried to keep his face from showing surprise.

"How'd it happen?" he said, trying to sound casual.

"Barbecue skewer. Up his nose. Terrible way to die," she said in verbal shorthand.

Charlie held back his reaction. "Weird," he said as if nothing was wrong. But his mind was racing. He and Elspeth had eaten skewered salmon for dinner. "Let's get the old bird into the chair so I can get her downstairs."

The policewoman said, "I can't do this. It's against regulations."

What can I do now, Charlie thought. He did not want to hit her over the head and he saw no other way to get Elspeth out of the room.

Elspeth came to his rescue.

"Are you calling me an old bird? I'll have you reported for this, young man," she said in a shaky voice. Charlie wanted to laugh. "Now get me to X-ray. I can get myself into the wheelchair. Constable, stay here and guard my room. I'll be back as soon as they will release me. I don't understand hospitals that wake people up in the middle of the night."

"I'll come with you," the policewoman said.

"You're not allowed in X-ray," Charlie said. "Only the patient and the technician." Why was she being so unbelieving? Probably because she had been well-trained and well-instructed.

"I'll wait outside," the policewoman said.

Since Charlie had no idea where the X-ray lab was, he had to try another tack. "OK, or do you want to go for a coffee? You could get me one too. I won't tell." He smiled as boyish a smile as he could. She frowned at him. So much for flirting.

"There's no way she could escape," Charlie said. "Not with her cast and being drugged. Take a break. It'll help you wake up. I promise I'll get her back asap. Where are we going to go in the middle of the night?" He sensed she was weakening.

"How long will it take?"

"At this time of night, fifteen minutes." After saying this, he wished he had given himself a bit more time. He smiled again. "You can trust me, not more than twenty." He hated getting this young woman in trouble but he was beginning to feel desperate. He wished Elspeth would step in. She lay with her eyes closed but he could sense she was following every word. He wondered if she was laughing at his weak attempts at seduction.

Finally the policewoman said, "I'm going to trust you, doctor. My job is on the line but I do need a break and coffee would be a godsend. Do you like yours white or black?"

"Black, two sugars," he said.

Elspeth opened one eye. "What now, young man? I want to go back to sleep."

"This won't take long, Ms Duff. Let me get the wheelchair."

After the policewoman disappeared, Elspeth said, "Charlie, you're positively wicked. Let's go. I think I can get in the wheelchair if you bring it over here to the bed."

After rescuing the crutches, they made the lift without anyone seeing them but the main floor of the hospital was another issue. They arrived in the emergency room, which was a buzz of activity.

"Where are you going?" a commanding voice said.

"This patient is being released to her family," Charlie said.

"Rather an odd hour, isn't it?"

"They've come all the way from Vancouver," Charlie said, hoping this would carry some relevance.

"OK but get back as soon as you can. We need the wheelchair. I expect she'll need the crutches. It's been a busy night."

Charlie wheeled Elspeth to the cupboard where he had

left his clothes. He only took time to take them off the peg and hurry out what looked like the entrance for people on foot. Once outside the door, he rifled through his pockets and found his mobile. He rang the Kennington Victoria.

"This is Charles Baillie Shaw. I need a taxi at the hospital. Send one right away, please. I'll be waiting by the emergency room exit." Then he whispered to Elspeth. "Can you walk?"

"If you give me your coat."

He looked and saw that under the blanket over her knees she only wore a hospital gown. He wondered where her clothes were. He should have looked before they left the room.

"Don't worry, Charlie, about my things," she said, seemingly reading his mind. "Richard says I have too many clothes. So the loss of a few isn't a problem."

He hastily put on his shirt and jacket and helped her awkwardly into his trench coat, as she stood on one foot, juggling one crutch. He looked down at her feet, which she had slipped into hospital slippers.

"You look gorgeous," he said.

She laughed. He loved her laugh, which was always joyous.

"Well done, Charlie," she said once they were ensconced in the back seat of the taxi. "Call the hotel and ask them to have Janet Church meet us with a blanket for me." She sighed. "That poor policewoman. I wonder if you can make things right for her tomorrow."

He grimaced. "I don't even like two sugars in my coffee. I don't know why I asked for them," he said, as if it were important.

8

Elspeth woke to pain. Her first thought was of her husband. She had not talked to him since arriving in Victoria although they had exchanged emails. Richard refused to text, as he said it was an affront to the English language, as little as was left to it in the twenty-first century. She would have to explain to him that she had been injured and was coping with another murder. He did not like what she did for a profession but one of the things he conceded on their marriage now over two-and-a-half years ago was that she would continue in her career. Elspeth suspected that he sometimes regretted this concession.

January light was coming in the window so she knew it was late in the morning. She turned to see if her mobile was at her bedside. Under it was a note from Janet Church. "Call me when you are awake," it said. She picked up the house phone and punched in 7-7-7. The voice that answered patched her through to Janet.

"Good morning," Janet said and paused.

"Good morning," Elspeth answered, trying to sound as if nothing had happened the night before.

"Shall we talk?" Janet asked.

"I think we need to. Will you come up to my room in half an hour? I need to talk to my husband and London first."

Richard's mobile informed her that he was not available. She wondered if he was already on his way to

Vancouver and asked him to call her back. Next she rang Pamela Crumm, who picked up instantly.

"My goodness, Elspeth. What havoc hath thee wrought?" Pamela misquoted.

"I assure you, I had nothing to do with Jason Ravensworth's death."

"Janet Church has already told me that you are a suspect. Good woman, Janet. Why did you bolt from the hospital?"

"I need to be here and get to the bottom of this. I can't do that from the hospital."

"Yer need ter take care of yerself, ducks," Pamela said in a fake Cockney accent. Then she switched back to her normal voice. "Eric will not be amused when he hears what has gone on. Luckily, he's in Hong Kong for the next few days. I've not told him what's happened there yet but I can't delay forever. Have the press got wind of the story?"

"Did Janet say they had?"

"Luckily not yet but some sharp reporter will get news of what happened."

Elspeth thought of Charlie and inwardly groaned. She hoped he would honour his pledge to stay silent.

"Has Janet Church told you what else is going on? About the Chinese delegation?"

"The Chinese delegation?"

"They've disappeared."

Elspeth sat up straight. Pain shot down her foot as she moved. She instinctively cried out in pain.

"When?" she asked, trying to ignore the arrows that were shooting through to her ankle and foot.

"They didn't come down to breakfast. Janet went and found their suite empty and their beds not slept in."

"Did she check the CCTV?"

"She sent along last night's tapes to the security department here. They are reviewing them now and will report back to me when they have finished."

Elspeth's professional mind clicked in. "Have them check on anyone seen with the Chinese in the hallways, particularly a fiftyish year-old American man. His name, so he says, is John C. Smith. I've suspected him all along. I'll go down and review the tapes myself. Pamela, I think I know now the reason behind this conference but I can't be sure until I see what the cameras picked up. Ta, ta. I'll be in touch."

"Elspeth, take care . . ."

Elspeth rang off before Pamela finished her sentence. The crutches that Charlie had given her the night before in the hospital were propped against the wall close at hand. She twisted herself about, taking care to protect her foot, and pulled the crutches towards her. She slowly lifted herself from the bed and made her way to the bathroom. Looking in the mirror, she saw dark circles beneath her eyes, but knew she did not have the strength to apply makeup to cover them. She performed the basic necessities. She noticed someone had taken off her hospital gown and dressed her in her silk pyjamas; Janet, not Charlie, she hoped. She hobbled to the walk-in wardrobe and selected loose-fitting trousers and a big heavily-weaved cotton shirt and a baggy woollen cardigan. She sat on the bench in the bathroom and dressed cautiously, only wincing when she drew on her trousers. She eschewed shoes; she would cope with this later. The slippers provided in the bathroom would have to do. She was making her way back into the bedroom when Janet Church's knock came.

Janet looked exhausted. Elspeth wondered if she had slept.

"Forgive my indisposition, which was quite unexpected, and which I regret. Tell me about last night," Elspeth said.

Janet grinned sadly. "I don't want to say when it's raining it's pouring but you get the point. I was just about to leave the hotel when you called from Mr Ravensworth's room. I called London and then the police as soon as I saw what had happened. You may remember my telling you that before the doctor sent you to the hospital."

Elspeth nodded although she wasn't sure.

"The police were here in fifteen minutes. In the commotion, I never thought to check the other members of the conference. I regret the omission now."

"I should have been there to help you."

"Your pain was very apparent. I couldn't ignore it. Besides you passed out."

Elspeth did not want to discuss what she considered to be a failure on her part. "Have you seen the security tapes? Who went into Jason's room before I got there?" she asked.

Janet twisted in her seat. "That's where it gets muddy. The tapes show a number of things going on outside Mr Ravensworth's room so it's hard to see who and when someone might have gone into the room."

"Tell me."

"After the Chinese delegation retired just down the hall from Mr Ravensworth's room, several people came into the camera's view. Besides, I couldn't identify them because we could only see their backs, and I don't know the members of the delegations well enough to pinpoint their identities from above and behind. I hope you can help there."

"Do you have the tapes for me to see?"

"In the security office. Can you make it downstairs?"

"Could you bring a wheelchair? I'm not very good on these crutches."

"I brought one up for you. I thought you would might appreciate one," Janet said like a true Kennington hotel manager. Comfort and Service, the mark of a Kennington hotel.

With Janet's help, Elspeth wheeled herself into the security office. The video technician had been alerted of her arrival and he had the tapes ready for viewing. The cameras were set to survey the hallways on all the floors of the hotel every ten minutes and also when any activity occurred. Elspeth sat patiently watching the scans, and occasionally asked the technician to stop the tape and rewind it.

The hallway outside Jason's room had been active during the evening hours. Most of the members of the conference who were housed on that floor went along the corridor at some point. Elspeth particularly watched the door to Jason's room. Before she and Jason had come up to his room, both members of the Chinese delegation came and went down the hall several times. Once Katherine Croft and John C. Smith joined them and they stood outside Jason's room talking for several minutes. Katherine left them and John continued talking, pointing up the hallway toward the back staircase several times. Chin Mei-su seemed uninterested and leaned against the door of Jason's room, but her fellow delegate Chao Kai kept nodding his head up and down rapidly. The three of them hurried on.

Several minutes later 'John C. Smith' reappeared and walked towards the lift. Two maids came and went, servicing the rooms. Soon Oh Seung and her husband appeared in the view. They too stopped at Jason's door. They seemed to be arguing. Takanori Sakurai was as usual on his mobile and his wife hurried along behind him. They seemed disinterested in any of the doors and went directly to their room nearby. The hallway was clear when Jason and Elspeth came out of the lift and went to his room. Elspeth watched him put his card in the slot, allowing the two of them to go in the room. The next activity recorded was Janet rushing to Jason's room. The cameras recorded the arrival of Janet and soon afterwards the police. Elspeth watched herself being ignominiously taken by a trolley to the lift up to her room on the next floor. The Russians were on the same floor and did not appear. The technician said they had not come in until well after two.

The next flurry of activity came at four in the morning. Four people, all wearing hooded coats, rushed down the corridor. Two were wrapped in blankets and the other two were shepherding them hastily along. Elspeth could not recognise the four and could only guess their identities, the Chinese delegation, John C. Smith and an unknown. The Chinese were obviously being spirited away. The blanket-wrapped figures were led to the emergency stairway. Was this the event that Jason Ravensworth had let slip to Charlie? A defection by the Chinese to the Americans? Or was it an abduction? If so, had Jason Ravensworth known this and did it have anything to do with his murder?

Elspeth asked the technician to find the tapes of the stairwell and the back door. A non-descript car with a driver in a baseball cap was waiting by the door and all four figures got into it, one at the front and the other three at the back. They sped away.

Elspeth wondered where the responsibility lay now. Certainly she would have to track down Jason's murderer but she felt the defection, if it was that, was beyond her purview. Yet what if the two events were connected? She could not positively say that the wrapped figures were the Chinese and that their liberators or perhaps captors were American. The number plate on the car was British Columbian although Elspeth could not read the letters and the numbers clearly. And why had the alarm at the back door not sounded and alerted the night security person? The alarm must have been disconnected but by whom? Was someone on the hotel staff involved?

Elspeth asked to see the tapes of the public rooms from eight o'clock the evening before onwards. She could find little of importance. She asked the technician to keep the tapes, rather than deleting them within the usual twenty-four hours, which was Kennington hotel policy.

She manoeuvred her chair out of the small viewing room and made her way to Janet's office. She noted that Janet had changed clothes and Elspeth suspected she had showered as well. All Kennington managers' offices had a full bathroom. Whatever Janet had done, she still looked exhausted.

"Did you sleep at all last night?" Elspeth asked.

"Briefly on the couch," Janet said, indicating an uncomfortable-looking but artistic Art Deco sofa in the corner of the room. "I feel responsible for what happened."

Elspeth knew her word held power because she reported directly to Eric Kennington.

"Go home and get some sleep," she said. "I'll hold on here and deal with the police, if they come back. It's all part of my job. I've done it many times before." Too many times, she thought but then she was compensated extremely well to handle such things. "No arguments," she added with a smile.

Janet looked relieved. "I'll think better if I can get a few hours' real sleep. Thank you. You may use my office as your own in my absence. I'll let the staff know you'll be here before I leave. Here's my home number if you need me."

After Janet's departure, Elspeth's mobile rang. She had programmed rings and knew that Richard would be on the other end of the line.

"Where are you, Dickie my dear?," she said.

"I am just leaving for the airport for my flight to Vancouver after being up all night with an Italian delegation. They enjoyed partying but had important information I need."

"Was the late night productive?"

"Terribly, but how are you, dear love?"

Elspeth was not above lying when her job required it, but she had difficulty in keeping anything from her husband. She gave him an abbreviated tale of what had happened to her and to Jason Ravensworth, also that Charlie was in the hotel and had helped her get out of the hospital. She did not mention the Chinese, however.

At first Richard voiced his concern for her but he chuckled at the escapade in the hospital. "Charlie always was a bit of a rogue," he said "but are you all right?"

"My foot hurts a bit but it will heal," she said, and then again groaned at her unintentional pun. "I'm up and active and need to clear my name with the police. I need to find out what happened last night and who was in the room when Jason and I entered. Obviously the whole thing was planned beforehand or I would not have been gassed. The murderer must have heard me and Jason talking after dinner and knew we were coming to Jason's room."

"Elspeth, my dearest, I wish I were there to help you. I know you can cope, but know I love you and regret you are in pain. Take good care of yourself. And keep me posted as much as you can. Ring me if you need any help that I can give from here. I'm just about to board now."

"Have a safe trip. I wish we were at home together," she said. She thought of the pleasure of being with him. The joy of their marriage, the second for them both, had not worn off.

*

Charlie woke with a start and for a moment forgot where he was. Then his hand ran over the fine Egyptian cotton sheet and his eyes focused on the heavy damask curtains that he had drawn across the windows the night before after he had returned with Elspeth from the hospital. Now what? he thought.

Jason's murder had changed things. Charlie's main

source was dead and he only had an inkling of why and what Jason's secret had been. Now his cousin was lying downstairs, incapacitated. If he wanted to pursue the story, one she would approve for publication, he would have to do his own surveillance. Where should he start? Breakfast first. He wondered if the Kennington hotels served breakfast at eleven, and then grinned at his naïveté. Of course they did, in his room or downstairs, his choice. He could get used to this luxury. Had Elspeth become inured to it? No one could.

After showering and dressing, he rang Elspeth's room but got no answer. He left a cryptic message for her, wishing her well and asking her to call. Next he called room service and ordered a sumptuous breakfast. So much for his budget. Perhaps in the end Elspeth might help him get a discount.

By noon, he was ready for action and made his way downstairs. He inquired at the reception desk if Elspeth had come down already, although he doubted she had.

"Shall I tell her you are looking for her?" one of the women behind the desk asked.

"Please. I'm Charlie Shaw, her cousin."

"Yes, of course, Mr Baillie Shaw," she said, using his full surname. Kennington hotel staff members were obviously well informed about their current guests.

Is there a quiet room near here where I can wait for her?" Charlie asked.

"No one is in the writing room right now. Perhaps you would like to wait in there."

Elspeth appeared in five minutes, wheeling herself into the room and shutting the door.

"Good morning, Charlie, or should I say afternoon."

"Aunt Elspeth," he acknowledged with a melodramatic

bow. "You are looking well, far better than the last time I saw you."

"Richard says you are a bit of a rogue but I am appreciative of your rescue last night. Are you willing to help me again today?"

"Do I have an exclusive?"

"Only if I approve it before you send it to your editors. But I need you to provide legs and eyes for me. This infernal chair makes getting about inconspicuously impossible."

"I'm in," Charlie responded. "What's the plan?"

"First tell me truthfully what brought you here to Victoria. Certainly it was not a dull conference on whaling."

Charlie looked at his cousin. Even sitting in a wheelchair, she carried herself with undeniable dignity but he always felt that inside she was laughing at herself.

"Well?" she said, cocking her head. "Surely you didn't convince your editors to foot the bill at a Kennington hotel for a rehash of the whaling issue."

"I'll come clean. Jason told me that an event of international significance was to take place here."

"Did he tell you anything more?"

"He said it had to do with the Chinese and they would not be happy."

She looked at him under raised eyebrows. "They? The Chinese delegation, the Chinese government or the Chinese generally? What's going on?"

"Both the Canadians and Americans were to be involved somehow. He said if I came here, he'd make sure I was the first to know. He suggested that when I was here I should stay alert to the Chinese delegation."

"Did you?" Elspeth asked.

"When I was running around yesterday afternoon after the wives, I also got on my computer to see who the Chinese delegation members were. We have our sources at the paper that go a bit beyond what most people could find on the internet. Both of the two Chinese delegates were rather more highly placed in the government of the Peoples' Republic than their titles here would suggest."

"And what were their positions?"

"Chao Kai was a deputy foreign minister for North American affairs and Chin Mei-su, his wife, is high up in the Public Security Bureau."

"Not particularly known for their interest in whaling, I presume," Elspeth said dryly. "I didn't know they were married. Charlie, do you have any contacts within the Canadian government?"

"Jason but unfortunately no longer."

"Any of his colleagues?"

"Not closely. Jason and I were friends. The others kept their distance because they knew I represented the press." Charlie thought for a minute. "Wait," he said, "I think I have a local source."

"Who?"

"Michelle."

"Not the protestor?"

"The same. Her father's a policeman. He's rather strict about her curfew."

"What sort of policeman, a police constable or inspector?"

"More like a chief superintendent."

"Do you think he might be approachable?"

"Michelle says he is a difficult father but I could ask her." Charlie was unsure if he wanted to but he also wanted to assisted Elspeth in any way he could.

"Charlie, what happened last night when you went to interview the protestors?" Elspeth asked.

Charlie told her, leaving out the more intimate details. Elspeth listened but Charlie could tell that she was scheming at the same time. He was beginning to understand the conference was more complex than he first had assumed. It obviously wasn't just rich meals, luxuriant rooms and the rehash of known positions.

After a moment she said, "Let's leave the chief superintendent out of things until we need him but I think you should continue to cultivate Michelle. We may need her father sooner or later. In the meantime, I have to face the police who were here at the hotel and establish my innocence. By now they must think that I have done a bunk. I need to set them straight and get them on my side. I just wish I remembered more of what happened in Jason's room last night and how I got hurt. I understand the room was torn up and therefore I must have been in the murderer's way. Jason must have fought for his life. I need the details. Charlie, will you stay with me when the police come? I'll introduce you as someone who is assisting me. I won't tell them you are from the press or that we're related."

Hoping that Janet Church had gone home to sleep, Elspeth picked up the house phone and called for the assistant manager, who was covering in Janet's absence. He came scurrying, obviously trying to impress the top staff member from the London office.

"Ms Duff, I'm at your service. My name is Ron Dillard."

"Ron, I need to talk to the police about last night. Have they been here this morning?"

"Janet has kept them at bay but I have Detective Inspector Clough's mobile number. We've followed policy guidelines about police presence in the hotel."

"Good," Elspeth said. Charlie watched her take command, which she did with natural ease. She must have done this many times before. Ron Dillard bowed to her authority. Seamlessly done, Charlie thought.

"Get Inspector Clough into the back rooms but make sure he doesn't come in the front door. I'll use Janet's office. Mr Baillie Shaw is assisting me on the case and will come with me." Elspeth's calm demeanour seemed to pacify the assistant manager.

While waiting for the inspector, Elspeth and Charlie went back into the private rooms of the hotel and into Janet's office. Elspeth ordered coffee for four but told room service only to provide minimal biscuits to go with it. The police were not to be treated as guests.

They waited for twenty minutes. Elspeth chatted about the family at Tay Farm but did not seem to hear his replies. Finally she came to the point.

"Charlie, normally I would be doing everything in my power to diffuse this situation and probably would be trying to find out who murdered Jason in order to clear the other guests. Most of the murders in the hotels that I have handled in the past, however, were not as physically violent as this one and I seldom have been suspected of duplicity before.

I'll have to ask your discretion, which I know for a journalist, is sometimes difficult. But your paper is a conservative one and more concerned with the world of business than sensationalism. Can you treat in confidence things that seem to have some bearing on Jason's murder, but which for the moment must stay under wraps?"

Charlie wondered what Elspeth could have learned between the time of her return from the hospital and their meeting after his breakfast. He already had put himself out on a limb with his editors, and could keep things quiet only so long at peril for his job.

"For the moment or always?" he asked.

"That depends on how things break. I wish it were different for you but you'll have to understand. Otherwise, I can't tell you what I know, despite my needing your help."

Charlie considered and then said, "Count me in. You can help me square with my editors."

"Last night the Chinese delegation was spirited out of the hotel, we think by a US agent who was posing as an assistant delegate to the whaling conference. Our security tapes confirm this. We have no idea why. Hopefully it was a defection and not an abduction. From what you have implied Jason Ravensworth may have known about this. In fact, it may have been the reason for his murder. My problem is that I have seen the security tapes of the incident but I can't prove anything beyond the fact that the delegates were shunted into a car at four in the morning. Either way, the Americans, and perhaps the Canadians, aren't talking. I can't afford to have this leaked to the press because I don't want the hotels to seem to be implicated. I have a call into

London but until I hear from them, I'm on my own. Lord Kennington will expect me to take charge."

A tap came at the door and Ron Dillard came in with a man whom Ron introduced as the detective inspector. A woman who called herself Detective Constable Mills accompanied him. Charlie hoped she was not a friend of the police constable he had duped the night before at the hospital. DI Clough did not look amused.

"Are you aware that you were in police custody last night, Ms Duff?"

Charlie watched Elspeth smile a beguiling smile. "I'm afraid I remember very little. I was heavily sedated. I hope I haven't caused a problem."

"You have," the inspector said uncharitably.

"Was I read my rights? Sorry, I just don't recall that I was. But I'm here now and I hope we can talk. Did Mr Dillard explain my position with the Kennington hotels?"

"He said you were from London."

Elspeth raised her head and looked the inspector in the eye. "I am a special security advisor to the hotel chain and report to Lord Kennington himself. My job is to make sure any infraction of the peace in the hotels is immediately quashed. We have a highly respected reputation to keep and no guest should question their security or comfort at any of the hotels. Inspector, I have as much need to find out what happened in Mr Ravensworth's room as you do. My injury is of little importance; finding the killer is of paramount concern to me."

Charlie wanted to chuckle at Elspeth's imperiousness underlying her clipped received pronunciation. He could see the inspector writhe at it but he was not completely cowed.

"Ms Duff, I must remind you that you are the chief suspect. When we came to the room, we saw that a fierce fight had taken place. You were injured and unconscious; Mr Ravensworth was dead. What else could we assume happened other than that the two of you had brawled."

Charlie expected Elspeth to say 'I never brawl' but she didn't.

"Of course that would be anyone's first conclusion. That is was not the case. Rest assured I want to cooperate fully with the police. I have as much stake in solving this case as you do. If you want to verify my credentials you can call Detective Superintendent Tony Ketcham at Scotland Yard. He is a friend and former colleague. I once worked for the Metropolitan Police."

Charlie did not know this and was as impressed as Inspector Clough seemed to be. Charlie's opinion of Elspeth rose even further.

"Let's cooperate," Elspeth said in a much more friendly manner. "Since I'm incapacitated, I have asked Mr Baillie Shaw to assist me. I know he is reliable and he will act as my legs as long as I'm in this chair. You can trust him. He has given me his word that nothing we say here will go beyond this room."

The inspector seemed convinced. Charlie let out a silent sigh of relief.

"Inspector, can you tell me what you found out last evening in Mr Ravensworth's room? Will you and your constable have some coffee first?"

9

Elspeth hated using her assumed façade of snobbery with the police but often it helped her cut out any doubt about her position in the Kennington Organisation. Detective Inspector Clough seemed sceptical of her words. He picked up his mobile and rang his headquarters, asking to confirm with Tony Ketcham Elspeth's former position with the Met. Elspeth knew Tony worked all hours supervising an anti-terrorism division in London and would be available. Only fifteen minutes passed before Elspeth's identity was established. The four of them in Janet's office sat and sipped coffee and nibbled at the skimpy supply of biscuits Elspeth had requested. The two members of the police looked doubtfully at Elspeth and Charlie. Their expressions changed when Tony Ketcham's reply was relayed to DI Clough. Elspeth tried not to feel smug.

"Now, inspector, can you tell me what you found in Jason Ravensworth's room. I only have vague recollections that it was rather torn up."

"Did you and the victim fight?" he asked.

"Fight? No, of course not." Elspeth was annoyed by his suggestion. He still seemed to believe she was a suspect.

"Then how can you explain your injury?"

"I can't. All I remember was that someone put a cloth of some sort over my face. The smell was sickly sweet, like something you would smell in a surgery. I woke up in the entryway of the room. I've no idea how much time passed or what happened in the interim. From the looks of the room, even at a cursory glance, there must have been a dreadful fight."

"Did you see anyone in the room before you, er, passed out?"

It seemed he still did not believe her.

"No one" Elspeth said. She needed to be asking the questions and tried to think how to turn the tables. "You must by now have some leads."

"You're our main suspect," he said.

"I want to assist you in every way possible," she retorted, "but I can't do so if you take me into custody. I hope we can develop a partnership in solving this crime as quickly as possible. We don't like violent crime to happen in our hotels. I can't help you if I don't know what you found in Jason Ravensworth's room."

"If you wish, Detective Constable Mills can go with you up there after our interview and you can see for yourself. Nothing has been disturbed except for the removal of Mr Ravensworth's body, which is in our morgue. The autopsy is scheduled for tomorrow."

"The instrument of death must have been the skewer. You don't need to ask. Janet Church told me about it."

"Ms Duff, we need your fingerprints. Detective Constable Mills has a kit in her bag."

Elspeth had had her fingerprints taken several times before but this time the process felt like an intrusion. DI Clough's tone of voice did nothing to alleviate Elspeth's sense that he was not going to look any further for a suspect. She stretched out her hands and subjected herself to the ordeal. She knew she had nothing to fear. In the past her prints had been recorded with an inkpad. Now they were entered on an electronic device and sent to the PC's handheld computer. The electronic method did not mitigate the indignity of the procedure.

"You can verify these with both Scotland Yard and the Kennington Organisation," Elspeth said when PC Mills was done. "I'll clear your query with our London office. Here's their email." She scribbled out a secure email address. "Use code XYZ space Police space Visitor. It's case and space sensitive," she added.

Although it was late at night in London, confirmation came back immediately from the Kennington Organisation's security office.

"I'll have to trust you for the moment but I want PC Mills to stay with you for the rest of the day," DI Clough said.

"Am I under house arrest?" Elspeth asked. "Don't you need to read me a warning?"

"Let's just say you are under observation. After your disappearance from the hospital last night, we don't want you vanishing today. And, PC Mills, don't be talked into going for a cup of coffee. Call me if you need relief."

Elspeth did not dare ask what disciplinary action had been taken against the policewoman in the hospital.

After the inspector left, Charlie helped push Elspeth's chair to the service lift and upstairs towards the room that had last been Jason Ravensworth's. PC Mills went with them. During the ride up, Elspeth plotted how she could get Charlie alone or at least speak to him out of the policewoman's hearing. Better yet, she could speak to him referencing things he would understand but PC Mills could not. She thought hard.

Cheerfully she said, "Charlie, do you remember the time we were in Washington, DC, when we met a woman named Katherine. When she heard we were Scottish, she said she had a friend who remodelled a croft. When we explained that it was not how we lived in Scotland, she looked at us as if we were from Japan or Korea or even Siberia. I remember your quizzing her about it."

*

For a moment Charlie wondered why Elspeth was talking such nonsense. He and Elspeth had never been in Washington, DC together. Still he recognised something strange in her voice. Was she sending him a signal?

"I remember vaguely," he said, hoping his reply would tell her that he did not completely understand her meaning.

"You must remember it. Think," Elspeth said.

PC Mills was walking behind them and seemed to have lost interest in what Elspeth was saying.

Think. Charlie thought of the words, not the sentences. Washington—Katherine—Croft—Japan—Korea—Siberia—quizzing. Yes, he got it. Elspeth wanted him to question Katherine Croft of the US delegation about the members of the Japanese, Korean and Russian delegations or perhaps talk to them directly. Elspeth could not do this while PC Mills hovered over her but Charlie was free to do so at any time. He was not a suspect.

"I remember," Charlie said. "I'd love to talk to that woman again. She did know a great deal for an American, although her concept of the East Asian countries was odd."

He came around in front of her and straightened the rug over her legs and winked. He watched Elspeth's body relax.

Elspeth had a passkey in her pocket and awkwardly fished it out. She handed it to PC Mills, who was obviously not sure how to use it. Charlie stepped forward gallantly and helped her. PC Mills smiled faintly at him and then stiffened her face, as if remembering she were on duty. Charlie wondered if he could charm her if needed but she might not be as malleable as the policewoman in the hospital. He decided to wait.

They entered the room, Elspeth going first because her chair needed to be wheeled in front of the others. She asked Charlie to stop in the entry hall.

"This is where I was attacked and where I woke up after I was hurt," Elspeth said addressing the policewoman. "Let me tell you what I remember."

Charlie looked up and saw PC Mills rummaging in her pockets. She drew a small hardbound notepad and a biro from it.

Charlie started to push the chair farther into the room but Elspeth stopped him.

"I want PC Mills to see things from my point of view and she can ask me questions later. Jason Ravensworth let me come into the room ahead of him. When I reached here, someone clapped a cloth over my face. Whoever it was possibly planned to use the cloth on Jason. My suspicion is that once the murderer realised his mistake, and not having a second cloth, he attacked Jason. Jason was a tall man and would have fought back, which makes me think the murderer was a man. A strong woman might have engaged him, but I doubt it."

Charlie wondered if Elspeth was putting suggestions into the policewoman's mind or if she truly believed what she was saying. Certainly Elspeth sounded as if she had enough experience in criminal matters that she believed her suppositions to be true. PC Mills was scribbling as Elspeth spoke. Elspeth clearly had the upper hand.

"It may have been that the attacker wanted to avoid a counterattack if I woke up and therefore he crushed my foot in the struggle. Or he may have done so after he subdued Jason and killed him. I'll be interested to hear what the postmortem says about the damages that were inflicted on Jason. Jason must have been unconscious or even dead when the murderer inserted the skewer into his brain."

PC Mills turned a page in her notebook and continued writing.

Elspeth continued. "You are probably wondering about the skewer as a weapon. It's hardly one's usual way of killing a person. Last evening at dinner, the restaurant served salmon on a skewer. You may check that but Mr Baillie Shaw, who dined with me, and I both ate it and others may have as well. The selection of the murder weapon must have been spontaneous but the use of the chloroform, if that is what it was, could not have been. It's hardly something you would find supplied to guests by the Kennington hotels, although the skewers were readily available."

Charlie expected PC Mills to say "yes, ma'am", which she did not do. The age difference between Elspeth and PC Mills, however, gave Elspeth the edge.

"Charlie, you might take a quick look around and see if you can see anything to help the police. Then, if you need to leave, please feel free to go. I can manage."

Elspeth had given him his leave, and, cryptically, his assignment. He left shortly afterwards.

*

Elspeth knew Charlie had picked up her signal and was relieved he could be of assistance while she diverted the police constable. She wished she could be with him when he questioned Katherine Croft and the others but he was an experienced journalist and knew how to draw information from his sources. She hoped he would ask the right questions.

She wheeled her chair farther into the room and surveyed the damage. She shuddered when she looked at the bed, remembering the last time she had. Jason's body had been sprawled across it in death. From her position on the floor, she had not seen the skewer thrust up his nose or that he was dead, only that he did not move as she had made her way painfully to the telephone and dialled 7-7-7. Now she took her time to look at the room and speculate about what had happened there. She had no idea if her ideas, so carefully recorded by the policewoman, were true or not. She wanted only to divert the police's attention from her.

The room was as she remembered. The furniture was strewn chaotically across the floor. One lamp was broken, the others tipped over. One side table at the bed was on its side, and one delicate chair had two legs broken off. The cushions on the sofa were in disarray and the duvet lay messily at the bottom of the large bed. The telephone

Elspeth had used was still lying on the floor, handset off. The fight must have been a fierce one.

Elspeth could see the policewoman looking at the damage.

"They've already taken pictures," Elspeth said. "I heard the detective inspector say so."

PC Mills nodded.

"May I get the maid to clean up the mess?" Elspeth asked.

"Would anyone want to stay here after this? I wouldn't," was the policewoman's reply.

"The management will make sure the room is completely refurbished before they give it to anyone. Of course, there will be no indication left of what went on here. Some people, particularly those from various cultures and religions, are affected by death differently. We've never had a problem."

"You've been involved in a murder in one of your hotels before?" the young PC asked. She swallowed hard.

"Unfortunately several. My job is to see that the culprit is found as soon as possible and that the crime not be leaked to the press. The latter is the hardest part. You would be amazed how many policemen are willing to let the media know about a juicy murder. You can understand, I think, that the Kennington hotels don't like the publicity." Elspeth hoped that by tacitly criticising police forces other than the Royal Canadian Mounted Police, the constable would think twice about letting the press know what had happened in the Kennington Victoria. Elspeth thought PC Mills had more to fear from Inspector Clough than from her.

"Is this your first murder?" Elspeth asked. She tried to sound motherly.

The policewoman nodded. "I've just joined the serious crimes squad. It's what I always have wanted to do."

"It's not always pleasant," Elspeth said.

"I'm beginning to understand," PC Mills replied.

While they were chatting Elspeth was making a visual reconnaissance of the room. She checked the doors. Other than the door leading to the hallway, there was a connecting door leading into the room next door. Elspeth tried to remember who was in that room. She needed to confirm with Janet Church that it was the Korean couple. Connecting doors always had a door at each side of the wall with a sound deadening space between them. The curtains were drawn across the windows. The room attendant had undoubtedly done so when she came into the room to straighten up for the evening, turn down the bed and ready the room for the night. The chocolates that usually lay on the pillow, chocolate made especially for the Kennington hotels in Belgium, now lay on the carpet and had been stepped on. Elspeth wheeled herself to the bathroom, which was orderly. The tape was still across the toilet and fresh towels laid out, all to Kennington hotel standards. Nothing there had been disturbed.

Elspeth moved back into the bedroom to the place where she had fallen. She looked carefully for any sign of the attack on her. She could see nothing.

"May I have a copy of the photographs?" Elspeth asked.

PC Mills looked disconcerted. "You'll have to ask the inspector."

"I'll do that," Elspeth said, thinking she had little chance of the inspector complying with her request. If she could get Janet Church alone, Elspeth would ask her to send a photographer to record the state of the room before it was made up for the next guest.

Elspeth went around the room one more time. Unlike fictional detectives, she did not find an all-important item that would later help her crack the case. She would have to use other devices, such as the CCTV tapes. If she could shake off PC Mills, she would ask the security department to brings the tapes to her room. She could put them on her laptop and review them again. Elspeth's mind was working furiously but no brilliant solutions came to it.

"I'd like to go back to my room," she told PC Mills. "I can wheel myself but I suppose you need to come along."

PC Mills assented. "I'm afraid we will be companions for the rest of the day, until I am off my shift."

"What time is that?"

"Six this evening."

Four more hours of precious time, Elspeth thought. She wondered what was going on downstairs at the conference and how Charlie was getting on.

10

Charlie went to his room to get his pocket recorder. He slipped it in the breast pocket of his jacket and was thankful that modern technology allowed the device to be small but the indiscernible microphone powerful. At times he had been able to pick up conversations in the background that allowed him to hear things that were meant to be private. A sound technician at his paper had installed software on Charlie's laptop that allowed him to isolate each conversation recorded. Several times in the past the *sotto voce* conversations had proven more valuable than the words of his interviewee.

He wished that Elspeth could have given him more specific instructions. He would have to improvise. He would assume the position as Elspeth's deputy but not mention his press credentials. He thought that was her intent.

When he arrived at the conference centre, Ron Dillard was supervising the setup of the afternoon coffee and tea service. The doors to the conference room were closed, which made Charlie speculate that the conference was still going on despite the absence of Jason Ravensworth, John C. Smith and the two Chinese delegates. If Elspeth was right that the conference was a front for the defection/abduction of the Chinese, what things were the other delegates discussing? He knew if he tried to slip into the room he would be noticed. Elspeth had indicated that he should talk to Katherine Croft, or so he assumed.

"What time do they break?" he asked Ron.

"I'm not entirely sure. They started this session late. The agenda says the break is at half past three but I can't verify that."

Armed with this knowledge, Charlie decided to make an entrance. If he created a furore, so be it. He cracked the door and all heads turned. The Japanese delegate, who was at the podium, stopped and said, "Who are you?" No politeness or finesse filled his words, just annoyance.

Charlie raised his head defiantly. In his job he was used to confronting arrogance. "Charles Baillie Shaw," he said. "I'm here at the behest of Elspeth Duff, who is incapacitated as a result of an injury. She has asked me to fill in for her. Please proceed."

Charlie saw an empty chair at the side of the room and made his way to it. He sat down and waited. The Japanese resumed his speech. The other delegates turned back to the speaker, although first several whispered to each other. Charlie breathed a quiet sigh of relief. He was in and accepted.

The speaker went on for another twenty minutes. Charlie watched. He noticed that only one person was at the desk for the Chinese delegation and that a smart, sexy young woman sat at the Canadian table along with an Inuit. The woman looked tense. She kept drumming the end of her pencil on the desk silently but impatiently. Charlie put her on the mental list of people to interview, thinking it would be a pleasure. He had been Jason's friend and would have an obvious reason to speak to her. Perhaps they could have drinks later. Then he remembered he had promised Michelle to meet her for an early dinner. Plans might have to change. He sighed. Business before pleasure.

He turned his attention to the American delegation and made eye contact with Katherine Croft. She smiled at him and he smiled back. Was it an invitation to talk? He hoped so. Her remaining aide leaned over and spoke to her at one point. The American Inuit was enjoying an afternoon nap, his head resting on his broad chest.

Katherine rose when the Japanese delegate finished.

"Ladies and gentlemen," she said. "Despite the unfortunate happenings of last night, I feel we have been able to make our positions here at the conference clear. We have one more session after the coffee break. I hope during that each country's chief delegate will give a ten-minute summary of their position that can be included in the final report. In the meantime, let's recess for fifteen minutes."

She rose as if what had happened the night before was only a minor interruption. She came over to where Charlie was sitting.

"Mr Baillie Shaw," she said. "How sad it all is. I felt I had to carry on because our sponsor needs to have value for money, particularly considering the cost of staying here. I intend to have my aide generate the final paper. We at the State Department are always cognisant of how much private foundations do to help us."

She spoke with such coolness that Charlie wondered if she felt anything at all about Jason's death or wondered about what had happened to the Chinese. Did she know the truth and was she trying to cover it? Diplomacy was sometimes duplicitous. Was it in this case? Or was Katherine Croft immune to intense feelings?

"May we talk?" Charlie asked. "Ms Duff asked me particularly to ask you to help her. As you may suspect her main concern is the wellbeing of the guests. Since Jason's death and her own injury . . ."

"Injury?" Katherine asked. "That's the second time you have mentioned it." She looked so concerned that Charlie thought her emotion was real.

"She was injured at the same time Jason was killed," Charlie said, hoping her was not revealing something that was not common knowledge to the conference attendees. "Her foot was damaged. We think it was done purposely by the murderer so that she would not interfere with his foul play."

"Did she see the murderer?" Katherine asked.

"No, unfortunately but she wants the murderer caught as quickly as possible, and wants to make sure the press does not get involved."

"That's where I know your name," Katherine said. She named his newspaper. "Don't you write on the United Nations?"

Charlie admitted that he did.

"Then you are press, not a representative of Ms Duff. Very clever, young man."

Charlie blushed. "I'm not here as a journalist. Truthfully. Elspeth Duff is my cousin and she has asked me to help. She's also made me promise not to publish anything about this last two days unless she approves it."

"I think you will need me to be added to that approval list. What has happened here is highly sensitive, particularly to the American and Canadian governments."

"Jason Ravensworth was a close friend. I don't want his name sullied by the media, even if I am a member of it."

Neither he nor Katherine had spoken of the Chinese delegation. Charlie wanted to find out more about them but judged that from Katherine Croft's reticence, she was either evading or purposely excluding the subject.

"May we speak in private?" Charlie asked. He was beginning to feel the pressure of time. The final session of the conference would begin in a few minutes. Charlie had no idea where individual delegates would go after the final speeches had been made. He speculated they might remain for the night and enjoy the last fruits of staying in a Kennington hotel, but also might leave quickly, particularly in light of Jason's murder.

"I need to use the ladies' room. See if you can get a quiet room while I'm gone," Katherine said and left him.

Charlie spoke to Ron Dillard, who nodded to a door opposite the doors into the conference space. "We use the room for set up," he said, "but there are a couple of extra chairs in there. Will that do?"

"It will have to," Charlie responded.

Ron unlocked the door and by the time Katherine reappeared, Charlie had set up two of the chairs and had Ron bring in two cups of coffee, cream and sugar. He also had appropriated a plate of biscuits from the buffet. The room had none of the panache of the front rooms in the hotel, but its privacy was overriding. Katherine smiled at his resourcefulness.

"I've been in worse places," she said and added "behind the Iron Curtain, when I was a junior officer. I assume there are no bugs here."

Charlie had not seen this light side of Katherine Croft before and hoped she was relaxing with him. But she quickly became serious.

"Charlie, the things that have gone on here in the hotel are far more serious than just the murder of Jason Ravensworth. Much of what happened last night was top secret and I cannot discuss it with you. It's unfortunate that Jason was killed but my colleagues and I think his murder had nothing to do with the other matters. Therefore I hope Ms Duff and you will confine your investigation to the murder only. I can't say more. I have asked that a member of our security force at State come out here to Victoria. He will be the one Ms Duff and you need to talk to and work with in solving the murder. I expect him at any time. In the meantime, I want the conference to wrap up smoothly. I hope you will respect my request to let the matter of the Chinese drop. Ms Duff and you are treading in deep waters. I don't want to see your going where you should not. I have read many of your articles and respect what you write. If your writing reflects your character, I believe I can trust you. I don't want to bring down the powers that be on either one of you."

She did not explain 'the powers that be' but the tone of her voice made Charlie believe she was speaking truthfully and that the threat was real.

"You have my word. I'll tell Elspeth as well," he responded. Inwardly he groaned. So much for his exclusive. "If I ever publish, I'll make sure my article is vetted by you as well as Elspeth. As you know my paper doesn't indulge in sensationalism."

"I know," she said. "I must get back to the others. Thanks for the coffee and cookies."

When she opened the door, Charlie saw that she had partaken of neither. He had seen the tough side of her, and felt she would follow through if he or Elspeth stepped over the line she had just drawn. Charlie wanted to talk to Elspeth but she was upstairs with her watchdog. Charlie could think of no way to encode what Katherine Croft had just said to him. Could he write it down and slip it to her? Then he had a better idea. He would find Janet Church and have her create a diversion. He must quickly think of one.

After the delegates returned to the conference room, Charlie went upstairs and asked the concierge if Janet was in her office. A voice behind him said, "Mr Baillie Shaw, I'm right here. I've just come in. Where's your cousin?"

He wanted to say 'incarcerated upstairs' but in such a public space he dared not.

"Come to my office," she said and led him there.

"I need to speak to Elspeth privately but she is being watched by the police," he explained. "Will you help me get a private word with her? Would you go upstairs with me, and engage the female pit bull for a few moments while I talk to Elspeth?"

"Better yet," Janet said. "I'll call the room and tell the police officer that Inspector Clough wishes to speak to her in person. Then I'll call the inspector and reverse the message. That way he will arrive here and she will come down to see him. That will give you five to ten minutes. Can you say all you need in that time?"

"If I have to," he responded. "Thanks for the help."

"Comfort and Service," she said and grinned.

Charlie went upstairs and waited in an alcove beyond Elspeth's room. He checked his watch. Fifteen minutes passed before PC Mills came out of the room.

She called back to Elspeth, "Don't go anywhere. I'll be right back."

Charlie could not hear Elspeth's reply.

He knocked softly on Elspeth's door once the policewoman was out of sight.

*

Even after almost two hours of trying to soften up PC Mills, Elspeth was amazed that the constable now trusted her enough to leave her alone. Where was Charlie now?

The knock came at the door and, with relief, she found him at her door.

Charlie poured out his news.

"Katherine Croft is serious," he said. "I think if we try to find out more about the Chinese, we will be in hot water."

Elspeth had been threatened before and did not accept the finality of Katherine's words. She knew even the most guarded secrets could be broken into if one knew the right people. Tony Ketcham had already vouched for her and she would use that connection if needed. She did not forget her husband, who was high up in the British Foreign and Commonwealth Office and the European Commission. Granted they both worked across the pond but information flowed between the Canadian and US governments and those in London and Brussels. Although she might not have personal channels to higher ups in both North American governments, people close to her did. Besides, Charlie must have contacts he had not yet considered using.

"All is not lost," she said, "but we have to be clever about it. Katherine might be right, however, in saying that Jason's murder is separate from the disappearance of the two Chinese. Let me get on my mobile while PC Mills is gone. Later both you and I should go to the bar and dining room and talk to as many people as we can, although I may be restricted by the police presence. This may be our last chance. If Detective Inspector Clough is here, I want to see him. Hustle downstairs and see if you can arrange for him to come up before you go back to the conference. I will sit here docilely. Then go downstairs and find out which delegates will be in attendance tonight. I want to speak to as many of them as possible, and get their reaction to the murder."

Elspeth had no intention of sitting calmly and waiting for the inspector. After Charlie left, she picked up her mobile. Her first call was to her husband. She wondered about his progress to Vancouver but her situation was sufficiently dire that she risked finding him in a public space.

He responded readily.

"Hello, my dearest. You sound like you you're on the ground," she said.

"I am. I just arrived and after the long flight need a nap."

"I wish I were there and in bed with you rather than stuck here in Victoria." She grinned as she said this. "Can you meet me in Victoria tomorrow? I thought you might have a few days off before your speech. You said you wanted to help anyway."

A long silence followed. "Elspeth, what are you up to?"

She laughed. "Skulduggery as usual but I need you. I'm

rather in a jam. Charlie's here but there is only so much he can do. Can you be here by tomorrow morning?"

He did not reply at first and Elspeth feared a negative answer. Finally he said, "I'll tell my hosts that something has occurred that will take the next two days."

"I'll have someone meet you at your hotel and take you across to Vancouver Island on the ferry. There's a cheeky young man who brought me here. I think I'll hire him for the weekend. He'll be at your hotel waiting for you when you're free."

Elspeth arranged the details with Spike quickly, and was about to make her next call, when someone banged on her door. The knock was impatient and the face of DI Clough was stormy after Elspeth called for the person to come in. Elspeth smiled sweetly at him and at PC Mills. She stood directly behind the inspector and looked chastised.

"Ms Duff, did you arrange to get my constable out of the way? I don't like such trickery!"

Elspeth thought quickly. Fortunately she had tucked her mobile under the blanket that covered her outstretched leg. "Trickery? I'm afraid I don't know what you mean. PC Mills asked me to stay here for a few moments and I've done so."

"Ms Duff, you are now definitely my main suspect. Your fingerprints were found on the murder weapon. Therefore I must warn you officially." He recited words that mimicked warnings around the English-speaking world.

Damn, thought Elspeth. She must devise some way to avoid going to gaol.

"I assume then I am no long just under observation but

under house arrest," she said. "I hope I can stay here, considering the state of my foot and that I have to use this chair to get about. Doesn't PC Mills have a handheld device that can video tape our conversation?"

Her request was a long shot, but it paid off, at least for the moment. PC Mills looked eager to reprieve herself.

Detective Inspector Clough frowned.

"This is highly irregular, but considering modern technology, I will allow it. PC Mills, will you set up the room," he commanded. When she was done, Elspeth's interview began after he stated the time and place of the interview and the participants.

"State your full name and address."

"Elspeth Fiona Duff." She gave the address care of the Kennington Organisation in London. He demanded her residential address and she gave him the location of her flat in Kensington.

"How long have you been in Canada?"

"I arrived two days ago," she said. It seemed a great deal longer than that.

"And the purpose of your visit?"

She explained the nature of her job with the Kennington Organisation.

"Did you know the deceased?"

"I met him the day I arrived. I didn't know him before that."

"What was your relationship with him?"

"He was a member of the conference that I was here to monitor. We met at the reception the night before the conference opened. He recognised me as he had seen me at a diplomatic reception in London. I didn't remember meeting him at the time but he knew my husband who is in the British diplomatic corps."

"Who is your husband?"

Elspeth considered her answer carefully. Should she use Richard's title? She could not judge how this would affect the inspector. Since Richard was in Canada, she decided to be precise.

"Sir Richard Munro. He is a senior member of the Foreign and Commonwealth Office in London and is currently on assignment to the European Commission in Brussels. He and I occasionally attend diplomatic receptions both in London and Brussels. Mr Ravensworth said he had met me in London but I don't remember the event." She did not add that she hated her role as Richard's wife and always withdrew as much as possible at these parties.

"When you met the victim at the reception here, did you interact at any length with him?"

"He introduced me to a number of the delegates and made small talk with them and with me, nothing more."

"Did you have any social interaction with the victim after the opening reception?"

"We had breakfast together the next morning."

"Why?"

"Why? I don't understand, inspector. I saw Mr Ravensworth sitting alone when I came in the dining room. I knew he was chair of the conference and thought it best I get to know him and explain to him my role at the hotel."

"Is that what you talked about at breakfast?

"Partly."

"And the other part?"

"I can't see why it's important," Elspeth said.

"We are trying to establish your relationship with the victim."

"I hardly knew him."

"Let's go back. What were the other things you discussed?"

Elspeth considered how she wanted to introduce Charlie. She stalled. "Chit chat, nothing more."

"Did anyone else join you at breakfast who can confirm that you were on amiable terms with the victim?"

"Mr Baillie Shaw joined us," Elspeth admitted. "He is, was, a friend of Mr Ravensworth from New York."

Elspeth was sorry she had answered more than the inspector had asked. She opened doors when she mentioned Charlie and New York. The inspector, however, did not follow this line of inquiry. He returned to Jason.

"Did Mr Ravensworth make any personal remarks to you?"

"Personal remarks? Of what kind?"

"Did he make a pass at you, Ms Duff?"

"Heavens, no."

"Did you make a pass at him?"

"If I made a pass at any guest, I would lose my job."

"Then you didn't. Is that what you are saying?"

"Yes. No, I didn't."

"When did you see the victim next?"

"I sat in on the two morning sessions of the conference, which Mr Ravensworth was leading. We spoke briefly at the tea break. Just a word or two."

"And at lunch?"

"I was occupied otherwise at lunch, on hotel business."

"When was the next time you saw the victim?"

"We spoke briefly at the end of the last afternoon session. He asked to see me in the bar after dinner and we set an appointment for eight o'clock."

"Did you see him before that?"

"I saw him at dinner but I did not speak to him before we met in the bar at eight."

"Tell me about what happened then?"

"Can you be more specific?" Elspeth asked. She did not want to give away more information than necessary.

"What happened between the time you met in the bar and the time you went to his room?"

Panic filled Elspeth. She had, after all, taken his arm brazenly in the bar and he had kissed her in the lift. Both actions would have been recorded on the security tapes. Eventually Inspector Clough would ask for them. Elspeth's mild flirtation could be interpreted as much more. In Inspector Clough's eyes she might have been initiating a tryst and then, when confronted by Jason in his room, might have fought him off and killed him. But this did not explain the chloroform or the skewer, both of which pointed to premeditated murder. Still, if the inspector did not believe Elspeth's claim that she had been gassed, she had no proof that she was unconscious when the murder took place or that the skewer might have been hers at dinner.

She also was faced with the dilemma of the Chinese delegation. She assumed that Janet Church had not told him about this but she could not be sure. Elspeth did not want to bring up the subject but had to give some explanation of why she went to Jason's room with him. She feared an evasion would not serve.

She paused. "I wanted to talk to him about security at the conference. I was. . ." She stopped, her mind fast at work. "I wanted to make sure that some of the tensions that had arisen among the delegates did not erupt into unpleasantness. I thought if I spoke to Mr Ravensworth out of the hearing of others, I could express my concern without being overheard."

"There are small rooms off the lobby. Why didn't you use one of those? The truth is, Ms Duff, that you wanted to get Jason Ravensworth into your bed, or his, isn't it? When he rebuffed you, you struggled with him and stabbed him."

"I'm not that strong," Elspeth said in her own defence. "In any case, I was gassed."

"There was no sign of this when we examined the room. If you were gassed, how do you explain the skewer?"

"Skewered salmon was on the menu at dinner. Anyone could have taken a skewer from the dining room and then pressed my fingers on it in order to leave my prints. Were there other fingerprints on the skewer? If I had brought the skewer from my dinner with me, there would be other fingerprints on it, the cook's, the waiter's and other people's from the kitchen. Have you asked the kitchen staff?"

"I'm asking the questions," he replied in a belligerent tone. Elspeth sensed he had not thought of questioning people in the kitchen. He must have been too delighted at finding her prints on the skewer.

Elspeth felt she may have bruised his ego and therefore softened her aggressive tone.

"Inspector, why don't we work together to find the real murderer? I have been trained, as you have, in investigating this sort of crime, and have a perfect track record of finding murderers in the hotels. I know how the hotels work, the ins and outs, which may be particularly useful to your search for the real killer. If you wish PC Mills to stay with me, she could assist me as well as keeping an eye on me. I can question the members of the conference in my role as hotel security without the onus of my actions being part of a police investigation. They are all aware that the police are involved but since they already know my role here at the hotel, they may tell me things they would not tell you. I can circulate without people asking me why. Surely that would be useful." She wanted to add that this would definitely help considering the evidence of the skewer against her, but restrained herself. "If at the end of the evening you still are convinced I'm implicated in the crime, you can take further steps against me."

He seemed to be softening. "I'll take this into consideration. PC Mills, you may stop the recording." He gave the time and the constable stopped the camcorder.

Elspeth took a deep and silent breath.

"Ms Duff, I may be making an error in judgement but for the moment I'm going to trust you because of the backing you have from Scotland Yard. The evidence against you is circumstantial, although strong. I'll give you a chance this evening but I want PC Mills to be in the room with you."

"Can she be in plainclothes? I think a policewoman in uniform will be disconcerting to the guests. I can lend her something. We're about the same build."

She turned to PC Mills. "If you don't mind. I assure you all my clothes have just come from the dry cleaners. They may not be your style, but they are appropriate for the hotel." Elspeth had seen the constable's admiring eyes on her clothes before.

"I wouldn't mind," the PC said to her superior.

The inspector looked at his constable. "Keep your eyes open. I don't want Ms Duff, or is it Lady Munro, to leave the hotel unexpectedly."

Having gained his point, Elspeth promised the detective inspector that she would not.

11

Charlie had put his mobile on vibrate and stepped out of the conference room to take the call oscillating in his pocket. He could hardly hear Elspeth's voice on the other end of the line.

"Come up to my room right away. I want you to divert PC Mills. She's in the bathroom changing now, but will be out any second now." Elspeth rang off suddenly.

Charlie's mind had wandered during the closing speeches of the conference. The only piece of intelligence he had picked up was that there was to be a final dinner but that conference participants were invited to meet in the bar beforehand. He bolted for the lift and arrived at Elspeth's room just as PC Mills was emerging from the bathroom. She had let her down her hair which was luxuriantly brown and wavy. Out of her uniform and in Elspeth's clothes, classical in style, she looked alluring. His smile must have conveyed this as PC Mills blushed slightly.

"Do I look OK?" she asked as a greeting to Charlie.

He swallowed. "You look gorgeous or am I allowed to say that to a policewoman? I'm Charlie."

"I'm Claudia," she said. "My friends call me Dee. Are you here to see Ms Duff?"

He looked at Elspeth who gave him an almost imperceptible nod. He assumed this was tacit approval of his flirtation with Dee.

"I am," he said. "I've been acting as her eyes and ears since she was incapacitated." He grinned as he said this.

"You work for her, don't you?" Dee said.

Charlie knew she could check the hotel roster, so he said, "Informally. Actually I'm a guest here. Elspeth's my cousin, although I call her my aunt. I've come up to see if she would be able to join me in the bar for a drink and then go on to dinner. We would be delighted if you joined us." He turned to Elspeth, who nodded again as if telling him to keep up the good work.

Dee seemed entranced. Charlie thought there might be compensation for his having to postpone his date with Michelle.

"I've been instructed to stay with Ms Duff. If she goes into dinner, so do I," Dee said.

"Aunt Elspeth, are you ready or do you need to freshen up?" Charlie asked. From the call to him, he knew Elspeth had her mobile concealed somewhere in her chair.

"Give me a moment," Elspeth said. She wheeled herself into the bathroom, leaving Charlie and Dee alone. Charlie decided to use this to his advantage. He rambled on to cover any conversation Elspeth would have on her phone.

"She's very sharp," Charlie said. "When I was a child, I couldn't get anything past her. I used to visit her in Hollywood. Her first husband worked there in the film industry . . ." He spoke in a loud voice. Occasionally he made Dee laugh. He had her hooked. Ten minutes passed before Elspeth emerged. She had changed her clothes and was on her crutches.

"I'm trying to be up and about," she said. "But, Charlie, bring the chair just in case I need to collapse into it." Charlie wondered if Elspeth might have hidden something there.

Elspeth hobbled but made good progress. Dee went over to help her but Elspeth brushed her off. "I'm fine really. I need to be able to circulate downstairs. Charlie, we need to find the real killer. We only have tonight. Dee is going to help us. It will be a real boost for her career because this is her first big case."

Clever, Charlie thought. Dee was no longer a minder but a co-investigator. How deftly Elspeth had changed Dee's role.

The bar was teeming with people, not only from the conference but also other guests in the hotel. Charlie was surprised at seeing someone he knew from New York. He propped the wheelchair in the corner and pointed this new guest out to Elspeth.

"Come and meet him," Charlie urged.

The new guest saw Charlie and met him and the two women halfway.

"Elspeth, meet Robert Kahn. Robert, this is my cousin, Elspeth Duff, and a friend, Dee Mills. I'm sorry for your reason here." In explanation Charlie added, "Robert is, was, Jason Ravensworth's partner. I was at their wedding last year in Montreal."

*

That, thought Elspeth, was a showstopper. She was accustomed to all sorts of relationships but she had never suspected that Jason Ravensworth would be in a same-sex marriage. Although the union was legal in Canada, she had not thought that Jason was gay. Certainly he had paid attention to all the women at the conference. Hadn't Charlie mentioned that Jason had stolen a girlfriend from him? Then she remembered that Charlie had said they both had moved on. Elspeth had not supposed that Charlie meant Jason had become attracted to men. Elspeth reddened at her feelings toward him. Elspeth had no bias against homosexuals, she had them among her friends in Hollywood, but Jason's relationship to Robert Kahn disconcerted her.

She held out a friendly hand. In cases of deaths in the hotel, the management was instructed to offer free rooms to the bereaved.

"I am sorry for the reason for your stay," Elspeth said. "I work for the hotel chain and if there is anything I can do, please let me know."

"It's a relief to see Charlie," Robert said. "I'm afraid it's been a rather hard time for me. Once the police release Jason's body, I plan to take it back to town where he grew up near Halifax for burial. Did you know him?"

"Only briefly. I'm glad Charlie is here as well."

Gathering her composure, Elspeth left Charlie and Robert together. Dee Mills followed her. Elspeth had no idea where to start her questioning. She still had no idea who the killer might be. She felt restricted both by the police presence and the secrecy of the departure of the two Chinese. Was the murder strictly for personal reasons? Or did Jason know something about the defection/abduction of Chao Kai and Chin Mei-su, and therefore needed to be silenced? The former motive would mean that the killer was probably in the room now; the latter that the killer was in the car with the two Chinese. The skewer being the murder weapon implied that the murderer was at dinner the night before. John C. Smith had not been but both Jason from the Canadian delegation and Katherine Croft from the American had been there. Elspeth would start with her.

Katherine was at the bar chatting with the Korean delegate, Oh Seung. Brittany Rogers, Jason's assistant, was lingering nearby but did not appear to be part of the conversation. Who should Elspeth question first?

Katherine Croft solved the problem. "Ms Duff, Oh Seung and I would like to speak to you privately. Is there any place we can go?"

Elspeth was faced with having to admit Dee Mills' role. She tried to brush her off. "Dee, would you mind if Katherine Croft, the US delegate, Oh Seung, the Korean one, and I had a word in private? It will only take a minute. There's a small room off the lobby with only one door. You might want to wait outside."

Dee frowned at Elspeth.

"I'd rather be with you. Orders."

Katherine looked questioning.

"PC Mills is my police escort," Elspeth said. "After the attack last night," she added.

"What we have to say is only for Ms Duff's ears," Katherine said in a voice that was used to being obeyed.

Dee Mills flushed but did not give way, until Oh Seung spoke quietly to her. "It's about my husband, nothing about the problem last night. I hope you will respect my privacy. In Korea we have trouble speaking before strangers."

Elspeth saw PC Mills relent.

"I'll wait outside, although I'm not comfortable doing so," she said.

Once the three women were in the small writing room, Katherine spoke first. "Oh Seung didn't want to speak to anyone but I convinced her that the hotel would want to know about Kim Bae's disappearance.

Elspeth gulped. "Disappearance?"

"Oh Seung hasn't seen him since last night. Tell her, Seung."

The Korean woman bowed her head. "I am ashamed to bring this matter to your attention when you are trying to cope with Jason's murder and the attack on you but Katherine insists. Last night my husband and I had a disagreement."

Elspeth nodded sympathetically. She had seen the two fighting on the security tapes.

"We became very heated and finally I told him I would sleep in Katherine's room. We have known each other for many years. I was posted to Washington ten years ago and we became friends then. She has visited me and Bae in Seoul and I have visited Katherine in Washington and her family in Rhode Island many times when I was travelling through the States. Last evening at about half past eight I left our room and spent the night in Katherine's. When I went back down to our room this morning, Bae was gone. I thought he might have gone to the airport. There is a late-night flight to Seoul, but I found his passport, his laptop and his wallet with his credit cards in our room. I thought he might come back during the day, but he didn't."

"She's very upset," Katherine said, putting her arms around her friend's shoulder.

"Bae did not want to come on this trip but I promised him a few days away from the children and his job in the ministry. He came reluctantly."

"Would you be offended if I asked what you fought about?"

Oh Seung raised her head defiantly. "What else but another woman?"

"Someone at the conference?" Elspeth asked.

Seung looked down and nodded her head. "Chin Mei-su," she whispered.

Elspeth was startled. Of all women, Chin Mei-su would have been her last choice, perhaps other than Svetlana Mihailova.

"I accused him and he denied it. But I heard him talking to her. They were in the corridor outside our room. He was speaking intimately. 'Don't let Chao Kai know' she was saying. Then they heard me. When I confronted him, he said he was innocent but had promised not to break Chin Mei-su's confidence not even to me. But I didn't believe his innocence. He has, how shall I say it, strayed before. I am away from Seoul frequently, and I know he has sought comfort elsewhere. In the past I have forgiven him but he never before has done anything to interfere with my work. That was why I was so angry with him."

"You have heard nothing all day?"

"No, nothing."

Elspeth bit the corner of her lip. "I can see why you are worried. Thank you for telling me. I'll see what I can do. I think I had better re-join my policewoman, but will make discreet inquiries and let you know if I hear anything."

Elspeth opened the door and found PC Mills sitting beside it and looking decidedly unhappy.

"I'm back," Elspeth said and grinned. "That didn't take long, did it?"

But inside Elspeth's stomach knotted. Instinctively she knew that Jason's murder, the rounding up of the Chinese and Kim Bae's departure had to be connected. But how? She thought of a shell game. Three people, all missing, but only two had been bundled into the car at four in the morning by John C. Smith and his cohort. Had she been wrong in assuming the two were the Chinese couple? Had Kim Bae and Chin Mei-su been the ones in the car and Chao Kai had gone somewhere else? Or had Chin Mei-su and Kim Bae's relationship been innocent, as he said it was, and the two had been used as a decoy to put off any investigation into Chin's whereabouts? Too many possibilities existed with the addition of Kim Bae's flight, if it had been a flight, into the mix. Kim Bae may just as well have gone to another hotel. But why would he leave his wallet and passport behind?

She smiled at PC Mills as if nothing had just happened.

"Man trouble," Elspeth said lightly. "Thank heavens my husband is too stuffy to look at another woman." He was too much in love with her, Elspeth thought. He had been since he was at Oxford and had met her in Scotland during the summer break forty years before.

PC Mills shook her head and smiled back. Elspeth wondered if the young woman could understand the marital problems of older women. Younger women were more concerned about catching a man than keeping him.

*

Charlie watched Dee and Elspeth come back into the bar, Elspeth on her crutches. Charlie had known his cousin long enough to see that something was amiss. How could he get her apart to ask what? Saying he would catch up after dinner, he excused himself from Robert Kahn's company and came over to Elspeth and Dee. "Robert's in a rough way. He wants to know and help," Charlie said. "Under similar circumstances, I would too," Charlie said. He looked at Dee Mills hopefully. "I hope it's OK with the police if Elspeth talks to him."

Dee nodded. "Under my supervision," she said.

"Charlie, please get me a sherry. They know what kind I like. Dee, would you like something?" Elspeth said.

"A diet cola with a slice of lemon, please. I'm on duty."

"Right-o," Charlie said and then wondered why he sounded so vacuous. Dee was having a heady effect on him.

When he returned from ordering the drinks, he found Dee and Elspeth talking to Takanori Sakurai and his wife. Takanori was fidgeting; his wife looked passive.

Mrs Takanori's voice was so soft that Charlie could hardly hear it over the chatter in the bar. She was speaking in Japanese. Takanori translated.

"I went right to our room after dinner. My husband had been working in the business centre. He told me he would be there. When I found him, he had a tray next to him and a half-eaten sandwich. I told him he had missed a very good dinner."

"What did you have for dinner?" Elspeth asked.

"Salmon. I liked the way it was cooked. I never ate warm salad before but I enjoyed it. Then I had the peach tart with clotted cream for dessert. My husband says I should eat less dessert. In Japan our diet is very healthy. When I travel with him, I sometimes indulge myself," Takanori translated, bobbing his head up and down, as if he agreed with her words.

"Did you hear anything in the night?" Elspeth asked.

Mrs Takanori shook her head.

"We slept very soundly. The hotel beds are very comfortable," Takanori said.

Two beds, not one, Elspeth thought. She had not seen Takanori come out of the room on the security tapes. Still, the Takanoris' room was adjacent to Jason's, on the other side from Oh Seung's. She must check again to see if there was a connecting door or any way that Takanori or his wife could have evaded the scrutiny of the cameras. She could not see them crawling through the mechanical system.

"Did you get up at all during the night? Forgive me for asking but I need to establish where all the guests were."

"No. My wife went to sleep early. I had work to do. My working at night does not disturb her. She is used to the light from my computer."

"Do you remember what time you went to sleep?" Elspeth asked.

"At about midnight, I think. That is the end of the business day in Tokyo."

"Did you hear anything in the hallway?" Elspeth asked.

Charlie thought he must have because of the many things going on outside his room. Charlie could not believe that the comings and goings in the hall were completely inaudible in the rooms along the hallway.

Takanori shook his head. "Nothing."

Charlie thought he was lying. If so, why? He watched Elspeth frown. Dee Mills looked up at Charlie as if to see his reaction to what Takanori Sakurai had said. She looked puzzled; Elspeth looked pensive.

"Thank you both," Elspeth said rising awkwardly and taking her crutches.

"Have we helped?" Takanori asked.

"Every bit of information is useful," Elspeth said. "The police and I are determined to wrap the investigation up as soon as possible."

Charlie followed Dee and Elspeth over to a table where the Russians were sitting. Elspeth greeted them.

"I thought you might skip the dinner," she said.

Svetlana, not Fedor, answered. "He convince me that dinner tonight is specially put on for us and will be very good. We plan to go out later."

"May I ask you a few questions? About last night," Elspeth said.

Both the Russians assented.

"What time did you get in last night?"

"Very late," Fedor said. "Maybe half past two."

Svetlana laughed. "We close the nightclub."

"We had a hard time getting a taxi at that time of night. The owner of the club finally had to call for one."

"When you came in, did you see anyone from the delegation?"

"No, we go right to bed," Svetlana said. "Fedor said he must work in the morning."

"When was the last time you saw the Chinese delegates?" Elspeth asked.

Dee Mills glanced over at Charlie. He cleared his throat. Why had Elspeth suddenly brought up the Chinese?

Fedor laughed inappropriately loudly. "The Chinese,

particularly that pair, don't know how to have fun. We saw them huddled together when we went out just after dinner. Then today they skipped the meeting. Probably called back to Beijing for enjoying themselves too much."

Charlie, who had recently been to Beijing, thought Fedor's impression of the Chinese was out of date. Charlie found Fedor pompous and ill-informed. He wondered if the Russian was simply stating a prejudice or if he had a reason to speak out particularly against the Chinese couple. He must ask Elspeth about her take on the comment, but wanted to wait until he could get her alone.

"Do you know them well?" Elspeth asked the Russians. Her tone was bland but Charlie suspected there was a reason for her feigned indifference.

"We have met several times. They do not like to mix," Fedor said. "Chin Mei-su is friendly but Chao Kai is a prig. He probably called a halt to so much luxury. He's a man of the old school."

Elspeth lowered one eyebrow. "I see," she said but her expression implied that she did not.

"Do you also know Oh Seung and her husband?"

"Oh Seung. Now there is a woman who is growing into middle age beautifully. I find her most attractive but she seems devoted to her husband."

Svetlana snorted. "You look at other womans too much, Fedor," she said in her broken English.

Fedor reached over and took Svetlana's hand. Svetlana, Charlie noticed, was not ageing well and had resorted to makeup to cover brown spots on her cheeks and lighten the wart growing at the side of her nose. The effort was only partially effective. Charlie thought of his mother, who eschewed dyeing her now greying hair but he had noticed more creams and lotions in her bathroom than after she had married Max Douglas-Forbes and that her haircut had improved. He guessed Elspeth had something to do with this, as she was ageing with flawless grace and probably was the only one who could bully his mother into taking more care of herself.

"We know most of chief delegates," Svetlana said, "although we not meet Katherine Croft before. Her predecessor he die last year."

"You sound a close group," Elspeth said.

"We are, in a business sort of way. We meet once or twice a year. Our stances change little but open discussion is always good. If only the Japanese would come down from their tall horse, we could all be more friendly socially I think," Fedor said.

"Did you know Jason Ravensworth well?" Elspeth asked.

"Not well," Fedor said. "We are sorry he died though. He had the possibility of a future leader in Canada."

"Have you met his partner?"

"No. He came alone always. I think he is ladies' man," Svetlana said. "He always flirt with them. I did not know he had partner. Poor women."

If only you knew, Charlie thought. He knew Jason was flirtatious but Charlie also was aware that this was intended to mask his sexual orientation. Jason had been forward-looking in uniting with Robert but his marriage was not yet common knowledge. Jason had often told Charlie that he was not ready to announce to the general public that he was gay. The subject still was considered a political liability and Jason never hid his ambitions to reach higher office in the Canadian government.

"Indeed," said Elspeth in response to Svetlana. She turned to Charlie, who remembered Svetlana's clamming up when he mentioned New York the day before.

"Are you off to New York tomorrow?" he asked Fedor. "I work near the United Nations. I might see you there."

"No, we are going to Ottawa but not New York."

Charlie was confused. Surely Svetlana said they, or at least implied, was going to New York. He must tell Elspeth this. Was Svetlana likely to venture out on her own? If so, why?

"Will you leave your address with the hotel so we can contact you if we need to ask you anything more about Jason Ravensworth?" Elspeth asked.

"We shall be back in Moscow in a week. You can reach me there. You have my address, which I put on my registration card." Fedor sounded curt. "I really have nothing to say about Jason Ravensworth's death. Svetlana and I were not here when it happened." How did Fedor know the time of death? But his tone implied that this was the end of the discussion, Charlie thought. Elspeth had other ideas.

"In a week I hope all the mystery around Jason's death will be solved. Perhaps you can leave me your mobile number in case I have any other questions."

"I put that as well on my registration card," he said, probably regretting he had done so.

Elspeth smiled sweetly. "Thank you. Enjoy your trip to Ottawa." She turned to Charlie. "Please fetch my chair. My foot's killing me." Her pain seemed real. "Then let's go upstairs; I need to lie down."

After obeying Elspeth's command, Charlie pushed her to the lift. She had him stop before the doors opened.

"Charlie, get on your computer and see if you can uncover all the meetings this group has had over the last four or five years. Find out who was at each one, particularly the people who also are here now. See if you can find when Jason was at the meetings. I'm convinced someone had a strong enough motive to kill Jason and it probably is one of the delegates. I'm discounting the Inuits because this is the first time, I think, they have been involved in the meetings. Check that too. Dee and I will see you downstairs in about an hour. I want us to mix with the conference members. Dee can help me the rest of the way up."

*

Dee Mills helped Elspeth to the sofa in her room but did not leave her alone, but rather sat on the easy chair nearby. Elspeth closed her eyes and wished the policewoman would go away because she needed time to think.

"Do you have any ideas on who killed Mr Ravensworth? Was it really one of the delegates?" Dee asked.

"Can you think of anyone else?" Elspeth said and knew she sounded irritated. She softened her tone. "It's been less than twenty-four hours. Considering my injury, I haven't been able to get about as much as I usually would."

"Did you really work at Scotland Yard?" Dee asked. She seemed awed by the fact. "The real Scotland Yard? Were you in the criminal division?"

"No, I worked mainly with white-collar offences. In those days they thought women university graduates were too effete to be involved with physical crimes, particularly with what was known as the criminal classes, although I have found since then that criminals are classless. Can you imagine that they told me I was too 'presentable' for the seamier side of crime but that I would be highly effective with people 'of my own sort'? That hardly would be tolerated today. I found the work interesting, however, and did get out in the field occasionally, even though the locations they sent me to were not dangerous."

"Why did you leave?"

"A man, what else? I met my first husband while he was working on a film near the Tower Bridge in London and I was assigned to see that the site was clear of onlookers. We were married six weeks later and I went back to Hollywood with him."

"That must have been exciting," Dee said.

"Actually it was rather humdrum. I spent most of my time raising our two children, although I did a bit of private detection on the side."

"How did you get the job with the hotels?"

"Pure chance. I was staying at one of the hotels when a theft happened. I tracked down the thief and Lord Kennington was so impressed he practically hired me on the spot. I was going through a divorce and the change was exactly what I needed."

Dee looked starry-eyed despite Elspeth's trying to make her life sound dull. But, Elspeth thought, if I can get her more on my side, perhaps she'll leave me alone.

"Do you need a break?" Elspeth asked. "I could stand a short nap and it would be nice to be alone. You can trust that I won't leave the room. In fact, you could do me a favour and go downstairs and talk to Brittany Rogers, the blonde Canadian woman. I think you two would get along. You might ask her about her relationship with Jason Ravensworth. Surely Inspector Clough would be pleased if you could turn up some information to help the investigation. Come back up just before the delegation goes into dinner at half seven and help me get downstairs."

Her strategy worked. PC Mills admonished Elspeth to get some sleep and left her alone. Elspeth could tell that the young policewoman was hungry to do something other than stay with a suspect. Before she left, Elspeth suggested a few questions PC Mills might ask.

The door had no sooner closed than Elspeth drew her mobile from her pocket. Although her foot hurt, she could work through the pain now that she had a chance to speak to London without the police hearing. She speed-dialled Pamela Crumm's private home number, even though it was now late in Britain. Pamela slept little and always came wide awake if disturbed in the middle of the night. Pamela had told Elspeth that this asset had been one of the things that had kept her good at her job as the chief manager of affairs at all of Lord Kennington's hotels around the world. Pamela was the detail person; Eric Kennington the man with the big ideas. This diversity produced an ideal business relationship, despite their sometime disagreements.

Pamela came on the line after the third ring.

"Elspeth, ducks, I've been thinking about you all day. Tell me what's happening there."

"I'm at a standstill. My foot being broken and the constant presence of a police hound dog are making me rely on others to do my legwork. Luckily my cousin Charlie, whom you may remember from Biddy's wedding in Scotland, is here and helping me. Don't cry out and say that he's a journalist. His paper is not inclined to publish sensationalism and I have made him swear to let me review anything he writes. He was here to cover the conference or so he says. He's being infinitely helpful."

"Make him keep his promise. Now tell me where you are in the investigation."

"I can't decide if the removal of the Chinese from the hotel has anything to do with the murder. The coincidence is uncanny if they are not connected, so my next move is to see if they are. I may need to go through official channels so I'll ask Richard to help. I think he served once in Ottawa when he was a junior officer in the FCO and may still have contacts in the government. Fortunately he is in Vancouver now for a speech. In the meantime, the Korean delegate's husband disappeared sometime last evening. Again a coincidence? I think there could be a link. It's a muddle. I've one more shot at questioning members of the delegation, a dinner in a few minutes. I'm trying to think who would be best to sit with."

"Try the American delegate," Pamela suggested.

"I hope I can continue to have contact with her. She said that the US State Department is sending someone out here after she leaves. I'm not certain why. After all Jason was Canadian. My hunch is that Katherine Croft, which is the US delegate's name, wants to make sure there are no repercussions from the defection or possibly abduction of the Chinese. I wish I knew which it was. I hope Richard can find out for me through official channels."

"What about the Canadians?" Pamela asked.

"Jason's aide is still here. She looks lost without him. I finally shed the policewoman who was minding me at least temporarily. I sent her off to question Brittany, who was Jason's aide. That's why I can talk so openly with you now. But she'll be back in a minute and of course Detective Inspector Clough of the Royal Canadian Mounted Police is hovering in the wings and still considering me the prime suspect in Jason's murder. I need to find something to put him off. I won't be defeated, Pamela. I just can't move as quickly as I'd like. I'll undoubtedly have to stay on a few more days, particularly if I'm arrested. I hope it's all right for Richard to stay at the hotel if I'm in gaol."

Pamela clicked her tongue. "You'll think of something. Richard's always welcome. And if Charlie Baillie Shaw is helping you, I'll call Janet Church and make sure his room is taken care of by the Kennington Organisation. That's the least we can do."

"You're a lifesaver, m'friend," Elspeth said. "Have you told Eric about this fiasco?"

"Not yet. He's on the plane back from Hong Kong and undoubtedly will take the weekend off. You have a reprieve until Monday. Use it well."

After a few more words with Pamela, Elspeth concluded the call. Then she dialled Charlie's mobile number. His response was cheerful.

"So you shook her off?" he asked.

"Only momentarily so I have to talk fast. First, Pamela Crumm is giving you a free room because you are helping me, with the proviso that you don't go to print without the

Kennington Organisation's clearance. I know, you already promised that. Secondly, get downstairs and join PC Mills. She is questioning Brittany Rogers and I want someone there to hear what passes between them. You can finish your computer research later. Come back to my room before dinner at half-past seven. Knock twice so I know it's you."

"Aunt Elspeth, you are a gem!"

Elspeth assumed he was referring to the free room.

"No, I'm getting to be a crotchety old lady, so off with you."

He laughed and rang off. Elspeth's foot now was in real pain. She rose to get a paracetamol when someone rapped on her door. She hobbled over to the door and opened it. Janet Church stood there and looked more ashen than before. Detective Inspector Clough was close behind her.

"We've found Kim Bae," Janet said. "His body has just been discovered stuffed in a linen cart in the mechanical room on the roof."

12

Charlie felt tremendous relief now that he knew the Kennington Organisation had agreed to pay for his room. With a light heart he took the lift down to the ground floor and joined the crowd in the bar. He looked around but couldn't spot Robert Kahn. He saw PC Mills with Brittany Rogers deep in conversation in a corner and thought luck was favouring him. He had met three beautiful girls in two days. He was usually not that fortunate. As he approached their table, Dee Mills looked up with a frown. She seemed to resent the intrusion. Brittany looked thankful for his arrival.

"May I join you ladies?" Charlie asked and sat down before they could deny his request. "Did I interrupt something?"

Simultaneously Dee Mills said yes and Brittany said no. Dee must have reached a sensitive point in her interrogation.

"Please continue," Charlie said.

"I will," Dee said ungenerously. "Brittany, someone must have been Jason's enemy. Do you have any idea who?"

Brittany looked close to tears. "Everyone liked Jason," she said. "I can't imagine anyone wanting to kill him."

"But someone did," PC Mills said flat-footedly. Charlie could see that the young policewoman had not learned the secrets of subtly drawing information out of a witness. "Did you know him long?"

Brittany shook her head. "No, this was my first assignment with him. Before last night I felt this was a coup for me, to be associated with Jason, whom everyone thought was destined for great things. Now this. I don't know how I can help the police. I really know nothing."

"Did Jason try to make your relationship more than an official one?"

Brittany squirmed and lowered her head. Charlie saw that the brown roots of her hair were beginning to show, but he knew that was the fashion. Brittany was a sexy woman. Jason would have noticed this but did he flirt with Brittany the way he did with other women? Brittany could not have known that Jason's attention to women was merely a front. Jason had previously told Charlie that he liked women but preferred men. Poor Jason, Charlie thought. He felt the sharp pain of losing a close friend, one with whom he had shared many happy moments.

"I, er, I enjoyed his company. He was always very attentive but there wasn't anything between us? No." Brittany ended on a defiant note.

"Was he attracted to the other women members at the conference?" Dee asked.

"Jason flirted with women but he never was serious," Brittany responded.

"Do you think this caused any of the women to expect more?"

Dee Mills, despite her greenness, was asking penetrating questions. Charlie wanted to take her apart and explain Jason's deception but this did not seem the right time to do so.

Brittany laughed brittlely. "Several may have."

"Who do you think may have? Please try to remember accurately. It may be important," Dee said.

Brittany was obviously being squeezed and she apparently did not like it.

"He seemed close to Oh Seung, the Korean delegate. She often looked at him with a knowing smile. I wondered if they had something going. Katherine Croft seemed to dismiss his advances. But the Chinese woman delegate secretly smiled at him several times. I don't know what that meant because otherwise she showed no emotion. "

"And any of the wives of the delegates?"

"No. Fedor's wife is a bit of a Russian tank. I didn't see Jason with her but I can't image anyone playing up to her. Mrs Takanori seldom appeared except at meals. Jason never spoke to her at all as far as I can tell."

The crowd in the bar stirred. Katherine Croft came over to Brittany and said that the delegates were about to go into dinner.

"Time to get Elspeth," Charlie whispered to Dee. Brittany seemed relieved when they rose.

*

Elspeth shifted her weight to one crutch and put her free hand on Janet Church's arm. She simply nodded to the detective inspector.

"Come in. It's better not to talk in the hallway." Elspeth said. She led them into the sitting area of her room and offered coffee, tea or a drink. Both declined Elspeth's offer. "Tell me what happened," Elspeth said as she sat down awkwardly on the sofa.

"The repairman went into one of the mechanical rooms on the roof to do a routine check," Janet said. "It was a scheduled maintenance, which is done once a week. Otherwise the mechanical room remains shut and locked. When he got inside, he was annoyed that one of the room attendants had put a laundry cart in the room. Then he choked when he saw a foot stuck out under the top layer of linen. He said he threw off the sheet and saw Kim Bae's body. He also said he vomited in the corner, which will need to be cleaned up after the police investigate. He obviously was quite shaken."

DI Clough added, "It seems we have another murder. Ms Duff, your hotel seems a dangerous place to stay. Does this sort of thing happen frequently?"

Elspeth bristled and said, "Every hotel in the world has unfortunate incidents. My job is to clear them up as efficiently as possible. Therefore, inspector, I hope you will allow me to do my job. I cannot continue to be under your close scrutiny and be effective. Surely you would like me to help in the investigation."

"Where is PC Mills?" the inspector said. He seemed to have just noted her absence.

"She has stepped downstairs for a moment. I was resting until you came and could not do so with her here. As you see, I've not run away and I have no intention of doing so. PC Mills has been a good minder. Please do not take her absence as a dereliction of duty. She had a chance to question a member of the Canadian delegation while I was sleeping." Elspeth laid heavy emphasis on the last word.

"You are still a suspect in Mr Ravensworth's murder," he said.

"Inspector, you must see that there's a connection between Jason Ravensworth's murder and Kim Bae's. I couldn't have committed the latter as I have been incapacitated since last night. I think you will find that the second murder took place after I was hurt."

"I will deal with PC Mills. The scene of crime team is up on the roof now and at any moment the coroner will do a preliminarily postmortem to establish the time of death. If he feels it was after Jason's murder, then you are free to get on with your job. If it was before, I will have to take you down to the station and detain you there."

So far Elspeth had been able to talk her way into staying at the hotel but the inspector's threat alarmed her. She should not have let PC Mills go. She glanced at the clock by the bed and saw that Charlie and Dee would be returning at any minute to get her for dinner. Elspeth had to stall.

"I'd like to wait here until you get the initial postmortem. I'm certain it will exonerate me." She tried to speak with more courage than she was feeling. She was also anxious to get downstairs to the last gathering of the delegates.

"Janet, you wait here with Ms Duff until PC Mills returns. I need to go up to the rooftop again but I'll be back." He did not say when. He left abruptly. Elspeth thought he came just short of slamming the door.

Janet blew her breath through her lips. "I can't believe this is happening at my hotel. We have to get you free, Elspeth. I can't cope with the murder investigation and run the hotel. Who's going to tell Oh Seung?"

"That would be my job if I could get out of here. I'd like

to see her before our inspector does. Do you know where she is?"

Janet picked up her mobile and called the reception desk and then the bar. She asked if anyone had seen Oh Seung, and then she looked up at Elspeth and shook her head.

"Can you try her room next?" Elspeth asked.

Janet did so but again with negative results.

"Any of the facilities—exercise room, business office, or even the hair salon?"

Janet tried and finally said, "She's having her hair done. She should be done in about ten minutes. That doesn't give us much time."

"I've an idea," Elspeth said. "When PC Mills returns, let's not tell her about Kim Bae's murder or that the inspector has been here and will be returning shortly. Let's say that I'd like to get my hair combed out before dinner and ask her to wheel me to the hair salon. If we're quick about it, I'll be able to see Oh Seung and get back up here in time to see the inspector and find out if I am off the hook. Will you call down and arrange it?"

After doing so, Janet rose. "I must get back downstairs. I'll sic Ron Dillard on the inspector. He said he wanted to be involved in the investigation but he doesn't know about the second murder yet. Now's the time to tell him. With your concurrence, I'll send him here first for instructions."

"Make it fast. Dee Mills and Charlie may be back at any minute and I'd rather speak to Ron alone."

Ron appeared at Janet's command.

Elspeth barely had time to compose her thoughts. She was so used to working alone that all the help she was summoning up made her change her normal modus operandi. Elspeth had always relied on her own sensibilities in her cases. Others might not have such sensitiveness to what was important and what was not, even if she gave clear instructions on what she wanted to do.

"Ron, find out as soon as possible what the pathologist has reported," she said after explaining the current situation. There will be a postmortem but I need to get the medical examiner's initial take on things. Tell Detective Inspector Clough that you're there to represent the hotel. You can truthfully say that there should be no disturbance to our guests. Make him aware that none of his investigations should take place in any of the public spaces of the hotel. If he wants to question Oh Seung, I want to be there. If you can schedule a meeting in the backrooms, call me. I'll convince PC Mills to come down with me. In the meantime, follow the police examination as closely as you can. Take your own pictures if you can convince the inspector that you are doing so for the security of the hotel or make good mental notes. And please don't offer the inspector the CCTV tapes. I have a copy here, but I don't want the inspector to see them until I can review them again."

Elspeth saw that Ron was intelligent and eager. She hoped he was tough. Toughness was a requirement of all hotel managers and Pamela Crumm would want to know how Ron responded and would note his performance in his record.

A double knock came just as Ron and Janet were ready to leave. Elspeth wrestled on to her crutches and was near the door when Janet opened the door.

PC Mills was laughing but her face fell when she saw the hotel manager.

"Has anything happened?" she said.

Clever girl, Elspeth thought. She could do well in the police if she stayed this alert.

Janet slid passed her and Charlie. "Stay in touch," she said to Elspeth.

"I have an appointment to get my hair combed out, Dee. Will you wheel me down in my chair?" Elspeth asked. "Charlie, come along and bring the crutches. Also bring my outdoor coat. I think I may need it."

Elspeth took them down the service lift to avoid anyone hearing what she had to tell them.

"Wouldn't it normally be the police's job to tell Oh Seung her husband is dead?" Dee asked.

"In the hotels, I always try to do it myself. It never is an easy job, even after doing it a number of times. But I usually can offer comfort that the police cannot."

"What are you going to say to her?" Charlie asked.

"I'm never sure until I face the person. It's different each time."

When they reached the hair salon, which was tucked out of sight of the main public rooms behind a discreetly signed door, Elspeth took a deep breath. Once more into the breach.

Oh Seung was finished with her appointment and was just thanking the hair stylist. "Elspeth, we must have the same idea. After a long day, a little pampering is called for."

Elspeth smiled and then frowned.

"Ms Oh, I have sad news for you. We have found your husband. I'm afraid he's dead."

Oh Seung looked at Elspeth as if she were speaking a language she did not understand. "Dead? But that's impossible." Her smooth face wrinkled.

"His body was found about an hour ago. The police are with him now. I came down to see if I could be of any help. They will ask you to identify him. Let me come with you."

Oh Seung still looked unbelieving. "Where is he?" she asked. "Are you sure it's him?"

"It's the staff's responsibility to know everyone's face and name," Elspeth said as gently as she could. "But they will need you to see the body to make sure."

"There has to be a mistake," the Korean woman said without conviction. "Where is this body?"

"It was found in a mechanical room on the rooftop. I think it may still be up on the roof. Do you need a wrap? It's quite cold outside. Let me go with you to your room to collect something warm. Dee and Charlie, I don't know when I'll be back down from the rooftop. Wait for me to come back down to dinner. If I'm not here by half-past seven, have dinner without me."

Neither of the two protested, seemingly willing for Elspeth to take on the uncomfortable task of accompanying the new widow. Elspeth had never become inured to the difficulty of the task of consoling the relatives of a murder victim. She knew that most of all they needed someone to help them manage the details of the death. She also knew that handling a death of an overseas national was complex. She would need to use the services of the Kennington Organisation in London and the Kennington Victoria staff to handle the physical details; she would try to manage the emotional ones.

Elspeth abhorred violent death and the realisation that murderers became so twisted in their thinking that they needed to resort to killing. Now two murders had taken place and must be related. She hoped Oh Seung could help her discover a motive. Elspeth also knew that she needed to tread delicately in case Oh Seung was directly involved in both deaths. Or was it murder? Elspeth could not tell what Oh Seung was thinking from her face, which was now like a mask.

"I would like to go back to our—my—room, before going up on the roof."

Elspeth suspected that Oh Seung's room could have been the scene of the second murder. Elspeth could not guess if Oh Seung thought the same thing. Possibly if she were the murderer, she might want to collect something that would implicate her or move something that would give away what actually has happened in the room. Elspeth suspected, however, that the room attendant had already made up the room and nothing would be as the murderer had left it.

Detective Inspector Clough had not said how Kim Bae had been killed. Surely if any violence had occurred, the room attendant would have alerted the management, or would she? Room attendants were taught to overlook oddities in rooms. Guests were allowed that much privacy. The room attendant would have made up the room at about ten o'clock in the morning and then come in to prepare the room for the night between seven and eight. This thought triggered something in Elspeth's brain. The tapes from the night before, of course! Something was wrong and she had seen it on the tapes. What was it? If only she could remember.

Oh Seung took Elspeth's arm as they got out of the lift. Elspeth could feel her unsteadiness, the only sign of emotion Oh Seung had displayed. Elspeth took one hand off her crutch and, in a balancing act, put it over Oh Seung's to steady her and give her reassurance. Oh Seung took in a long breath as they approached her room.

"Do you think he died here?" she asked.

"Let's wait to hear from the police. I still don't know how he died or how he got to the roof. Once we find out, we'll have a better idea."

"Can we go somewhere to talk? Not here," Oh Seung said as she stepped into her room.

"Come to my room," Elspeth said. "It's on the next floor up. We can speak privately there."

Once Oh Seung was settled on the sofa, Elspeth offered tea.

"I'd rather have a gin and tonic," Oh Seung replied. "A diplomatic shortcoming, I'm afraid. Let me get it from the mini bar. Will you have something?"

"I'd love a sherry although with my medication, I probably shouldn't. Go ahead. Take what you want."

Oh Seung took a long time getting her drink. Elspeth watched her. Oh Seung's back was rigid and she dropped the ice tray. Before she returned to her seat she took a long drink from her glass and added another miniature bottle of gin.

"How may I help you?" Elspeth asked. "I'm not the police and can keep a confidence when necessary."

Oh Seung took another swallow and visibly rolled the clear liquid around the back of her throat. Was she summoning up courage?

"Kim Bae and I were arguing about Jason Ravensworth," she said and stopped as if waiting for Elspeth's reaction.

Elspeth stayed silent and looked up questioningly.

"My husband thought Jason and I were having an affair," the Korean woman said. "He accused me of having broken it off and then having brought him to the conference as a foil so that I would not have to face Jason. I was drawn to Jason but it never materialised into anything. He flirted with all the women. I don't think he considered me differently from the others. Bae didn't believe this after he saw me and Jason talking at the opening reception and then later in the lobby, where he put his arm around me. Jason liked to touch women but I never thought it was an invitation to get into bed with him."

"He was very attractive," Elspeth said. Many gay men often are, she thought. As a middle-aged woman, she blushed inwardly at her own reaction to Jason's charm.

"Is that why you left your room and slept in Katherine Croft's?"

"He ordered me to get out. Bae is, was, seldom angry, but he was angry last night. Nothing I said helped. Do you think the police may blame me for his death? I can claim diplomatic immunity but it will put a stain on my career. Our foreign minister doesn't like us to be involved in anything that smacks of impropriety. I've come a long way up in the diplomatic corps and don't want to lose everything because of what happened last night. The problem is that I'm involved, even if just peripherally. Do you think this will break in the press?"

"Not if the Kennington Organisation has anything to do with it. Right now, I would advise you to act like the grieving widow and tell no one else about your disagreement with you husband. Is Katherine Croft the only other person who knows?"

"She knows we fought but not why. I told her the same story I told you earlier, that we were fighting about another woman. Katherine didn't ask for the details. She's a close friend but has the grace not to be a prying one."

Elspeth sympathised. "Thank you for telling me the truth. You can trust that I'll keep your confidence. That's part of my job as well as my natural inclination. Too many secrets have been spread about that have adverse effects on the innocent, which I have to assume you are. Is there anything else you want to let me know before we go up on the roof?"

Oh Seung finished her gin and tonic and shook her head.

"May we talk later, after we get back down?" Elspeth asked.

Oh Seung nodded. "Please," she said. "I don't want to confide in anyone else. I felt I could trust you with the truth."

"You can," Elspeth replied rising. "Now let's get the difficult part over with."

The police had laid a body bag out on the rooftop. Detective Inspector Clough was clustered among a group of people in protective clothing that must have been the crime scene investigative officers. He looked up when the two women came off the lift. He broke away from what he was doing and came over to them.

"You shouldn't be here," he said, obviously angry.

"I've brought Kim Bae's wife to identify the body," Elspeth said, leaning on her crutch. "Let's do it quickly. This can't be easy for her."

When the body bag was opened Oh Seung whispered, "That's my husband. May I go now?"

"Ms Oh, we're treating this like a murder. I'll have to question you," the inspector said without sympathy.

Elspeth jumped in. "Ms Oh is distressed by all this. She also is an official of the South Korean Ministry of Foreign Affairs and Trade, which gives her diplomatic status. Perhaps, detective inspector, you would allow me to talk to her unofficially. I believe she will answer any questions to help with your investigations without the threat of being taken to the police station."

"All right, if you must, Ms Duff. I want to know where she was last night between seven o'clock and ten."

Is that the time of death?" Elspeth asked.

"The coroner thinks so but his results are preliminary before the full postmortem."

Elspeth calculated quickly. The missing time she was in Jason's room fell into the inspector's time frame. She still was not cleared of guilt.

"Since we were travelling on official business, my husband was using an official passport," Oh Seung said. "I hope this does not complicate matters. I would like to take his body back to South Korea with me if our consulate in

Vancouver can arrange it. I will be leaving on the first flight I can get to Seoul so that I can be with our children before anyone else can tell them about the tragedy."

"I don't know about your rights as a diplomat," the detective inspector said. "I'll have to check with my superintendent."

Michelle's father? Elspeth thought. She hoped so and that Charlie could secure her an introduction outside the official channels. She wondered where Charlie and Dee were now and if Charlie could break free in order to see Michelle later in the evening.

"If there is anything else you would like me to ask Ms Oh, please send me a list. In the meantime we will be in my room. You can send a written list of questions there. Speak to the manager. She can get help you get the list to me. In the meantime, I think Ms Oh deserves some privacy and some time to arrange for her trip back to Seoul," Elspeth said to the inspector. She spoke with authority.

Once Elspeth and Oh Seung were back in the lift, Oh Seung let out a long sigh. "Well done," she said to Elspeth.

"I think it best if you do come to my room. I can have dinner sent up for us, if you wish."

Oh Seung shook her head. "I'm not hungry. Let me have another drink."

"I'll send down for proper ones," Elspeth said. "Then let's talk a bit more. The inspector may ask a policewoman to sit in on my interview with you. I'd like us to get any sensitive information out of the way before that. I want this case solved quickly, as I'm sure you do."

"If it were only over," Oh Seung said, leaning back against the wood panelling of the lift. This whole conference has smacked of irregularities from the very first. I should have refused the assignment on instinct."

Elspeth's interest was piqued. As they entered her room, Elspeth said, "What irregularities?"

"There wasn't any purpose to the conference and the Clifton Trust is a suspected CIA front. I only accepted a place at the conference because I was trying to impress my boss. I'm due for a promotion soon. Now this has happened. I'm not sure where this leaves me."

Elspeth ordered drinks and three Kennington hotel portions of snacks, which in the end might serve as their dinner. Oh Seung was a source she did not want to lose. The information about the Clifton Trust was too vital for Elspeth to ignore it.

"Do you think Jason Ravensworth knew about the Trust?"

Oh Seung held Elspeth's eyes. Elspeth could not read the look.

"I don't know," Oh Seung said finally. Somehow Elspeth did not believe her.

"Do you think the CIA had anything to do with Chao Kai and Chin Mei-su's departure?" Elspeth asked.

"What do you think?"

"Now that I know about the Clifton Trust, what other explanation can there be? Did you know the Chinese delegates?"

"South Korea and the People's Republic of China do co-operate, although it most often has to do with North Korea and with trade matters."

Elspeth was not put off by the non-answer to her question. "What were the two Chinese like?"

Oh Seung shrugged slightly. "They were always a bit closed down. Chin Mei-su was the friendlier of the two. I don't know if Chao Kai was reticent by nature or if, as a high official in government, he was just careful. She worked for the PSB, Public Security Bureau. Strangely, in my experience, they tend to be less guarded. Her job, I think, was to monitor him and therefore she could be more open with diplomats from outside China. She would join in a social event, where he would draw back. She has a good sense of humour."

"What was her relationship with Jason Ravensworth?"

"Jason only recently began attending our meetings. He liked to joke with everyone, but particularly Chin Mei-su. They seemed to have similar senses of humour."

"Therefore Jason might have used this relationship to arrange for their defection to Washington," Elspeth said to the air.

Oh Seung did not deny this.

Elspeth persisted. "Do you think Jason may have been the contact between the CIA and the Chinese delegates?"

"I have no idea," Oh Seung said. This time Elspeth did believe her. Elspeth suspected that to pull off a deception such as the spiriting away of the Chinese required a great deal of secrecy as well as split second planning.

Elspeth changed her tack.

"Do you have any idea why your husband might have been killed? I need to have a plausible story for the police if

I'm going to help you. Spouses are always the first suspects."

"He was here because I wanted him to come. Our relationship in recent years had been up and down and I wanted to start to repair that. But I didn't have an affair with Jason, despite Bae's insistence that I did. Bae didn't like Jason's way with women."

"Did Bae know that Jason was gay?"

Elspeth might have hit Oh Seung with a cricket bat. The South Korean drew back with a jerk.

"Gay?" she said. "You mean a homosexual? I can't believe that! Not Jason."

Elspeth was astonished at the intensity of the reaction.

"He's married to a man named Robert Kahn, who's come from Montreal to see to Jason's affairs here now that he's dead. Why does that surprise you?"

"He seemed so . . . otherwise," Oh Seung said. "He hid it well."

"I have heard from a reliable source that Jason put on a front with women to cover his true feelings. But a source I trust attended Jason's wedding a year ago. Jason fooled quite a number of people. He wanted to keep his private life quiet. Although gay marriage is legal in Canada, Jason was aware there is still some opposition to it. That could have hurt him politically."

Their conversation was interrupted by a knock on the door.

"Let me answer," Oh Seung said, regaining her composure.

A middle-aged woman with short cropped brown hair, stern eyes and a slightly receding chin stood in front of the door when Oh Seung opened it.

"Detective Sergeant Bastien," the policewoman said in a voice as clipped as her hair. "I'm relieving DC Mills, who has just gone off duty. She'll be around in a minute to get her clothes. I'm to stay with you tonight."

"I think you must be mistaken," Oh Seung said in a haughty voice. "Who do you think I am?"

"Ms Elspeth Duff," the sergeant said, looking a little puzzled.

Elspeth could see Oh Seung grin. "Do I look like an Elspeth Duff?"

The constable grimaced. "Is Ms Elspeth Duff here?"

"She's inside. Perhaps your superiors did not tell you that she has been injured and walks with pain."

"Oh," said Sergeant Bastien, the word voiced expressionlessly.

Elspeth watched this interchange. Obviously after PC Mill's lapses, Elspeth was being given a more senior watchdog. Elspeth rose and took her crutches and faked more difficulty of movement than was necessary.

"I'm Elspeth Duff. Ms Oh and I are having a private conversation. Please wait outside. There is only one door so I won't escape."

"I was told not to leave your side. I also have an envelope for you from Detective Inspector Clough."

Yikes, Elspeth thought. The inspector had cadged a Kennington Victoria envelope, possibly taken from the writing room just off the lobby. He had gone into the hotel's public spaces, which Elspeth had asked him not to do, meaning a game for control was taking place between the two of them, Elspeth thought.

"He said I was to take notes," the sergeant insisted. "I can't do that outside in the hallway."

Elspeth saw that she had no choice but to ask the policewoman in. Elspeth sensed that Sergeant Bastien would not be as pliable as PC Mills or the unfortunate constable at the hospital.

"Then come in," she said without adding 'please'.

Elspeth tore open the envelope and skimmed down the list. She looked up at Oh Seung and said to her, "These questions are all straight forward. Shall we begin?"

Seung settled back down in the chair she had just vacated, and pushed her glass of gin and tonic out of view of the newcomer. Elspeth made no offer of drink or snacks to the sergeant.

Elspeth cleared her throat and began. The sergeant took out her note pad and a pencil and a small voice recorder.

"It is now seventeen minutes past seven in the evening of January 12, two thousand and nine. The people present are Detective Sergeant Bastien of the Canadian Royal Mounted Police, Elspeth Duff of the Kennington Organisation and Oh Seung, a member of the South Korean diplomatic corps. Elspeth Duff will be doing the questioning of Oh Seung. It should be noted that Ms Oh has diplomatic immunity and is answering these questions of her own free will. She has not been read a warning nor is she required to answer any of the questions. The interview is taking place in Room Three Seventeen of the Kennington Victoria hotel in Victoria, British Columbia."

The sergeant frowned at this long preface.

"Please state your full name, Ms Oh."

"Oh Seung. My surname comes first and my given name second. I have no other names."

Elspeth had not warned Oh Seung only to answer the question asked.

"And your address?"

"Care of the Ministry of Foreign Affairs and Trade, Seoul, South Korea."

"Are you a guest here at the Kennington Victoria?"

"Yes, I am.

"Which room are you occupying?"

"Two ten, on the second floor.

"Who is or was staying with you in that room last evening?"

"My husband. His name is Kim Bae."

"Was he with you between the hours of seven and ten last evening?"

"No, I was away from our room after dinner."

"Did you see him at all during that time?"

"No."

Good. Seung was giving short answers.

"Were you on good terms with your husband?"

Elspeth looked up and caught Oh Seung's eye. She waited to see how Oh Seung would reply.

"My husband and I are generally on good terms."

Not really the full answer, Elspeth thought, but she did not follow up.

"When did you last see your husband alive?"

"Just after dinner. I'm not sure what time exactly."

"Did your husband have any enemies in the hotel?"

"None that I know of."

"Can you think of any reason someone would want to kill him?"

"None."

"Was he acquainted with other members attending the conference?"

"No, I don't think so, except Katherine Croft, the US delegate. He first became acquainted her when I was posted to Washington. That was before we were married ten years ago. He has met her only twice since when she visited me in Korea."

Elspeth wondered how this would sound to the police. If Kim Bae knew no one other than Katherine Croft, the most likely murderer was either Oh Seung or the US delegate—or Elspeth herself. Since Elspeth was reading from the list, she could not skew the questions in Oh Seung's favour.

"Did he have enemies in South Korea who might have followed him to Victoria?"

"Not that I know of. He was a government official in Seoul and was highly thought of. He was scrupulous about his ministerial affairs, both to protect me and because that was his natural way of doing things. He insisted on old-fashioned propriety. He was a devout Christian and not the type to accumulate enemies."

Elspeth finished the page of questions and read the statement at the bottom. It read: "The police reserve the right to question you further. Do not leave the country before clearing your departure with them."

Elspeth could think of no way to shed Detective Sergeant Bastien. Oh Seung left Elspeth with a questioning frown, almost a plea to help Elspeth. Elspeth nodded her head slightly.

13

Charlie and PC Mills stepped out of the lift on Elspeth's floor. Dee Mills jerked to attention and dragged Charlie back into the cab.

"Oh, no," she said. "It's the vulture. Poor Ms Duff. She's in for trouble."

"The vulture?"

"Detective Sergeant Bastien a.k.a. the vulture a.k.a. the Wicked Witch of the West or W3. Charlie, you have to get me out of here and somehow get my clothes back from Ms Duff's room. I can't show up at the station in her clothes."

"Come up to my room," he said, his room being one of the cheaper ones and located at the top of the building under the mansard roofs. "We can go there and devise a plan."

Dee reddened. "I'm on duty," she warned.

"Strictly business," he said. "We can't continue riding up and down on the lift all night."

He wished now that he was neater about his things. He had strewn his few possessions to fill every corner of the room. Even the room attendant's tidying up could not counter his disorderliness. Charlie hoped Dee was not compulsively neat by nature. The room attendant had folded some of his clothes and put them on the bed. His papers, however, remained in a chaotic state on the small desk that held his computer.

"I had a deadline," he said limply.

"Deadline?"

Charlie had forgotten that Dee did not know he was a journalist.

"Back to my office in London. They always want reports as soon as things develop. Elspeth insists on it as well. Here, have a seat on the sofa. I'll get something out of the minibar."

"Diet cola for me," she said.

"Crisps?"

She looked confused.

He corrected himself. "Potato chips?"

"I'm on a perpetual diet. There's too much food around the station and I always give in, in moments of stress. What are we going to do, Charlie?"

"You're going to stay here until I can fetch your clothes. I'll go back down to Elspeth's room and talk my way into getting them. What time are you due back at the station?"

"As soon as possible. They don't like us working overtime these days. There's too much pressure on the budget."

"Before I go down, Dee, tell me what Brittany Rogers told you. Elspeth will want to know and you won't be able to tell her in person if W3 is with her."

"You're right. Brittany was pretty guarded but I'm getting better at questioning with a velvet glove. Brittany said this was her first assignment with Jason Ravenscroft but after we talked a bit of girl talk, she loosened up and said she found him very sexy. I think she may have thrown herself at him but from what she said he wasn't biting. She did say she hoped it was a temporary impasse. Life married to a diplomat was better than being an aide in the Canadian

Foreign Service, which she described as a bastion of old white men subtly covered up in politically correct language."

"Did she say why she thought Jason was murdered?"

"She was about to say something when you came up."

"So I came at an inopportune moment. Forgive me. I hate blundering in. Did she say anything else that might be important?"

"She said all the women delegates had the hots for Jason. That was her wording."

"Do you think any of them knew he was married?"

"Married? No. In fact I think she didn't know he was."

"I see," said Charlie. He did not expound on the nature of Jason's marriage.

"Did Brittany say anything about the purpose of the conference?"

"That she thought whaling was a dull subject but that Jason seemed excited about attending it and therefore she was willing to be included."

Charlie was at heart a reporter and could not resist probing further. "Did she say anything about the sponsor of the conference?"

Dee knit her brows. "Sponsor?" she asked.

"Find out more about the sponsor," Charlie said and then wished he had not.

"Is that a clue?" Dee asked innocently.

Charlie liked Dee well enough to say, "It might be. Now let me go get your clothes. I'll be back in a second—or two."

Grinning he left the policewoman still in Elspeth's clothes. They suited her better than the dark blue of her uniform, probably now hung up neatly in Elspeth's walk-in wardrobe. Before he left, he went to his shaving kit and extracted a box.

Charlie found Elspeth with a sour look on her face. He knew her well enough to suspect she was plotting some way to get rid of W3. Charlie to the rescue, he thought.

"Elspeth," he said, remembering to drop the Aunt before her name, "here is the Percocet the doctor left for you."

Elspeth looked up but did not move her face in any way. "Thank you, Charlie. The pain in my foot seems to be getting worse. It should help, although it tends to put me to sleep. I'll wait until after dinner." She pocketed the box before W3 demanded to see it.

"I'm Charlie Baillie Shaw," Charlie said extending his hand to W3 to distract her. "I'm helping Ms Duff in her capacity here at the hotel. You must be the policewoman taking PC Mills's place. Competent woman, Constable Mills. While Elspeth was asleep she extracted some invaluable information on the murder. I was there with her. She's quite an expert at questioning. I predict a great future for her in the RCMP."

"Constable Mills still has a lot to learn, like not exceeding her orders," the sergeant said.

Charlie turned to Elspeth, who raised an eyebrow as if to say, 'see what I have to put up with'.

"May I offer you both a drink, or coffee if you wish, sergeant?" Elspeth asked.

"Coffee," W3 said. I don't plan to sleep tonight."

"Nothing for me," Charlie said.

Elspeth rang room service and ordered strong coffee, which arrived in less than five minutes. In the meantime Elspeth excused herself and went to the bathroom. When she returned, she played the perfect hostess.

"Sugar and cream?" she asked the sergeant.

"Both. Three sugars.

Elspeth turned her back to the sergeant and busied herself with the coffee. Charlie could see her pour powder into W3's coffee. Ten minutes later the policewoman was nodding off on the sofa; fifteen minutes later she was sound asleep.

"How many pills did you grind up?" Charlie asked.

"Three. I didn't dare do more. I don't know what the lethal dose is and I don't want to be charged with the death of a policewoman. Drugging is bad enough. Now let's get down to the dining room. Perhaps we can catch the delegates during their dessert."

Charlie demurred. "I promised Dee I would retrieve her clothes. She's waiting in my room and needs to get back to the station before her shift is up."

"In the box under my clothes hanging in the wardrobe. I thought it best to conceal them. Be quick about it, Charlie. And do get my things back. I'm rather fond of the trouser suit and the scarf. I found the material for the suit in Brussels last autumn and the scarf is from Paris. Richard bought it for me after a difficult case. He's very sweet that way."

So Richard did have some soft qualities. Charlie thought he must get to know Richard better.

14

When they reached the dining room, Elspeth was disappointed. The delegates at the dinner were arranged in a rectangle of tables and she could see no extra seats. Katherine Croft was sitting between Brittany, who was looking tense, and Greg Allen, who was eating large mouthfuls of his meal and only occasionally looking up at his superior. Katherine and Brittany were engaged in deep conversation. Elspeth wondered what they were discussing, something serious because neither smiled. Mr and Mrs Takanori were talking to each other in Japanese at the exclusion of all the others. He looked impatient; she resigned. Svetlana Mihailova fidgeted with her napkin, twisting it by its corner. She had finished her meal; Fedor had not. He asked for more. She shook her head and said something inaudible and probably in Russian. The Inuits were bunched together, speaking in their native languages, which must have been similar, and laughing when it seemed they found they had so much on common. They were the only relaxed people at the table. Obviously the closing dinner was not being a success.

Elspeth wheeled in her chair and motioned to the waiter.

"Will you set a place for me next between Ms Croft and Mr Allen?"

He nodded and took her order, roast chicken with fresh salad and no starch. She often had this meal and knew it would be good and slimming.

She turned and addressed the group as a whole. "For the Kennington Organisation, I want to apologise for the disruption to your conference. I hope after dinner, you will all enjoy a drink in the bar paid for by the Kennington Victoria." Elspeth had the authority to offer such things if it helped her in her work. She hoped it would be an inducement for the remaining delegates to stay in the hotel. She also knew that W3 would probably be conscious in an hour or two so she would have to work quickly in order to be back in her room by then.

Once her place was set, she turned to the US aide.

"We haven't spoken before. I see your colleague has left the meeting early. Did he take ill?"

Greg looked uncomfortable. He stared at his whipped potato, which was prepared with herbs, butter and double cream and set back in its skin. Elspeth saw his prominent Adam's apple go up and down. Elspeth had learned over time that such features were a hindrance if one wanted to lie.

"He was called away unexpectedly."

"That must have been difficult for you—to do both your jobs." Elspeth smiled sweetly as she said this.

His Adam's apple went up and down again. "We have different jobs. I work directly for Katherine." He did not explain John C. Smith's affiliation.

Elspeth pressed harder. "Did something go wrong that both Mr Smith and the Chinese left at the same time? We at the Kennington Organisation are always trying to please. If we did something . . ."

She waited.

His neck mottled with redness that spread up to his cheeks. "No, it was nothing to do with the hotel," he said, as if the words were choking him. "It was other business."

Elspeth became aware that Katherine Croft had stopped talking to Brittany and was staring at Greg. He flushed further.

"Ms Duff, we need to talk after dinner. In the meantime, Greg, finish up your meal and get back to the report." Katherine's order was crisp.

Elspeth wondered if the report really existed or if the command was a warning for Greg to keep quiet. He took a large forkful of potato and retreated into silence.

Charlie came into the room soon afterwards and came over to Elspeth.

"Mission accomplished," he whispered in her ear. "I checked W3. Still out."

"Thanks, Charlie. Have some dinner. I'll join you shortly."

Elspeth sat back in her chair. The voices in the room slowed to murmuring and finally stopped in an awkward moment. Katherine Croft rose.

"Ladies and gentlemen," she said. "After dinner you all are free to go. Ms Duff had offered drinks in the bar, if you wish. I will be going upstairs to finish my packing. Despite the difficulties, I think we have accomplished enough to satisfy our sponsor and I will be making a full report to him when I get back to Washington. I wish you all a safe journey home, although we may see each other as we leave. Thank you for coming."

She sat down abruptly. No one clapped. Conversation resumed as their desserts arrived. Elspeth did not stay for hers.

She found Charlie in the main part of the dining room sampling a large plate of rare roast beef. As he was wiping a dribble of jus from the corners of his mouth, Janet Church came up to them.

"May I see the two of you? I've more news on the events on the rooftop. Mr Baillie Shaw, please finish your meal. Would you mind eating dessert in my office? The conversation may not be too savoury."

Janet let them into her office shortly afterwards.

"Where's your police guard?" Janet asked once they were settled.

Charlie grinned. "She dozed off. Hard work, being a member of the police."

Janet burst into laughter. "That's the first funny thing I've heard all day. How did you accomplish that?"

"Mum's the word," he said merrily.

Elspeth was less amused. She knew her time was short.

"Tell us what you learned from Inspector Clough."

"He thinks Kim Bae died about eight o'clock last night. He was smothered, probably with a pillow. There were threads from the tassels from a pillow on the sofa in his room caught under his fingernails. The inspector though that Mr Kim probably struggled to get some air before he died. He speculates that Kim's murder must be a man who was quite strong. Mr Kim was tall and appeared to be in good condition."

"I saw him in the exercise room yesterday doing weights," Charlie said.

"At some point the killer put Mr Kim in the laundry cart. Because Ms Oh said that she did not return to her room until this morning, the cart could have been taken up to the roof at any time from eight o'clock until Ms Oh entered the room. I'm having our security technician checking the tapes again. I've made a copy for you, Elspeth, if you can find a way to view them without your minder seeing what you are doing. I don't want her impounding your computer. I'm also sending a copy to London. Inspector Clough hasn't asked me for a copy yet I'm sure he will. I want to have us review what happened first to mitigate any damage they may cause the hotel. No news of Jason Ravensworth's death has reached the press as of yet and I hope it never will."

"It may," said Charlie, "unless you have the government clamp down on the report, saying that the matter is classified and cannot be printed. Do you know anyone in the Canadian government who can help us?"

"The Chief Justice of the Supreme Court and her husband have stayed here several times. We have the contact information on the computer. I propose that it would be most effective if Lord Kennington called her."

Elspeth squirmed. There had to be a point where Eric Kennington needed to know all that had happened at the Kennington Victoria but Elspeth hoped it was later rather than sooner. She explained that Lord Kennington was not in London and that he did not like to be disturbed at the weekend.

"But perhaps my husband knows her," Elspeth suggested. "He's rather high up in the UK Foreign and Commonwealth Office."

"Can you reach him?" Janet asked.

"He's in Vancouver now and probably is catching a few hours' sleep now after his flight from London to Vancouver, where he is giving an address. He should be here in Victoria tomorrow afternoon." Elspeth said. "Let me try his mobile, even if it does make him a bit testy. If that doesn't work, I'll call Pamela Crumm. She may know someone and she doesn't mind being awakened. She'll also want to know about Kim Bae."

Elspeth was right. Her husband was annoyed when she made her request.

"Elspeth, can't this wait until I get to Victoria? Surely nothing will happen before then if it hasn't happened already."

Unfortunately Elspeth had her mobile on speaker mode so that Janet and Charlie could hear Richard's irritation.

"It probably wasn't a good idea to call him," Elspeth said after she rang off.

Charlie screwed up his face. "He's probably right. If the press hasn't heard the story by now, they probably are too late for tomorrow's papers and most parts of the Sunday papers are probably already being printed. But I'll keep checking the internet to see if anything breaks there."

Elspeth straightened her back, which was stiff from sitting in the wheelchair for so long.

"I'd better get upstairs before the sergeant wakes up from her nap. Janet, can you have room service bring me up a trolley with dirty dishes on it and a big pot of tea with two cups."

"Dirty dishes?" Janet asked.

"So the sergeant will think I had dinner in the room and didn't come downstairs."

After instructing Charlie to try to get in touch with Michelle, Elspeth went back to her room. She found the sergeant stretched out on the sofa, snoring contentedly. Just wait until she wakes up, Elspeth though. She might be in trouble but she suspected that the sergeant would be in even greater trouble. She had fallen asleep on the job. When room service arrived with the rigged trolley, Elspeth put her finger to her lips. "I'll ring down when I need you to collect this," she whispered.

She was propped up in her bed sipping tea when the sergeant finally stirred. Elspeth hurriedly logged out of the security tape, having seen several things she had not paid attention to earlier.

"Did you enjoy your nap?" Elspeth asked. "I hope room service didn't disturb you when they brought my dinner. There's some tea left. Will you have a cup?"

W3 looked nonplussed. "Was I asleep that long? I can't think what came over me. But I see you've been a good girl and stayed tight. A cup of tea would be a life saver. Two sugars, no lemon—or milk," she added for her British prisoner.

Elspeth smiled and poured out the tea.

*

I've done it. I've gotten away and no one has come after me. Now I can get on with the rest of my life. Victory is mine!

15

Sir Richard Munro had come to his wife's rescue many times before. He supposed this was the price of marrying someone who was not always out of danger in her occupation. His first wife Marjorie had been safe but dull. Elspeth was frequently exasperating, irritating and unpredictable but never dull or safe. Had he not loved her so much, he might have considered confronting her. Yet he knew she had a fragile inner core that she covered with her grace, sophistication and intelligence. A person who did not know her would be surprised by this vulnerability. When she called and asked for help, he always came, although sometimes it caused him great inconvenience. Such was the price he paid for being married to Elspeth. It was not quite the marital bliss he had imagined.

He stretched out in the back seat of the limousine, glad that Elspeth's recently acquired wealth meant they always travelled in luxury without seeking recourse to their expense accounts. He was tired, particularly after Elspeth's late evening call.

When they ascended to the passenger deck, the driver offered to bring him tea or coffee from the canteen on the ferry. He shook his head and went back to thinking about Elspeth. He wondered why she was so accident prone but then remembered that she was frequently put in life-threatening situations in her job. Once her injury had been almost fatal; her current broken foot seemed minor in comparison. She would make all sorts of protests that she could handle herself and had often done so before. He smiled. Dearly beloved Elspeth. He was looking forward to seeing her. Their careers so often took them in opposite directions. He had not told her but he daily thought of retiring from his job at the Foreign and Commonwealth Office. He had just turned sixty-two and he wanted a change in his life, something less stimulating than the high levels of diplomacy he now had to handle. The FCO was making noises about offering him the post of high commissioner at one of the large countries on the sub-continent but he could not see Elspeth in the role as his wife there. Marjorie would have been delighted and fitted the role perfectly. He would be filling the same role as Marjorie's father had when Marjorie was a child. Marjorie would have been in her element; Elspeth would hate it. Such a position would require a full-time wife and Elspeth would never consent to that.

He thought about going back to Scotland where he was born and where his brother still ran the family estate. He wondered if he could convince Elspeth to retire too. They had no money worries now that Magdelena Cassar's bequest was settled, Elspeth being one of the chief beneficiaries. They could buy a house near Loch Tay or Loch Rannoch, where she could be near her ageing parents and see them live out the rest of their lives. He could take up fishing seriously and write a book about his life and career. In any case he had the house on Malta that Magdelena Cassar had willed to him and where they could spend time during the worst of the Scottish winters, although Richard suspected that Elspeth loved the cold, wind and occasional snow. The prospect of retirement filled the rest of the ride with pleasure. Now he just had to find a way to approach Elspeth on the subject. He knew how much her job meant to her, but she was not getting any younger. He must think of something that would make retirement as exciting for her as her current job. More thought on the subject was definitely needed before he approached his wife with his new plan.

He had been met at his hotel in Vancouver by a large Cadillac and entertained during the drive by a young Canadian driver with spiked hair and a large tattooed dragon head emerging from his cuff. Did the dragon go all the way up his arm? Richard wondered. Where did she find the lad and the ostentatious black car?

Richard asked the cheeky young man's name and was told it was eponymously Spike. What odd names young people had these days, monikers that had no dignity. But Spike was an engaging driver and Richard liked him almost instantly. Trust Elspeth to find someone like Spike to take him to Victoria by mid-afternoon. Richard had served in Canada as a junior officer in the FCO in the nineteen seventies but he had never ventured further west than Calgary. On the ferry ride he was bowled over by the beauty of British Columbia's coast and islands, and was sorry when the trip ended. Spike informed him that Ms Duff had taken care of everything and that he would be at their service all weekend. Richard wondered what Elspeth had in mind.

Elspeth had mentioned that she had hurt her foot yet he was surprised when he saw her in a wheelchair with a policeman behind her when she met him at the door. Spike opened the car door for Richard. Elspeth's disgruntled look changed into a big smile. She threw up her arms to him as he emerged from the limousine and bent down to kiss her.

"This is Detective Sergeant Flannigan of the Royal Canadian Mounted Police," she said. "He's minding me. Come inside. I'll tell you more."

Richard knew that the hotel staff would care for his luggage. He took control of the chair from the policeman and manoeuvred it through the lobby according to Elspeth's instructions. Janet Church came across the lobby when she saw them and introduced herself.

"Sir Richard, welcome to the Kennington Victoria. Elspeth tells me you will be staying for the weekend. I've made sure all your preferences have been taken care of and your bags will be taken up to Ms Duff's room. Will you come have some tea in my office?"

"Minding you?" Richard whispered once they were out of hearing of the public rooms. He turned to the sergeant and spoke in his most imperious voice. "I hardly think my wife needs minding. She is a highly respected investigator and holds a top position in the Kennington Organisation. There never has been the least hint of any wrongdoing in her past. I would like to speak to my wife and Ms Church alone. You may wait outside. I guarantee you that my wife will not try to escape."

He could see the corners of Elspeth's mouth twitch. She had sometimes skirted the law, perhaps more times than Richard knew. But Richard's tone worked. Sergeant Flannigan withdrew after Janet Church offered him coffee in the staff room. He insisted that he be called when Elspeth and Richard were ready to leave the office. He stumbled over Richard's title, calling him Sir Munro. Titles were difficult for the uninitiated.

Richard drew his chair next to the wheelchair and said, "Now, Elspeth my dear, tell me what's going on."

"The Mounties think they 'have got their man' or in this case 'woman'—me." She explained in some detail the circumstances around Jason Ravensworth's murder, the subsequent discovery of Kim Bae's body and the reason Detective inspector Clough thought she was the murderer. "I was in Jason's room and I could have taken part in the fight that occurred at the time of the murder. The inspector doesn't know it yet but Kim Bae may have been murdered about the same time as Jason, particularly if I read the CCTV images right. I could have killed him too because I have a passkey and could have gone to his room quite easily. I have found some holes in Inspector Clough's case but I haven't come up with a fully plausible explanation of what did happen. To clear myself I think I have to find out what did. It's such a bother to have a policeman with me at all times. Charlie and I have had to go to all lengths to evade them."

"Charlie?"

"Charlie Baillie Shaw."

Richard looked perplexed. "What's Charlie doing here?"

"He's covering a story or was covering a story until the murder. Now he's assisting me. Dickie, I need you to help me too. Charlie has to go back to New York tomorrow. As of yet, he doesn't have a story for his paper. I need to give him one that's plausible but doesn't implicate the Kennington hotels in any way. I thought you could help us."

"What story was he after?"

"He said he had a tip about something big happening, what I think was a conference set up to cover up a defection. No one has said so directly but there have been enough hints to make me feel the story probable. That's where you come in."

"Come in? How possibly?"

"Can you use your connections in Washington and Ottawa to find out about the defection? My best guess is that both the US and Canada were involved and that Jason's death had something to do with it. But I have no access to either government and I doubt they would tell me anything anyway. You must know someone you can contact so I can confirm that it was a defection."

"Who defected?" Richard asked.

"I think the two Chinese delegates. They were spirited out of the hotel in the middle of the night, the night Jason Ravensworth was murdered. Jason was Charlie's friend. Jason let on that the conference might lead to a big story, which was probably the disappearance of the Chinese delegates. Jason must have known about the defection but could not tell Charlie directly. Charlie trusted Jason and came out here on a journalist's hunch. I was as surprised as you were just now to see Charlie here but he has been useful."

From the way she said it Richard guessed that Elspeth's term "useful" covered more than Charlie's becoming an errand boy.

"Elspeth, explain."

"Perhaps when we get upstairs, if we can get rid of Sergeant Preston of the Yukon. Surely he will allow us a few intimate moments."

"I hope you will tell me more about the Chinese and why you think they are connected to the murder," Richard said with a grin.

"It's too coincidental that the murder and the defection took place within hours of each other. Jason must have known something that made him dangerous, and, somehow Kim Bae got in the way too."

"Now tell me about Kim Bae. Who was he? Elspeth, your mind is far ahead of mine and I'm not following you. I still don't know what crime you are suspected of and why you have a policeman at your side?"

Elspeth blew out her breath. "I'm so excited to see you, Dickie. Let me tell you what has happened in the last forty-eight hours in detail." She did so but he felt she was skimming over some of the details. He knew Elspeth often resorted to stretching the limits of legality. He disliked this trait in her but quietly admitted that at times her deceit got the intended results. He turned to Janet. "Ms Church, you must wonder about Elspeth's movements. My wife is a clever woman but sometimes she doesn't use conventional means to solve her cases. Lord Kennington tolerates this because he doesn't care about her methods as long as she gets the results he wants. I suspect, he doesn't often know the full extent of what Elspeth has been up to."

Janet glanced sideways at him. "Sir Richard, you must realise that Detective Inspector Clough is a bit heavy handed. I've worked with him before and he can be like a bulldog. He fixated on Elspeth at the beginning and refuses to allow her much latitude. I'm impressed at her agility in getting round him."

Richard turned to Elspeth who raised her head and nodded at him mischievously as if to say 'see'. Richard laughed.

"I didn't come here without knowing Elspeth was in some sort of trouble. I'll use as much influence as I can to get Inspector Clough out of Elspeth's sights. I know the British consul-general in Vancouver. I'll see if I can get diplomatic immunity for Elspeth. Normally that only applies if she accompanies me on business. Before I left Brussels, I made sure I had some business in Vancouver that would require Elspeth's presence. I, too, can use a bit of magic when needed."

"Sir Richard, you're a wonder," Janet said.

"Dickie, you are a gem. When do I morph into Lady Munro?" Elspeth said simultaneously.

"Tomorrow at a reception at our consulate-general in Vancouver. As you know, I'm giving a short speech on international money laundering. I've given it before so didn't need to prepare anything. The group will be small, mainly from the diplomatic community, a few government officials and some of the top business men and women here in British Columbia. Ms Church, will you get Inspector Clough here so I can explain? I have my wife's diplomatic passport with me. She doesn't use it when working for the Kennington Organisation."

*

Bless Dickie to find a way, Elspeth thought. His eyes were steely as he spoke. She thought he must have half-disapproved of what he was doing. He knew how much she disliked playing the diplomatic wife but at times like this any device for shaking the police guard would be a godsend. She rose from her wheelchair and hobbled over to kiss her husband. Her foot instantly felt better but she was glad for the stiff cast that the doctors had put on at the hospital. She also was happy that she had brushed over the escape Charlie had devised there.

When Detective Inspector Clough arrived at the hotel, he was not amused.

"Ms Duff," the inspector said, "or should I say Lady Munro?"

"I don't use my title except at diplomatic functions. I prefer my own name."

The inspector started again, "Ms Duff, I have no choice but to release you but I still feel you are implicated in Jason Ravensworth's murder and possibly that of Kim Bae. Your diplomatic immunity is seriously hindering this case. You are the obvious perpetrator. If you think you are as clever as Ms Church thinks you are, then find me the murderer, or murderers. You are free to go tomorrow but I want you to stay in touch."

The sergeant looked relieved. Obviously Elspeth's ability to dodge their watchful eyes had spread among his colleagues.

Now that Elspeth was able to move freely, her mind changed into a different gear. She had resources Inspector Clough did not. He might view the tapes but he did not understand the workings of the hotel. She had no intention for the moment of telling him what she had seen on the tapes. She might have if he had treated her less harshly. When the inspector left Janet's office, Elspeth let out a huge sigh of relief.

"Now I can get to work seriously. Have any of the delegates remained?"

Janet shook her head. "Someone came this afternoon who said he was from the US State Department. He said he was working with Ms Croft to wrap up the last details of the conference. I assume he is here about the murders but I'm confused as to why a US diplomat rather than a Canadian one should do the mopping up."

A tap came at the door and Charlie Baillie Shaw poked his head around it.

"Uncle Richard! How long has it been? My mother's wedding to Max, I think. How are you?"

Richard rose and shook Charlie's hand. "I hear you are helping Elspeth."

"I am, as much as I can. Everything's quite dreadful. I've lost a good friend and don't have a story. My editors are not going to be happy because I have a feeling the whole story of Jason's murder and the causes of it are going to be quashed by some sort of government security measure. I have to go back to New York tomorrow empty handed and very saddened. I'm glad you're here to take my place at Aunt Elspeth's side."

Charlie looked around at Elspeth and looked puzzled at her standing up.

"My foot never was as bad as I made out," she said. "I was eliciting sympathy particularly from the police but now that I'm free, I can manage with the help of a cane or at least one crutch. I didn't want the police to know. Richard's arranged for me to have diplomatic immunity at least while he's here."

"Have you told Uncle Richard everything?" Charlie asked.

Elspeth frowned at Charlie. She hoped he was savvy enough to stay silent about some of their activities.

"As much as is necessary," she said. "Charlie, what happened last evening with Michelle? I haven't seen you since dinner. I hope you had a long sleep."

Elspeth explained to Richard who Michelle was. "I thought we might need her father's influence to get rid of the police in the hotel. Her father's a detective superintendent in the RCMP."

"I haven't met him. Michelle said last night he was leaving today for an important conference in Vancouver on international money laundering which takes place tomorrow," Charlie said. "He's in terrorism, not ordinary crime, that is if murder is an everyday crime. In any case, I couldn't think of a way to ask for an introduction. Michelle says she keeps her social life as private as possible so he won't interfere. I couldn't think of a way to bring up Jason's death or that you are being suspected of his murder." He looked a little embarrassed.

Elspeth did not ask what he and Michelle had talked about. Charlie's love life was none of her concern.

"Charlie, can you get back to checking about previous whaling conferences and who in our party was there? I think the information is critical to our investigation."

Charlie grinned. "I know when I'm not needed. How about dinner together tonight?"

Richard saved Elspeth. "Perhaps I do have a story for you," he said. "I'm speaking in Vancouver on international money laundering, probably the same one Michelle's father is attending. The international economy is one of your subjects, I know because I follow your articles. Come with us. I may have things to say that your paper would be interested in. We have a very engaging driver who will take us by ferry. But it is black tie. Can you manage?"

Jane Church broke in. "Let the Kennington Victoria be at your service. Mr Baillie Shaw. Give me your measurements and I'll have the tuxedo delivered to your room by five."

Comfort and Service, Elspeth thought. Where else but a Kennington hotel?

"May I bring a date?" Charlie asked, without specifying whom he had in mind. Elspeth suspected it was Michelle.

"If you wish," Richard replied. "Others will have partners along as well. I'm not discussing anything classified. In fact, I think what I have to say does needs to get out to the responsible press."

Elspeth and Richard rode up the lift together without the sergeant who had been guarding her.

"I haven't said hello properly," he said and drew her in his arms. Elspeth kissed him back with customary intimacy and then remembered Jason kissing her in the same lift less than forty-eight hours ago. She shuddered and Richard noticed.

"My dearest, what was that for?" He looked concerned.

Elspeth pulled his arms around her. "A sudden shadow over my soul for all my crimes and misdemeanours," she said laughing.

The staff had arranged Richard's things and a welcoming folder lay on the desk of their room. He touched it with familiarity and looked up at Elspeth.

"This case seems to have upset you more than most," he said.

She admitted that it had. Was it Charlie being there and that he was a close friend of the victim? Was it her own clumsiness in her investigation so far? Or was it that she had no idea as to who the murderer might be? Inspector Clough was right in his blunt sort of way. This tangle of facts had made her work almost impossible. To whom could she speak about the disappearance of the Chinese? Brittany Rogers seemed an innocent and probably could provide no help in Elspeth's understanding of Jason Ravensworth's role in the conference. In any event, Katherine Croft had probably left by now. She was abrogating her responsibility to a State Department official who had just arrived at the hotel. He had not booked in but had come for lunch and asked at the bell desk if he could spend the afternoon at the hotel. Elspeth wondered why he had come and what he was doing. Why had the Royal Canadian Mounted Police been so inept up to this point or were they working with the State Department representative? She felt she had lost control.

Richard took a seat on the sofa, and Elspeth stretched out with her head on his lap. He stroked her forehead and ran his finger down her nose. He smiled lovingly as he did so. Normally this would have soothed her. Now it did not.

"It doesn't make any sense," she said, as much to herself as to Richard. "It would seem that Jason was part of the group that was involved in escorting the Chinese out of the hotel in the early hours of the morning, he and John C. Smith." She explained who John C. Smith was. "One would think that the Chinese Public Security Bureau might be interested in the defection of two of their delegation but Chin Mei-su from the PSB was apparently one of the people slinking out of the hotel. Who would want to kill Jason? And why?"

"Perhaps someone from outside the hotel?" Richard suggested.

"That doesn't feel right to me. I was almost constantly with Jason during the two days of the conference. To my knowledge, he didn't meet anyone who was not attending the conference during that time. In any case, there are the tapes taken by the CCTV cameras. Every person in them can be identified as a hotel guest or a member of the hotel staff. I personally viewed the tapes from the night of the murders and went over them again a second time—after Kim Bae's death. The first time I was looking for people going in and out of Jason's room from the time we went in until early the following morning. No stray people were about in the hallway. The only anomaly about the time of Jason's murder was an extra staff member pushing the cart that was to be used for Kim Bae's body. About ten o'clock, one of the room attendants pushed the cart out of Kim Bae and Oh Seung's room. Was it really a room attendant? I think it must have been the murderer posing as a member of the hotel staff. No one else was about in the hallway each time the linen basket was used. Now that I am no longer being watched, I can ask Janet openly to have the security technician view all the tapes from the time the delegates got here until yesterday morning to see if Jason met anyone or if a staff member was behind the cart. It will be a tedious job."

Elspeth knew she was rambling but it was a relief to be able to talk openly and set up a plan. Richard looked down at her lovingly and took her hand, which he kissed.

"You're distracting me," she said and smiled at him. What pleasure to think about something other than the murder!

Elspeth had loved three men in her life. The quixotic Malcolm at Cambridge, the adventuresome but unreliable Alistair, her first husband, and now Richard, who was solid and stuffy but in private was more ardent than the other two combined. Of the three Elspeth thought she loved Richard the best because, unlike the others, she could ask him for help and he was there when she needed him. He did not always approve of her methods but none the less he provided constant and loving support. He would follow her into danger and never reproved her for her tenacity. She knew he loved her but she sometimes wondered if she stretched his love too far. But she gave in to him passionately and he always gave back in kind. Furthermore, she could always trust him.

An hour later, Elspeth left Richard asleep in their bed, and quietly left the room. Her precious moments with her husband had revitalised her. Using only a cane she walked with resolve if not with her usual grace. She must confront the man from the US State Department.

He was in the writing room off the lobby where he was engrossed in typing something on his laptop.

Elspeth introduced herself. "Katherine Croft told me you might be coming. In my position as security advisor to Lord Kennington in London, I have full authority to help you in every way possible." She hoped that by seeming cooperative she could find out his real reason for coming from Washington. Politeness was always an effective tool.

"Phil Watkins," he said standing and putting out his hand. As he did so he closed his computer.

Elspeth returned his handshake. "Mr Watkins, what is the reason for your visit? Perhaps if I knew, I could expedite your stay. It is Saturday, after all, and I'm sure you want to get back home as soon as possible. Does your visit have anything to do with the unfortunate events here over the last two days?"

Phil Watkins had acne scarred skin and chewed fingernails but also intelligent eyes. Elspeth knew enough successful diplomats to think that he would always hold a post behind the lines, not at glittering receptions. He seemed one of those bulldogs that kept embassies going but did not present the public face of his country.

He put his hands to his temples. "I'm not too sure what I am allowed to tell you."

"Has it to do with the Chinese? You needn't worry about my integrity. I work with confidences every day and I'm married to a diplomat. I understand the need to know and when it is necessary to remain silent. If you tell me what you want to know, perhaps I can facilitate your visit."

He considered for a long time. "Married to a diplomat?" he said as if he had not heard clearly.

"Yes, to Sir Richard Munro. You can check him on your computer if you like. He's quite high up in the British Foreign and Commonwealth Office. I'm cleared as well, both as his wife and because I once worked for Scotland Yard."

Finally he spoke, "I'm here to find out if anything was left behind."

"Such as . . .?"

Elspeth began to suspect that Mr Watkins of the US State Department was not from there at all. Was he from the CIA? If he were, he would of course not admit it.

"Would you like to see the rooms the Chinese were in? They were cleaned after the delegation left but have not been reoccupied. Hotels in colder climates do not run at full capacity in the wintertime, except perhaps in ski areas, even as in lovely a place as Victoria."

"Yes, I'd like to see the rooms," he said.

Elspeth led Phil Watkins up to the second floor and down the corridor. Using her passkey, she opened the suite where Chao Kai and Chin Mei-su had stayed. Everything was in perfect order and up to the high standards of the Kennington hotels. Phil Watkins looked impressed.

"How the other half lives," he said with a half-smile.

Elspeth did not respond.

He went into the room and began to search all the drawers, both inside and underneath, the desk, and behind the furniture. He took a chair and mounting it examined the tops of the curtains and top of the armoire.

"Would you like to have the mattresses turned over? I assure you that there will be nothing as the room attendants turn the mattresses between each guest. It's a difficult and heavy job but Lord Kennington insists. If anything were hidden there, they would have found it. If you tell me what you are looking for, perhaps I can help?"

"I'm not sure," he said. "I haven't found anything yet. Can you show me the room where Jason Ravenscroft was killed?"

Elspeth called housekeeping before they left the suite and asked that the rooms they were in be tidied again.

"You really do take a lot of care, don't you?" he said.

"We do," Elspeth said.

They went on to Jason's room. Phil Watkins went through the same routine as he had in the Chinese delegates suite. Again he came up empty handed.

"Everything here is new," Elspeth said. "When tragedies happen in a room, we change everything in it. There is a certain amount of discomfort by the staff if they have to come into a room where murder is committed. We try to be sensitive to their feelings. As you can imagine, we pay them well and respect for their feelings. That way we get the best staff and keep them."

"Did the police have anything to say about disturbing the crime scene?" he asked.

"I'm sure that they photographed every nook and cranny. You could contact Detective Inspector Clough of the local police force. He could possibly show you the photographs."

"No, I prefer to work on my own," he said.

Definitely CIA, Elspeth thought. "Would you like to see anything else?" she asked. "I can show you the back stairs that they took when they left."

"How do you know about that?" he countered.

"The hotel has closed circuit cameras. They were seen leaving. We are particularly interested in the side entrances at night, although more usually to see if anyone manages to get in, not if anyone goes out. I've reviewed the tapes myself. Four people left the hotel just after four o'clock yesterday morning. They were the two Chinese, your man John C. Smith and another person who was unidentified. They were met by a dark coloured car with BC number plates and a driver in a baseball cap. But you probably already know all that."

His face remained passive and he provided no confirmation or denial.

He examined the back staircase as thoroughly as he had searched the room. At the bottom he shook his head but did not explain to Elspeth why. He drew in his eyebrows, which ran in a line across his forehead.

"Did your cleaning staff find anything in the rooms?" he asked. "Anything at all?"

"Not to my knowledge. Unlike many hotels, we send back anything we find to the occupants of the room after we confirm that they have lost it, or provide a service to return it if they have checked out. I can't speak for Mr Ravensworth's rooms, however. The police may have recovered something and kept it for evidence. If you give me your card, I'll let you know if anything turns up."

"That won't be necessary. You can contact Katherine Croft." He might just have well added, "because tomorrow Mr Phil Watkins will no longer exist".

"Mr Watkins, if we have finished, I need to ask you to leave the hotel. Here's my card, including a mobile phone number that has voice mail. I check it frequently."

She led him back down to the lobby and out to the front door. She offered him a taxi at the Kennington Organisation expense. He accepted. Later the taxi driver told the doorman that his passenger asked to be dropped in front of the Empress Hotel, had walked away and turned a corner.

How odd, Elspeth thought. He did not ask anything about Kim Bae. What could the American have been looking for?

16

Richard put out his hand for Elspeth after taking her cane. She emerged from the limousine and straightened up. How exquisite she looked. He adored taking her out in public. So many eyes turned when he did. Men smiled; women admired. Elspeth, as always, had dressed to perfection, having chosen a bold checked Thai silk frock in tan, soft orange, red and light coffee colours which were accented with burnt orange. It had a full pleat at the front, allowing Elspeth to hide her cast under her full-length skirt. She wore the ruby pendant he had given her on their first anniversary, simple stones mounted in a heart of platinum on a short chain. Her every bearing shouted comfort with her body, in the way that well-bred Frenchwomen carried themselves. Richard smiled, knowing that Magdelena Cassar arranged for her to be taught deportment many years before and had transformed her from the ragtag tomboy he first knew into the woman of the world that was now his wife. Elspeth acted perfectly at diplomatic functions, although he knew she abhorred them. She now gave in to attending these receptions with good grace. She took his arm as they walked up the stairs to the building where he was speaking. He helped her take off her coat and turned to see who else was in the room.

Charlie and, as Elspeth had suspected, Michelle, were waiting just inside the door. Michelle's attempt at chic was very modern. Her dress was a fraction too low cut and a bit tight, in the latest style, presentable but not expensive. Richard preferred his wife's more classic taste. Michelle looked nervous when introduced to Richard, who took her hand gently and said he was so delighted to meet her. He professed that Charlie was his favourite among his wife's younger cousins. "Don't tell the others," he said with a grin and a half-wink. Michelle softened.

The four of them moved into a reception room that was abuzz with about fifty people, more than Richard had anticipated. He would have to modify his speech slightly to address so many. He spoke easily and changing his manner would present no difficulty. He had given the same speech several times before. He recognised no one in the room. He had met the British consul-general who had invited him, although he remembered him only slightly. Soon his host came up and introduced himself. The consul-general eyed Elspeth approvingly. Richard made the introduction.

"Lady Munro, this is a pleasure. We had no idea you would be accompanying your husband. I'll see there's another place at the main table." He raised his hand and motioned to a waiter. The deed was swiftly done.

They circulated during the cocktail hour. Elspeth held her own, although Richard knew she was uncomfortable in doing so. He was amazed that small talk did not come easily to her, considering her job. She always countered that she seldom made small talk in her job unless she was using it as a tool to probe a witness or suspect.

They soon made their way around to where Charlie and Michelle were talking to an older man. He looked pleased and had his hand possessively on Michelle's arm.

"Meet my father, Detective Superintendent Henri Gilbert," Michelle said. "This is Sir Richard Munro, who is speaking tonight, and Ms Duff. She works at the Kennington hotel in Victoria."

Superintendent Gilbert's eyes widened. "Not Elspeth Duff?"

Richard watched Elspeth flush. How had the superintendent known Elspeth's given name?

"This evening I'm in my role as Lady Munro. I'm Sir Richard's wife as well as working for the Kennington Organisation in London," she said.

"You've given the Victoria police officers quite a run," he said.

"Have I?" she said coolly. "I hope I've been able to help them with their investigations. It's been a bit of an ordeal with my broken foot." She stuck her cast out from under her long frock.

Richard wanted to laugh at Elspeth's response but he kept his face impassive.

"My wife is very good at her job despite any infirmity. Fortunately she was here in British Columbia when I was scheduled to talk," Richard said in his most correct manner.

Elspeth looked at him gratefully. They moved on.

"I don't think the police are very happy with me," she whispered in his ear. "I hope he doesn't pick up that Charlie is my partner-in-crime. I'm now not too sure if I can call the detective superintendent if I need to divert Inspector Clough's attention from the hotel."

Before they were seated for dinner, however, Elspeth dragged Richard back to speak to the detective superintendent. She had obviously been plotting how to take best advantage of this new acquaintance all the while she had been at her polite best with others in the room.

"Superintendent," she said warmly. "Before we sit down to dinner, I wondered if I might invite you to the Kennington Victoria for breakfast tomorrow morning. Our breakfasts are quite spectacular. Bring your wife and Michelle as well. Charlie can join us. Perhaps I can make up for leading the police apace."

He looked at her askew, as if assessing her intent. She looked back pleasantly and expectantly. Finally he agreed and they set a time. Richard wondered what she was looking for at the breakfast but he did not have time to ask.

At the head table he was placed next to the British consul-general and one of the top bankers in Vancouver. Elspeth sat at the end next to a man Richard did not know. She fell into conversation with the man as they ate their meal. Richard hazarded a guess that Elspeth was not playing the passive role of Lady Munro but was quizzing the man about something that had to do with the two murders.

Richard's speech was followed by numerous questions. Richard and Elspeth did not return on the ferry to Vancouver Island and Spike's eager care until well after half past ten. She settled back in her seat and said, "The evening was more worthwhile than I expected." She leaned over and kissed him on the cheek. How good it was to be with her again. He put his arm around her and kept it there most of the way back from the ferry terminal to Victoria. She rested her head on his shoulder and did not protest.

*

Elspeth considered what she had accomplished. The entire evening she had played his wife as well as she could but she had not let that interfere with continuing the investigation. She thought Detective Superintendent Gilbert was now in her pocket. The man next to her at dinner was the US consul-general in Vancouver. She had led their conversation around to the CIA's cooperation with the Canadian Security Intelligence Service. She thought she had done this subtly by speaking of her own experience with terrorism in her case in Malta several years before. He seemed fascinated with her story and spoke more openly than perhaps he should have. Elspeth wondered if he was involved in any way with the events in the hotel over the last three days. At the end of their conversation she was still not certain. However she had obtained from him the name of the head of the Canadian desk at the State Department in Washington. She had shamelessly said she would be in Washington shortly.

She snuggled more comfortably into her husband's arms and let out a sigh of contentment.

"Happy?" he asked.

"Mmm," she responded. "Dickie, when do you have to be back in Brussels?"

"Wednesday, which means leaving on Tuesday. Why?"

"How do you fancy a trip to Washington tomorrow?"

He shook his head, as if he did not hear correctly. "Washington? My dearest one, what are you scheming?"

"I want to know for sure what's happening with the Chinese delegation. Perhaps no one will tell me in Washington but I'm going to try. Dickie, surely you have connections with the Secret Intelligence Service in London that can open doors for us."

"Elspeth, it's Sunday in London."

"And probably the best time to find someone at home," she said, rising up and looking at him directly. "All we need is a toe in the door."

"If the Chinese did defect, their whereabouts will be top secret. I don't think they will like interference."

"Can they block a murder investigation?"

"They can block anything. You must know that. Why your persistence?"

"Jason's murder cannot go unsolved. Inspector Clough will go plodding on and in the end will continue to blame me and curse diplomatic immunity. The real killer will go free. I think Jason was murdered because of the defection but I can't sort out why. Kim Bae must have interfered, somehow, and needed to be disposed of. The people who organised getting the Chinese out of the hotel will know the connection between their disappearance and Jason's presence in the hotel. By now I think we can assume that the conference had been set up as a ploy to get Chao Kai and Chin Mei-su first to Canada and from there to the US."

Richard put his hand to her cheek. "Had you ever thought that Jason discovered the plan and tried to stop it? The CIA probably cannot launch operations in Canada without some sort of cooperative agreement. It could be that Jason, as a representative of the Canadian government, stumbled across the plan and unfortunately became involved."

"Are you implying that John C. Smith might have murdered Jason? I hadn't thought of that. You see John C. Smith was a tall man. Nowhere on the security tapes showed him near Jason's room."

"Or Kim Bae's? Didn't you say their rooms were adjoining?"

"I've considered that the murderer came through Kim's room. There was a connecting door but only the top hotel staff would have the passkey to unlock it. The code on the passkeys is changed every day. But you're right; the killer must have had a passkey. I'll have to ask Janet how that's possible. The tapes show a room attendant pushing the laundry bin that had Kim Bae's body in it. That someone must have had easy access to any space in the hotel. The person with the laundry bin looked and walked like a woman. John C. Smith could have, I suppose, changed his gait. I'll look again when we get back to the hotel."

"What about the fourth person who left with the Chinese?"

"If only I knew who that was. Obviously he or she was an invader, someone who got in the hotel without being a guest, perhaps someone John C. Smith let into the hotel earlier. Oh Dickie, I'm tired of rewinding the security tapes. Perhaps I can get London or the security technician at the hotel to select the unusual parts on the tapes the afternoon and early evening of the day of the murder for me to review."

"Are you sure you want to go to Washington?" he asked.

"Yes. We could be there Monday morning and we can storm the citadel. I need to find out about the Chinese, and if Chin Mei-su particularly knows anything about the murder."

He laughed and kissed her. "It may be more difficult than you imagine to break into the secrets of the US government," he said, "but we can try. Now let me think who I know who can open a door for us."

*

Despite the pleasure of lying in bed next to her husband, Elspeth could not sleep. Her task seemed insurmountable. She could return to London and say that the Canadian police had taken over and that no mention had been made in the press but she was not certain how long the press blackout would last. The murder of a senior diplomat was a hot story and some clever journalist would eventually sniff it out. It could not be suppressed forever and Lord Kennington would not be happy with her for abandoning the case and failing to prove the hotel had nothing to do with it. He would grumble; Elspeth's job was to see that he would not. The task of keeping the reputation of the Kennington hotels pristine was a complicated one. Never before had she been involved in a case that had so much governmental secrecy around it. She was not certain if a short trip to Washington would help, yet with Richard at her side she might get to the bottom of the disappearance of the Chinese. A long shot at best.

*

Charlie was flushed with pleasure at spending such a glamorous evening with Michelle and at no cost. Elspeth was footing the bill. Janet Church had delivered the dinner jacket, trousers and black tie and to his amazement it fit as if it were bespoke. He wiggled in his costume and felt grand. In his social circle casual dress was more the thing but dressing up gave Charlie a sense of dignity. He hoped it would impress Michelle.

For Charlie the evening was also a chance to help Elspeth. From the way Henri Gilbert greeted Elspeth, Charlie know that the superintendent had followed the case in the hotel. Charlie had to tread lightly. He wanted to appear to be Michelle's innocent date who by chance was staying at the Kennington Victoria. He wondered how far he could push Michelle's father by feigning casual interest.

The superintendent gave Charlie a lead-in.

"Michelle tells me you are a journalist and interested in the conference that just took place at the Kennington Victoria," he said.

"Yes, I'm covering the conference for my paper," Charlie responded and named the prestigious journal that employed him. "Among other things I cover environmental business issues for North America and at the United Nations."

"It's odd, the superintendent said, "for you to be in the same hotel as Sir Richard Munro and Ms Duff. Is there a connection?"

"Pure coincidence. Aunt Elspeth, who is really my cousin, works for the hotels and has done for years. I was staying at the Kennington Victoria to get a story when I met her. What a great surprise that she was there. She travels all over the world for her work, you see."

Michelle's father frowned and looked hostilely at Charlie. Charlie was telling the truth but he felt like a schoolboy who had just told a whopper. He thought that

Henri Gilbert had probably reached where he was in the police by seeing through people's lies.

"She's an incredible person. Everyone in the family says so. I've never seen her at work before. Usually we meet on the family farm in Scotland, where my mother and stepfather live."

"Has she shared with you what has been going on in the hotel?"

Charlie swallowed and considered how much he should tell. If he admitted to helping Elspeth, he might make the superintendent suspicious of his role at the hotel. Charlie decided on another tack.

"Jason Ravensworth was a close friend of mine. We're in the same group of friends in New York. Jason suggested that I come to the hotel to get the story on the conference there. His death has hit me hard. I hope your force can catch the killer soon."

"The case is complicated," Henri Gilbert said. "It's not my department but anything this big gets around the police. Inspector Clough is a plodder but he will get there eventually. Tell your cousin that. Young policemen and policewomen still have a lot to learn from him. They may be seduced by the elegance of the hotel but posh surroundings or not, the underlying principles of detection remain the same. Get all the information you can from people at the scene, look at all the physical evidence and shift things around until everything makes sense. Often it's the process of elimination, discarding the impossible and seeing what's left. Clough's good at that."

"I'll tell Aunt Elspeth," Charlie responded to this avuncular speech.

"And what, young man, are your intentions toward my daughter? She is quite dazzled by you."

Blush rose slowly up Michelle's cheeks.

Charlie reached over and took her hand. "We get on famously. I hope to see her again, although I have to go back to New York tomorrow afternoon. But that's what social media and texting is for."

Henri Gilbert laughed. "Distance is no object in the modern world of dating. I'm very protective of my daughter. The world these days has too many pitfalls for the young and I don't want her to fall in any of them."

They did not mention Elspeth or Inspector Clough again, but after the speech, the superintendent shook Charlie's hand. "I'm sorry about your friend," he said. "Trust us. We'll find out the truth. And treat Michelle well. She's still young and to her you are an older man with a lot of experience. She's a bit starstruck right now. Don't hurt her."

"No, sir," Charlie said the way he would have to his schoolmasters. He had a feeling that any continuing romance with Michelle would be heavily monitored. He turned to Michelle who had her jaw stuck out and was glaring at her father.

Afterwards, when they had returned to Victoria on the ferry in the superintendent's large saloon car, Charlie asked Michelle to join him for a drink at the hotel.

"Stay safe," Henri Gilbert told his daughter.

"Yes, Daddy," she said, her voice conveying her subsequent rebellion.

Once back at the Kennington Victoria, they sat in the bar sipping their drinks and Michelle threw herself back on the settee. "You see what he is like," she said. "Wait until you see my mother in the morning. You would think she would be meek. Quite the contrary, she mows her own path. I have some of her stubbornness. Do you mind?"

Charlie would have not minded anything about Michelle at this point. Out of the corner of his eye he saw Elspeth and Richard return to the hotel. They were deep in conversation and did not see him.

"Michelle," Charlie said, "is it OK with you that we do stay in touch?" Her smile was her answer. "I'm thirty-three and I guess you are about twenty."

"Twenty-two," she said. "I took a year off before going to university. I went up to the Arctic Circle to work with the Inuits. I think that's why I joined the protest. The Inuits need whaling. Many of them still live by their traditional ways and eat traditional diets. It's amazing that in the twenty-first century, some of the Inuits have little contact with the modern world. Last Thursday was the first protest I ever was in. I don't think we were very successful."

"There were four Inuits at the conference. They spoke softly but eloquently about their needs. The ones at the meeting, however, seemed well up on the latest technology. I saw one tapping away at his iPhone and showing photographs to one of the others. Did you enjoy working among the Inuits?"

"In my village, which was well above the Arctic Circle, the people were gentle and kind. I think they found my blonde hair strange. One young girl came up to me all the time and stroked it. I showed her how to do a French braid, which she had always wanted to do. I tried to teach the women new things by enticing them with tea and cake. They were not particularly interested in what I had to teach, but absorbed enough that I considered my time there worthwhile. Did I enjoy my time there? Let's say I found it educational rather than inspirational. I don't need to go back."

Charlie was unsure how much Michelle knew about the murders. Her father had mentioned them at dinner but, as Charlie thought about it, the references were oblique. Charlie had mentioned that he missed Jason, so Michelle must have known that someone named Jason died. But did she know anything else? He decided to be direct.

"Did your father tell you what has happened here?"

"He said two people died and the police were investigating, that's all. Your cousin must be involved. You said she is the security advisor here. She was amazing when we marched in here. We were ready to come back the next day and get more sandwiches."

"A way to a protesters heart is through his stomach," he said.

She grinned. "If it's Kennington hotel sandwiches and desserts."

Charlie paused and then said, "You see the thing is that the police think the two deaths here were murder. They suspect Aunt Elspeth because she was in the room when one of the men was killed—my friend Jason. It's bad business really. I've been involved a bit."

"How thrilling."

"Actually I find it quite awful. I don't know how Aunt Elspeth stands the work she does. Family lore has it that she's solved a number of murders and was almost murdered twice. After one attack she was in hospital in a coma for a long time. My mother said Uncle Richard saved her life when she was coshed over the head. Aunt Elspeth and Uncle Richard married a year later. They had known each other since he was at Oxford and she a teenager but each had been married before."

"How romantic," Michelle said with a sigh. "Love in late middle age."

Charlie wondered how Elspeth would feel being described as late middle-aged. He thought of her as timeless.

"It was rather romantic," he said. "But she won't use her title unless Richard makes her. Like this evening. She spent her first marriage in California and is quite egalitarian." Charlie did not mention that his mother was titled and used her title with ease working on her farm on Loch Tay, where she had lived all her life. If things did progress with Michelle, as he hoped they would, he would have to introduce the rest of his family to her. Would they approve of his choice because he knew even on short acquaintance that Michelle was the one he had always hoped to find?

"I know that at breakfast tomorrow morning the murders will be discussed. I just wanted you to know beforehand."

Michelle chuckled. "Maybe I have a wicked mind but is your cousin trying to milk my father for information from the police?"

Charlie laughed in response. "Probably but I also think she wants to have a connection with the police that's higher up than Detective Inspector Clough. She's found that the police suspecting her and putting 'minders' as she calls her police guards on her has hampered her own investigation. She has an exacting boss in London. She's aware that he will want her to resolve things here at the hotel before she returns there this coming week. Her deadlines are more vital than mine, probably because I work for a sedate newspaper that is more interested in heady analysis than breaking headlines."

Michelle looked at him oddly. "Why do you continue with a job that sounds so dull?"

"It's not dull at all. I like my job because it makes me think of what's behind the news, what really makes things tick, and not just the daily splash. When I sit down to write an article, I have to engage my brain, not just write the immediate who, when, how and where, but why. Our readers want to have the articles in our paper help them understand the news as well as just straight reporting. I write to help the decision makers make informed judgements. That may sound dull on the surface but it gives one a greater responsibility."

Her eyes were filled with awe. "Do you really do that?"

"I try."

"Are the murders here of any importance to your paper?"

"They may be, as the underlying cause of them may be something that will change how the powers-that-be think and what issues will become important to them. In any case, Aunt Elspeth has made me swear that I won't publish

214

anything detrimental to the hotels. Lord Kennington, her employer, holds a lot of sway in the City of London. If our newspaper were to indulge in some sensational article about happenings in one of his hotels, he would be on the phone immediately to the owner of my paper."

"Your world sounds complex," Michelle said, "and exciting."

"I often forget in my daily routine in New York how important what I write could be. If I did think of the consequences, I would seize up."

She leaned over and took his hand. She turned it over in hers. "Charlie, would you introduce me to your world? I dreamed about such things when I would go out and view the northern lights, deep in the arctic and far away from anywhere I had ever been before. Someday, I thought, someday I will be part of the bigger world of people and I will make a difference."

Nothing in the world would have suited him better. He would invite her to New York. He just had to get her father to agree.

17

Richard dressed quickly, letting Elspeth use the bathroom at her leisure afterwards. He loved watching her dress. His first wife had never let him view this ritual but Elspeth never seemed to mind. As she put on her makeup, she would first screw up her face at her image in the mirror and then turn to him for approval. His smile was always enough to make her satisfied. She always dressed with such care, even for such a casual event as breakfast at a Kennington Hotel.

They met Charlie in the lift. Charlie looked tired but his face was beaming. Richard knew the signs; he did not need to ask. Charlie was on his way to meet the woman of his life.

Elspeth looked at Charlie. "Late night?" she asked.

"Detective Superintendent Gilbert imposed a midnight curfew. We didn't quite make it but he was asleep when we got to Michelle's home. Aunt Elspeth, I want to invite her to New York. I thought I might do it this morning."

"I see no difficulty in you doing so. The detective superintendent probably won't make a scene. But, Charlie, do it in a way that won't upset Superintendent Gilbert. Do you have a woman friend in New York who would put Michelle up? At least nominally?"

"Brilliant," Charlie said. "I hadn't thought of that. I was wondering how I could foot the bill for a hotel, even one much less magnificent than this one."

The three of them met Michelle and her parents in the

lobby. Michelle introduced her mother as Faith Fitzhugh. Her pale blue eyes twinkled at Richard as he shook her hand.

"Sir Richard, are you trying to bribe my husband with this invitation?"

"I'm not but my wife may be," he said. He introduced Elspeth by her own name. The two women ought to get along, he thought. Both have an independent streak or so he assumed from this initial meeting.

Henri Gilbert put his hand softly on Faith's and said, "Please don't mind Faith. She is absolutely delighted to be here. A policeman, even one high in the force, can't afford such luxury."

Elspeth, who always was quick, said, "We wanted to meet Michelle's parents. Charlie's mother is my first cousin, and will want to know all about Michelle. Is that too blatant?"

The comment brought a deep blush across Michelle's face. How clever of Elspeth to turn the breakfast into something personal rather than official, Richard thought. It also cleared the way for Charlie. Elspeth had implicitly told Henri and Faith of Charlie's feelings towards Michelle and hopefully given them some comfort in accepting the meal as being more than a bribe.

Richard remembered the first time he had a breakfast at a Kennington hotel, in Malta when he and Elspeth were working on a case together. That was several years before and he had eaten many such breakfasts since but they never failed to impress him. The buffet alone was sumptuous and featured both British and Canadian fare. He noted that the only person who held back was Elspeth. He wondered how many of these breakfasts she had eaten before and if the abundance of food no longer attracted her.

Conversation at their table was lively. Michelle and Charlie were in their own world and hardly spoke to the others. Faith and Elspeth seemed to have hit it off instantly. Richard was left to talk to Henri Gilbert. As a diplomat, Richard conversed easily and put the detective superintendent at ease. Henri had many questions about Richard's speech the night before.

When they all except Elspeth had filled fresh plates with dessert, Elspeth finally turned to Henri Gilbert.

"Charlie is very taken with your daughter. I think he would like to see more of her. I hope you don't object if he invites her to New York."

Charlie turned from Michelle and looked at Elspeth, thanks in his eyes.

"I can assure you that Charlie is thoroughly honourable. I have a daughter too and know how protective one can feel when they're Michelle's age," Elspeth said.

Henri looked at Elspeth. "I know very little about your family," he said.

Richard became wary. He hoped Elspeth would not put on the snobbery act she had done at her son's wedding in order to put down her ex-husband, who had a starlet on his arm.

"We're quite respectable," Elspeth said. "Charlie's mother is a gentlewoman farmer and runs a large farm on Loch Tay in Scotland, and his stepfather is an advocate, which is the Scottish word for a barrister. I'm the only one of my generation to run away from Perthshire. My family wonders why I do what I do. Charlie's mother, Biddy, once helped me on a case and she said running a farm is much easier."

Richard relaxed. Elspeth's family's aristocracy was not flaunted.

"Have you worked for the Kennington hotels long?" the superintendent asked.

"For over ten years."

"Do you often get involved with the police?"

"Of course I try not to be," she said. "Lord Kennington likes things solved quietly and prefers that I present the police with an answer to any criminal activity rather than leaving it to them. Yet I have worked closely with the police many times. In all criminal situations, I like things wrapped up quickly before the hotel gets mentioned in the press. Usually I'm successful, which is why I keep my job."

"Do you think you'll be successful in this case? Just between you and me, Inspector Clough had reached an impasse now that you seem to be cleared."

"Am I cleared? Marvellous," Elspeth said. "Now I can get on with my investigation here at the hotel. The thing that bothers me most is why Jason Ravensworth was killed. I can't find a motive."

"What are the common motives? Sex, money, jealousy, revenge and now increasingly fanaticism. Somehow I can't imagine fanaticism at a hotel like this," he said.

"I once handled a case where extremism was the reason behind a crime but usually the murderer is close to the victim. Haven't you found that true?"

"I've never worked in capital crimes, but still have a fascination for them. My beat right now *is* terrorism."

"Extreme Islamists?"

"No, mainly French separatists. As a French Canadian myself, I can understand the concerns of people of my background but you see I have married an Irishwoman from Belfast. Elspeth, discount Inspector Clough for the moment. If you find out anything important, call me and I'll see that it gets into the proper channels."

"Thank you. May I ask a direct question?" Elspeth said. "Does the Canadian Secret Intelligence Service cooperate with the clandestine services in the States?"

"These days often."

"Do you know someone in the SIS I could talk to here in British Columbia?"

Elspeth said this intentionally. Social conversation between Henri and Elspeth had disappeared. Richard felt that they had reached the real reason for the invitation to breakfast. He stopped talking to Faith in order to hear Henri's answer.

Henri paused in the midst of a bite of lemon tart topped with fresh strawberries, blueberries and whipped cream. He looked up at Elspeth and considered her for a long time.

"Perhaps," he finally said. "Why don't you tell me what you want to know?"

Henri's circumspect answer impressed Richard. It was neither yes nor no.

"I want to know something about the early morning activities here in the hotel just hours after Jason Ravensworth's death and if and how they are connected. I need to know if Jason was involved in these activities or if he was trying to prevent them. It's quite that simple," she said.

Henri slowly took another bite, obviously savouring its taste, before answering.

"Would it do if I asked?" he finally asked.

"It would be a start."

"When do you need to know?"

"The sooner the better, of course."

He put down his fork. "Tomorrow morning will have to do. This is a delicious tart. It's diet time all next week." He patted his comfortable stomach. "I've never had a brunch like this before. Truly spectacular."

*

Elspeth had to be satisfied with what Henri Gilbert said he would do for her on Monday morning, but felt that once again she was losing control to the hands of the Royal Canadian Mounted Police. Inspector Clough might be plodding but Detective Superintendent Henri Gilbert was not. Still Henri had become an ally not an obstruction, of which she was glad. The information about the defection and Jason's part in it was vital to Elspeth solving the murder. In the meantime she had the afternoon and evening ahead of her. She would have to put off the trip to Washington a day and hoped Richard could still accompany her. What could she do now that would be most effective?

After breakfast Elspeth decided to look at the tapes again, this time without the prying eyes of the police behind her. Richard came up to where she was sitting and put his hands on her shoulders. He gently massaged her taut muscles.

"If you do that much longer, I'll have to stop what I am

doing and jump into bed with you. Dickie, will you look at the tapes? A fresh pair of eyes will help. I have an idea. This afternoon, let's walk through the murder scene, using what we see on the tapes as a guide."

He continued to rub her shoulders and she was as good as her word. Middle age does not destroy passion, she thought.

When they rose, Elspeth went back to her laptop.

"Let's start in the lobby," she said, "before dinner the night Jason was killed. Dickie, I'll look at the tapes and you take notes."

The process was painstaking and tedious but when they were finished, they had a timeline of where each of the delegates were during the evening, at least when they were in public spaces or hallways. The motions of the delegates on the tapes were awkward and unworldly. The camera view was from the ceiling so all the figures were foreshortened. Elspeth had many times before rued the fact that there was no audio. Conversations, not just movements, would have added so much.

She leaned back in her chair. Frustration set in. The tapes revealed little that she had not already known or posited. John C. Smith had followed the Chinese and after dinner had disappeared into their room with them. Oh Seung and Kim Bae had been arguing in the hallway. Katherine Croft had gone to her room and Oh Seung had arrived there shortly after the Koreans could be seen having their spat. Gregory Allen, Katherine Croft's assistant, was in the business centre most of the evening. Brittany Rogers must have been in her room working on Jason's report because she did not appear on the tapes after Jason had sent her from the bar. The Russians were nowhere to be seen. The Japanese had gone into their room together, each ignoring the other. The Inuits were in the bar long after Jason's murder.

Viewed in their entirety, coordinated by time and laid out for examination, the tapes did not give up the secrets of the murders.

Suddenly Elspeth saw an incongruity. It was so hidden, that she couldn't be sure it had any relevance. At first she did not want to point it out to Richard for fear she was mistaken.

What should she do next? She could hardly go to the police and say, I think I am beginning to see how the murder was done, or at least I think I have a positive clue. Their first questions would be how and by whom? Then the all-important question, why? She could not say she had seen an anomaly on the tapes, particularly when she had not previously shown the tapes to the police.

Richard was always sensitive to her moods.

"You've found something, haven't you?" he asked.

"I'm not sure. Perhaps. It's only a scrap, not even enough to make a fuss about. But one person went in the door to Kim Bae's room and came out of the door of Jason's room with no explanation as to how they did so. The connecting doors between the two rooms are locked and can only be opened on each side separately. Even room attendants have to go around and open the connecting doors from each side. Their passkeys are updated every twenty-four hours or immediately if one is mislaid. This policy was put into place so the room attendants would not interrupt someone in a room by going to the next room when a guest was in it and wanted privacy. For a person to go through the connecting doors, that person would have to have a master passkey or would have to go in each room individually. Most of the rooms in our hotels have connecting doors so that individual rooms can be made into suites at a moment's notice. The doors are left open if the suite is used and locked on both sides if the spaces are made into individual rooms."

"What does that mean?" Richard asked.

"That there may be more than one murderer or a murderer and an abettor, one on each side of the connecting doors. Before I thought the same person had done both killings. But who? Could it be that there was an accomplice who had a key for both sides?"

"Does each guest have a key card or is each room given two?" Richard asked.

"A guest can choose how many keys they use. The preference is logged into the computer for future visits."

Elspeth rang down to the front desk to find out. The receptionist said Jason had one keycard and the Koreans two.

"Elspeth, how do you account for, the person who chloroformed you being in the room when you and Jason came in?"

"I can't—yet."

"Could it have been Jason himself? Could he have needed you out of the way to meet Kim Bae?"

"How then were they both murdered? Jason was stabbed; Kim Bae smothered. They couldn't have killed each other, unless Jason was not dead after he was stabbed and fought with Bae, smothering him and then returning to the room, in the process locking both doors, one from each side. That would be an incredible feat."

"Highly improbable but not impossible," Richard said. "Did anyone check to see if one side or the other of the connecting doors was unlocked?"

Elspeth shook her head as if to clear it. "Then what was the motive? Who knew Oh Seung had gone to Katherine Croft's room? What's more, Kim Bae was not part of the conference. Let me call Charlie. I hope he hasn't left the hotel for the airport. Did he say what time he was leaving?" Elspeth asked.

"He didn't tell me."

Elspeth picked up her mobile, as the line was secure, unlike the hotel phones.

Charlie was obviously napping when Elspeth's call came through.

Elspeth knew Charlie had a late night the evening before, but she hoped he had finished the homework she had assigned to him. "Charlie, did you finish your research on past conferences?" Elspeth asked.

"Mmm," he said unintelligently. Then he seemed to come to consciousness. "Yes. I put it in a spreadsheet. Let me email it to you?"

The email came through a few moments later. Elspeth brought it up on her laptop. Charlie had listed the six whaling conferences. Elspeth went through it methodically.

Before the conference this last weekend, all the American delegates had been different. The two Chinese had been at four of the six. Oh Seung has been at all six. Jason had been at two and Brittany had been with him only at the last of these. Fedor had been at all six, as had Takanori. The Inuits had only been at the current one.

Elspeth emailed Charlie back. "Can you check about spouses, particularly Kim Bae?" she asked.

Charlie rang her mobile fifteen minutes later. "He was only at the last one before this one."

Therefore, thought Elspeth, Bae would know Jason at least slightly. Had something arisen between them that would make them want to kill each other? What could possibly have driven them to such extremes? Elspeth still preferred to find another murderer. Who, who, who? And why? The murders, (or at least Jason's) must have been premeditated. The unlocking of the doors must have been arranged beforehand. Elspeth wondered if Kim Bae could have been set up, and if he saw what the murderer was doing, he had been killed as well to keep him silent. An unnamed person on the tapes had gone in Bae's room and come out of Jason's. What was the significance of that?

She remembered Oh Seung had told her that she thought Kim Bae was carrying on with Chin Mei-su. Elspeth had from the beginning thought the Chinese were involved in the murders, but was now almost certain that Chin Mei-su could have been the mysterious person who went in one door and came out the other. Elspeth hoped that Superintendent Gilbert could get her a contact in the Canadian Secret Intelligence Service to find out where the Chinese had been taken. For Elspeth, the clock was moving too slowly as she waited for the superintendent to get back to her, and too quickly because Richard would be leaving soon. She needed Richard for his contacts as well as his good advice. If the Chinese had been taken to the States, could Elspeth get access to them? She also knew that on Tuesday or Wednesday she would have to face Lord Kennington and explain why she had not solved the murders. One murder in a Kennington hotel was bad enough; two were totally unacceptable.

Elspeth groaned audibly and Richard came and put his arms around her shoulders.

"This case seems to be getting you down," he said.

"I can't get my head around it. I wish I had the evidence from Kim Bae's postmortem but I expect it isn't complete yet. Do you think I can pry it out of the police?"

"Henri Gilbert could probably help."

"If I knew for sure when Kim Bae was killed, I could juxtapose it with the coming and goings on the tapes," she said. "If Bae was killed a significant time later than Jason, that would complicate things and the connection between the murders would be harder to establish. Dickie, do you think it possible that we have two unrelated murders on our hands?"

"I think it's highly unlikely. Carry on, my dearest. I've never seen you defeated."

She rose and put her arms around him and her head on his shoulder. "Thank you, Dickie, for being here and for being you."

18

Several times during their cases together, Richard had seen Elspeth struggle with the imponderable. He knew fretting did her no good. He must find a diversion for her that would let her subconscious mind mull over the problem but would occupy her conscious mind with lesser thoughts. He could see Elspeth was perplexed, not just with the conundrum of the murders but also with what she would tell Lord Kennington when they met next. Elspeth's problem was that she was too agile at solving most mysteries and therefore when she could not crack one, she berated herself unreasonably. He wondered why she continued working if doing so caused her so much anxiety. With Magdelena Cassar's legacy, Elspeth had a great deal of money, more than any one person could spend in a lifetime. She did not need to work. In fact, she had not needed to work since the day she married Richard two and a half years before. Some inner obstinacy kept her doing so; some defiance of spirit that made her want to be independent from other people's wealth. Elspeth often had said that she needed the stimulus of her job but increasingly Richard had noticed that the job had ceased to give her much enjoyment.

"The sun seems to have come out," he said, looking out the window at the bright winter day. People below the window drew their coats more firmly about them to protect from the wind but Richard felt Elspeth needed the break from the hotel, wind or not.

She looked up at him as if she had not heard.

"Shall we enjoy the sunshine while it lasts? We could bundle up and walk along the waterfront," he said. He secretly hoped the coldness of the air and her infirmity would bring her physically closer to him.

"Are you trying to divert me?" she asked.

"Yes, my dearest. You are fretting."

"I am," she replied with a laugh. "A walk would do me good, even if it's near freezing outside and I'll have to limp along on this bum foot."

They walked along the quay without speaking. This alone made Richard's trip to Canada worthwhile. Elspeth seemed to relax and began to walk confidently with only the aid of a cane. She had put a plastic bag tidily over her cast to keep it dry. She laid her head on his shoulder and tucked her free arm in his.

He wondered if this was the moment to mention retirement.

"I've been thinking," he began.

"A dangerous occupation," she responded.

Good, he thought. She has regained her irreverence.

"What would you say to going to Scotland and building a small house somewhere on a loch? Perhaps Biddy and Johnnie would let us renovate the old barn down at the bottom of the farm on Loch Tay. I've always loved the view towards the highlands from there."

"My grandmother's favourite," Elspeth said. "We could go there for long weekends."

He took her gloved hand in his. "I had thought of something more permanent," he said.

A gull came by and squawked harshly at them and headed for a boat coming into the harbour.

"Permanent?" she said as if amused. "You aren't talking of leaving the FCO, are you?"

"Rather something like that."

"What would you do all day whilst I was away?"

"I had thought you might not be away."

She stopped and turned to look at him. "You mean that I would retire too?"

"Neither one of us is getting any younger."

"Dickie, you're just over sixty, and I'm not yet even there. Aren't we a wee bit young to retire? Didn't you hate retirement the last time you tried it?"

"The circumstances were a bit different," he stammered. "Marjorie's death was a bit of an ending for me. When she died, I didn't see how I could carry on."

"And then you met me again. Oh dear. I have been a bad influence, haven't I? But why this sudden urge to retire again?"

He was not sure how to tell her. Normally words came easily to him, but in the face of Elspeth's incredulity, he felt tongue-tied.

"I had thought I might take up fishing seriously."

"And?" she asked.

"And write my autobiography."

"What would I do? Lord Kennington would not be amused if I wrote up my exploits for him and I loathe any blood sport."

"I'll catch and release," he said lamely. "Fishing, I understand, brings great peace of mind."

"Have you tried it recently?" she asked. "I think after a few days you would find it a great bore. A weekend fishing is one thing; a lifetime of fishing is quite another."

"There are many things I'd like to record about my life," he responded, now feeling defensive.

"Couldn't you do that from our flat in London? All the resources would be at hand. You could pop over to the FCO whenever you needed a reference."

"So you don't like the idea," he said.

"Of retiring? No, not yet, anyway."

"Do you still like your work with Lord Kennington?"

"I'd never considered another life. Not only that, we'd lose the flat in London."

"Couldn't you buy the lease from the Kennington Organisation?"

She stopped and turned around so that she could look him directly in the face. "You've been thinking a great deal about this, haven't you?"

He admitted he had. "I no longer get any thrill out of what I do. I haven't told you because I just figured this out before I left Brussels. I've been offered the high commissioner's post in New Delhi. When Marjorie was alive, I would have taken it for her sake. But I know you would hate it there and, honestly, so would I."

"And fishing in Scotland sounds better?" Elspeth asked with a wry smile on her face. "Or is it that you think I would make a fuss?"

"I'd thought you might," he said. "Even if you would want to go to India again, which I assume you don't, I don't want that much pompous formality in my life anymore.

Being high commissioner in a major country often involves more ceremony than substance. The minister in the high commission does most of the real work. If I were to go to India, I think I would prefer to be the minister but I wasn't offered that position."

"It's quite a coup for you, isn't it?"

He smiled. "Yes and no. I'm honoured, of course, but know for sure several other people were offered it first, people of higher standing than me."

She drew his arm closer to her. "Still, Dickie, I think you should be honoured, even if you have decided to turn the job down. You have decided against it for certain, haven't you?"

"Yes, my dearest. I have already told them so. I didn't want you to feel guilty that my decision was made as a result of your reaction to the offer."

She looked up at him, first questioningly and then with love. He knew he had made the right choice by saying no to the assignment.

*

Elspeth's mobile's insistent blare shattered the mood. She knew from the designated ringtone that Pamela Crumm was on the other end of the call. It was well after midnight in London so it must be important.

"Pamela?" she said.

"Are you aware of what is going on at the hotel in Victoria and on the international press wires?" Pamela said without a polite greeting.

Elspeth had seldom heard Pamela be so blunt.

"No. Richard and I are out for a walk or in my case a hobble. We only left the hotel twenty minutes ago. What could possibly have happened in that space of time?"

"Eric got off the plane from Hong Kong-and the media was waiting for him—*The News of the World, The Times, The Telegraph, The Guardian* and several American television networks, not to add the CBC, ITV, Channel Four and the BBC. They asked him if the three main news items about his hotel in Victoria were connected. Since he had no idea what these were, he threw his scarf around his face and fled, muttering "No Comment", which only seemed to make the media more determined to pursue him to his waiting car with cameras, microphones and flash photography following in his wake. I won't repeat his words but I think you have a great deal of explaining to do. I assure you he won't be pleasant when he rings you."

Elspeth jerked back physically and Richard caught her arm.

"You are lucky that he asked me to call you first. He's gone home but will be in the office at nine in the morning — one in the morning your time. You'd better be ready. This time, Elspeth, you are in very deep trouble. I can protect you only so far."

Elspeth could feel the blood run down to her feet and squeezed her eyes together in disbelief. She swallowed, her throat instantly dry. It took her a moment to find words.

"What am I to do?" she rasped out. "Pamela, help me."

"Everything you can do to protect the hotels. Eric's on the rampage and you are at the centre of it. You have nine hours to find a solution. I suggest you do so. And, by the way, he wants you here as soon as you can get here, or even before that. I can't find flights for you that get in before day after tomorrow. He therefore is going to send his personal jet. Elspeth, come back with the solution to the murder of Jason Ravensworth. That will be your only reprieve. I'll let you know when the jet is scheduled to land in Victoria."

Pamela rang off with no words of kindness or sympathy. Elspeth knew that her strong friendship with Pamela would always be superseded by the needs of the hotels. Pamela had always made that clear.

As if he had heard Pamela's message, Richard led Elspeth to a nearby bench and seated her on the icy surface. She felt no physical cold but she was frozen inside. She repeated Pamela's side of the conversation to him.

"This could destroy my career," she said. "Eric was not happy with my solution to my last major case at the Kennington Chelsea. Now this."

She felt tears come to her eyes, which she tried to drive away.

"Let's get back to the hotel," Richard said practically. "We'll beat this, my dearest. He hasn't won yet."

Richard did not have to identify the 'he'.

"Oh, Dickie!" she said. "What will happen now?"

"Do you have any choice?" his unruffled voice responded.

She wiped her nose on the back of her glove and fleetingly hoped she had not ruined its fine leather.

When they arrived in front of the hotel, two doormen were fending off a mass of the press. Richard helped Elspeth up the stairs. She staggered on her cane and turned to face the mob. Inspiration filled her.

"Ladies and gentlemen," she said raising her head defiantly. "I am from the Kennington Organisation in London. We will be hosting a press conference in two hours' time. Please come back then. I will leave instructions with the doormen as to where you should go. It will take us until then to get things set up. In the meantime, will you please allow our guests unfettered access to the hotel."

"Brilliant," Richard whispered in her ear as they made their way through the press.

"I have two hours to think what to say," she said. "Help! The wolves are at both the front and the back door, Eric at one end and the paparazzi at the other."

"All of my career I have found that staying calm and facing a problem directly saves the day," he said.

"Oh, stop being avuncular," she snapped. He looked hurt. She reached up and touched his cheek. "I'm so sorry, Dickie. I shouldn't vent my spleen on you. What am I going to do?"

"Come upstairs, ring Janet Church and have her set up a room for the press conference. Then have a long and very hot bath. Something will come to you. You always rise to the occasion. This can't be as bad as Cyprus or Singapore. I don't see that you are in danger of losing your life the way you were in those two places."

"Keep calm and carry on!" she said in a quirky voice.

"Exactly," he said with a laugh. "Together we'll think of a way to keep the wolves at bay."

When Elspeth stood up in front of the media two hours later, she felt little more prepared than she had earlier. She had dressed in a severe business suit and grey-blue silk top and a gold choker, which would look well on television, and had applied more makeup than her usual soft touch. As she mounted the podium Janet had set up for her, she looked up at Richard, who was standing at the rear of the room. He nodded encouragingly. Janet, who was beside him, looked anxious. Richard whispered something in her ear.

"Ladies and Gentlemen," Elspeth said, although she felt they were not. "I am here to give a brief statement about the events of the last few days and then will take limited questions. Let me introduce myself. I am Elspeth Duff, and work as a special security advisor to Lord Kennington, head of the Kennington Organisation in London. I am here in Victoria as a representative of Lord Kennington and the Kennington Organisation as well as the Kennington Victoria hotel. Let me tell you briefly what has happened here in the hotel. Thursday evening two guests died in their rooms. Death is not uncommon in hotels that cater to older people of means. The two people who died this week were both attending a private conference here. Because of the sudden nature of the deaths, the police were called in. They are in the process of conducting their investigation and you will have to question them as to their findings. I am not at liberty to disclose the names of the people who have died. Their next of kin have been notified but they have not given the hotel permission to release their names. At Kennington hotels, we are rigorous about the privacy of our guests. I cannot tell you any more in respect to that policy nor can I comment on the police investigation. I have no information to show there is any connection between the deaths."

A general murmur crossed the room. Elspeth looked above the masses of cameras, and avoided eye contact with anyone on the floor. Richard had advised her to stay aloof.

"I will take a few questions, but there is little more I can add."

"What about the Chinese?" a voice yelled out.

Elspeth looked in the direction of the voice and answered as coolly as she could. She answered truthfully, since she could only conjecture about what actually had happened. The security tapes were no proof of anything.

"I have no direct knowledge of anything happening to any of our Chinese guests," she said, trying to control her delivery.

"They say two high-up Chinese officials defected to the US when they were staying here. We heard they were spirited away in the night by the CIA," one of the reporters said.

"I have no confirmation of this. I suggest you try to contact the US State Department, if indeed this is true."

"Doesn't the hotel bear some responsibility?" a female television presenter asked.

Elspeth watched the cameraman next to the woman zoom in.

"We cannot be responsible for the individual activities of our guests. Our job is to see that they have a comfortable and safe stay. We regret that there is any perception that we have not done so. The hotel has taken every step to ensure that the families of the two people who died are cared for. I'm sorry not to be able to provide any further information. You may contact our publicity department in London for any further developments in regard to the hotel and our security policies."

She gave them an email address, which she wrote in large letters on the whiteboard Janet had provided her.

"I hope you all will enjoy the bar we have set out for you at the back of the room. In respect to the other guests, please do not go beyond the area we have set aside for you."

Richard winked at her and smiled. To Elspeth's relief, few stayed on for drinks. She assumed that most fled to their respective papers or television networks. Elspeth walked sedately to the manager's office, followed by Richard and Janet.

Elspeth let out a huge sigh as they entered the room.

"That wasn't as bad as I thought it was going to be," she said. "Janet, I hope I have diverted the press from any further interest in the hotel."

"You were magnificent!" Janet said. She came across and gave Elspeth a huge hug. Elspeth returned it gratefully.

"Now I have to deal with London and his lordship," she said. "That will be less easy."

Elspeth picked up her mobile and dialled in Pamela's private number. Her friend answered immediately.

"I've done damage control." Elspeth said. "Now what?"

"Eric's jet will be at the airport in Victoria at six tomorrow morning your time. Have something ready for Eric when you return. He isn't interested in a plaster on the wound. He wants your explanation on what happened and he wants results. I sympathise, Elspeth, but this time I can't help you. I don't know if there is anything that can."

"I'll try to think of something before I get there. By the way, Richard is with me."

"I've already told the pilot. Both of you are expected. You'll land in London before ten in the evening our time. Eric will see you at nine Tuesday morning."

Spike had them at the airport at half past four. Elspeth tipped him generously. He carried their bags into the terminal. "Geez, so this is where the rich travel from. Someday! You folks have been great. Call me if you're ever back in BC."

The steward showed Richard and Elspeth to the back of the plane, not to Eric Kennington's private sitting room at the front. Elspeth wondered if this was the first indication that she was demoted in rank. The steward told them he had ordered breakfast according to their personal preferences, which were stored in the plane's computer. Elspeth thought of her usual lean fare and said, "I'll have orange juice first. Bring me some crepes made with orange marmalade and dusted with sugar. Put some strawberries on the side and I'll have a cup of hot cocoa with whipped cream on top."

Richard glanced at her oddly.

"Sensual gratification," she said. "If this is my last trip on this plane, at least I'm not going to nibble away at yoghurt and a piece of toast. They have everything in the galley to make up my request. The cook is a retired chef from one of Eric's restaurants and does marvellous things with a few basic ingredients. Think up something delicious and fattening for lunch. I'm definitely in a dangerous mood."

Richard laughed and brushed her cheek. "I'll remember that."

Those were Elspeth's last cheerful words for the whole trip. She sat in a space age lounge chair and stared into space. How could Eric blame her for what had happened in Victoria? How could she speak to the Chinese, particularly Chin Mei-su, to find out their connection to Jason and Kim Bae? How could she solve the murders if she was continually hampered in her movements? And mostly, why was she called back to London so summarily?

Richard had a book, which he read without looking up or disturbing her thoughts. "If you want to talk, let me know," he said.

She did not want to talk; she wanted to make sense of everything that had happened in Victoria. The hum of the aircraft and the direness of her situation finally gave her a fierce headache. She took two paracetamol and dozed off to sleep.

19

"Lord Kennington will see you now," his receptionist said. Usually Pamela was there to greet her but the door to Pamela's office was firmly shut.

Eric Kennington did not rise to greet her.

"Sit down," he said.

She did. He rose from the chair at his desk and put both fists on it.

"Elspeth, you have let me down, you have let the hotels down, you have let Janet Church down and you have let yourself down."

He went to the window and looked out and down. Elspeth knew this was a bad sign. She sat rigidly and said nothing.

He turned towards her. His eyes were steely. "I don't know what has happened to you. Your last case at the Kennington Chelsea ended in disaster, and this one is worse. I have always trusted you to behave with dignity and propriety. I have always assumed you would protect the image of the hotels by your grace and intelligence. I have always expected you would solve the problems I gave you by using your wit, not by devious tricks. Do you have an explanation?"

She swallowed hard but think of nothing to say. Finally she bleated out, "For what?" It seemed this was the wrong thing to say.

She saw his face redden with anger. "For your ridiculous behaviour in Victoria. What else do you think I am talking about? You have disgraced the Kennington Organisation! And you have disgraced me! I will not put up with it!"

Elspeth winced. She felt she had been slapped. She raised her head defiantly but knew the blood had gone from her face. Finally she said, "What would you like me to do?"

"I wanted to fire you. Pamela has convinced me to give you six months to think things over. You may contact her later for details. Now leave!"

Elspeth rose with as much dignity as she had left. Not sure where to turn, she made her way across Lord Kennington's vast office and out into his reception area. She closed the door gently although she felt like slamming it. No one was in the reception area. Elspeth did not know where to turn. She sat down in one of the chairs and choked down her tears. She had never been spoken to in the way Eric Kennington just had, not even after her most devious escapades as a child. He had no right; but he had every right. She had failed him. She never had done so before.

She sat there breathing in and out, trying to compose herself before she had to go out on the street. She wanted Pamela to open her office door but she did not. Slowly Elspeth rose, took a handkerchief from her shoulder bag, and blew her nose. She went to the small coat cupboard to the right of the receptionist's desk and drew her tweed coat off the hanger where she had left it. She went to the lift and pressed the button for the express lift to the ground floor. Her spirits fell as quickly as the car descended to the ground floor.

She flagged a taxi and gave the address of the Kensington flat where she and Richard made their home.

20

Richard opened the door to Pamela Crumm. He had been expecting Elspeth so was surprised at this unexpected visit. Pamela's small frame hardly filled the lower half of the door opening. She did not look happy.

She was greeted and seated and had refused a cup of tea. He came around to face her.

She said, "I thought it best if I came here and let you know what has probably just transpired between Elspeth and Eric. He is angrier than I have ever seen him. Most of all he feels Elspeth has let him down. Richard, perhaps he is being too harsh. Elspeth until now has done brilliantly. Eric always expected the moon and she always gave it to him. He can't accept her failure."

"Has she really failed?" Richard asked. "Surely given time . . . "

"The papers this morning are filled with the double murders at the Kennington Victoria and the disappearance of the Chinese. Elspeth was shown on the BBC morning news. Granted, she carried herself off well but the media has found out that she was or possibly still is a suspect in at least one of the murders and that she has not cooperated fully with the police. Eric didn't take this well."

"What will happen to Elspeth?" he asked.

"Eric wanted to fire her. I convinced him to give her six months suspension from her job."

"You are a true friend, Pamela."

"In this case, I'm not. I know how valuable Elspeth is to the hotels. She will be very hard to replace, if she can be at all. But Eric doesn't forgive easily. I have my work cut out for me. I owe it to Elspeth and to you. But mostly I owe it to the smooth running of the hotels. We need people like Elspeth."

Richard heard the sound of a key turning in the door. He rose quickly and was at the door as Elspeth entered. He took her arm and felt her rigidity.

"Pamela is here," he said softly.

Elspeth walked into their sitting area. Her face was ashen.

"Hello, Pamela," Elspeth said without inflection.

"I thought we could talk without interruption here," Pamela said. "I'm glad Richard is here too."

"Have you told Richard?" Elspeth asked.

"Briefly."

With blank eyes, Elspeth sat down on the sofa opposite Pamela. Normally Elspeth's features were sharp, which before had given her a look of distinction. Now the shadows of their angularity made Elspeth look haunted. Richard's heart bled. He did not know how he could help her. He hoped Pamela could.

"Thank you, Pamela, for giving me a reprieve." Elspeth gritted her teeth.

Pamela shook her large, bespectacled head. "I wish it were a reprieve; it's not. He's doing this as a favour to me. I don't ask for many. Now you and I have to convince him that things will change."

Elspeth tried to speak again but her voice cracked.

Richard rose and poured Elspeth a brandy, despite her dislike of drinking the harsh liquid during the day. She took it and sipped it slowly.

Finally she gained her voice. "I seem to have done a great deal wrong."

Pamela nodded.

"How did he know what had gone on in Victoria?"

"He had a call from the Royal Canadian Mounted Police. They were not happy with you."

"Detective Inspector Clough," Elspeth said slowly. She set her jaw. "The rat," she said through her teeth.

Richard sat down close to her and put his arms around her shoulders. "Pamela is here to help."

"I can stay only a moment," Pamela said. "Come to dinner tonight at my flat, both of you."

"Unfortunately I have to leave for Brussels this afternoon. In any case I think that you and Elspeth need to talk alone," he said.

"Take care of her, Richard. I'll see you at half seven, Elspeth ducks." Pamela said. These were the first friendly words she had spoken since the crisis in Victoria had erupted. She echoed Richard's words. "We aren't defeated yet."

*

Elspeth sprawled on Pamela's low custom-made sofa. She knew the posture was ungainly but it reflected her mood.

"What am I to do?" she cried out.

Pamela had a practical mind. "Go to Scotland with Richard. He suggested you renovate a barn at Tay Farm. If Biddy agrees, put your mind and heart into it and forget Eric for the time being. Enjoy Biddy and Max's company. Let the six months pass without thinking of Eric or his concerns."

"What about the flat?"

"Richard suggested you could buy out the lease. I can see it happens. Let me do my work here in London. A time will come when Eric will demand to know where you are and why you aren't at his immediate command. Let it happen."

"Do you really think so?"

"I can't always judge his moods, particularly lately. I never have spoken to you about his family but his wife is ill, possibly terminally. It weighs on his mind and he isn't always rational. I don't know what happened between you this morning but I assume it was extremely unpleasant. I'm not asking you to forgive him."

Elspeth scowled. "I don't feel forgiving at this point. No employee, in fact no person, should have to tolerate what he said to me this morning."

"I know," Pamela said with a frown, as if she too had been the brunt of his anger. "Do you think you can go to Scotland and put all of this out of your mind?"

"I want to solve the case in Victoria, not for his sake but for mine. The dastardly Detective Inspector Clough will undoubtedly botch the job and leave the dangling impression that I'm guilty. I can't bear the injustice."

"Let it go, m'friend. The harm has already been done."

"But I know I can rectify it if given a chance, even if I am in disgrace. The murderer is out there and probably laughing at our ineptitude. Two people have died. I just can't let the killer succeed."

"Do you think you are close to a solution?"

"If only I could talk to Chin Mei-su. I think she's the key."

"I doubt you ever will be allowed to. If she has defected, they will be keeping her under wraps for a long time. Can you get around the problem without her?"

"Maybe. If only I could get all the details straight."

Pamela served two cocktails but did not say what was in them. Elspeth took a large sip and knew the mix was as strong as it was tartly sweet.

"I call it my power punch. Here's to a better future."

"Yes, indeed," Elspeth said. The concoction was already going to her head.

21

Richard had watched Elspeth brood for three months. She took part in the design of the barn at Tay Farm and spoke for hours with the architect from Edinburgh about the floor plan, elevations, interiors and materials. She wandered the farm with Biddy and joined in merry dinners with Richard, Biddy and Max. She took to taking long walks, usually with Richard. They spoke of the days of their youth and laughed a great deal. They went into Perth to see Johnnie and Madeleine Tay and their new son, the heir to the Tay earldom, and to speak expectantly about the next child who already was on the way. They bought bicycles and toured Perthshire and enjoyed the freedom of no structure to their lives. Twice they went to London to discuss with Pamela terms of the turnover of the lease to the London flat and finally signed all the documents. Elspeth found an old diary that her mother had written as a teenager and started reading it with curiosity and amusement and found a mystery in it. Elspeth frequently went over to the Duffs' home on Loch Rannoch and for the first time in Elspeth's life her mother and father talked about their life before they were married. Elspeth wondered why she never had asked about it before.

But Elspeth's mind was always half in some dark land of its own. She did not seem to want to talk about her feelings and Richard did not prod her. He felt that she knew he was there if she needed him. The day would come.

In April the unexpected happened. Biddy announced that Charlie was coming home and bringing the 'love of his life'. Her name was Michelle Gilbert. Biddy pronounced Michelle's surname in the English way. Elspeth gently corrected her.

"For once he seems to be serious," Biddy exclaimed when she showed Richard and Elspeth Charlie's email. "He wants me to meet her and also meet her parents. They're from Canada. Charlie says you know them. You didn't tell me."

"I've never been sure with Charlie how serious he is about his women," Elspeth said with a crooked smile.

"What's she like?" Biddy asked.

"Very pretty. More intelligent than she seems at first. And quite young." Elspeth said.

"Do you like her?"

"I met her under strained circumstances," Elspeth said.

Biddy and Elspeth were as close as two sisters might have been. As cousins, they were close in age and Elspeth had spent much of her childhood at her cousins' home at Tay Farm. Richard assumed that Elspeth had told Biddy all about Canada and its aftermath but obviously she had not mentioned Michelle or her parents, by name anyway.

"What about Michelle's parents?" Biddy asked.

"Their names are Henri Gilbert and Faith Fitzhugh. He is distinguished and she lively. I think you'll like them. After brief acquaintance I do. When do they arrive?"

"Next weekend. Trust Charlie not to give me much warning. Do you mind if I put them in rooms in the main house next to you?"

Richard and Elspeth were staying in a wing of the grand house at Loch Farm. Normally this was shut up as Biddy and her husband Max stayed in the old farmhouse wing. Biddy opened the rooms for Richard and Elspeth when they came to stay.

"Of course that's fine," Elspeth said. "Soon Richard and I will be out of your hair. Our architect says that the plans will be ready for the beginning of construction by the end of the month. She has recommended a local joiner, Dougal Cameron. Do you know him?"

The discussion went off on to the renovation of the barn. Richard left the two women talking and made his way up to the farmhouse. Max's large BMW was just coming down the drive. They greeted each other and made their way inside.

Max Douglas-Forbes, QC, Biddy's second husband, and Richard had struck up a close friendship despite the striking difference in their natures. Both were inclined to escape from Elspeth and Biddy when the cousins were nattering away and oblivious to the rest of the world. Richard had probed Max on the workings of the Scottish legal system and Max had reciprocated by asking Richard about his career in the Foreign and Commonwealth Office. They also went fishing together along the Farm's private burns and along their private shoreline of the loch. Richard had also discussed Elspeth's hidden depression with Max.

"I'm a bit worried that the Gilberts' arrival will stir up things for Elspeth. Henri Gilbert is with the Royal Canadian Mounted Police and although he was not directly involved in the case at the Kennington Victoria, he knows what happened there. I'm afraid the memories of that time will only exacerbate her already bad memories," Richard said.

They were sitting in the morning room of the farmhouse and sipping whiskey. The windows, contrary to the room's moniker, looked out to the west and the high mountains beyond Loch Tay. The late afternoon sun was setting and casting golden ripples across the loch. Richard stood and watched the wind swirl patterns into the light. He loved this place, where he had first met Elspeth over forty years before, but he now felt unsettled because of his wife's hidden despair.

"I wish she would talk to me," he said. "She puts on a good front but deep down she seems to be suffering."

"Perhaps she feels she has let you down," Max suggested. "Or herself."

"I keep wondering if I should help her go back and try to reconstruct the crime. I've never seen her fail yet. I don't know why the solution to this crime is so elusive."

"Have you asked her?"

"I fear she will snap my head off."

"Perhaps Charlie coming here with Michelle and her family will help rather than hinder. You might suggest that Elspeth talk about the crime with Michelle's father to get an update on the developments in Victoria. Would Elspeth have heard if the crime was solved?"

"I expect the hotel would have and by extension Pamela Crumm. I'm sure she would have told Elspeth."

"Has Elspeth asked her?"

"Not to my knowledge. Pamela told her to let the issue rest."

"When do you plan to be in London next? Can you

approach Pamela by yourself? After all, she is a family friend."

"I'll be there next week. I can try."

"Best it be done before the Gilberts get here."

Richard took a long drink of his whiskey soda. "Perhaps you're right."

Richard was good to his word to Max. He left a message for Pamela at her home and invited her to lunch at his club in London. He told her Elspeth would not be along. Pamela rang his mobile later in the evening and left a message accepting his invitation. She was waiting for him when he arrived at the club.

Richard had requested a quiet corner in the dining room. He suggested some of the specialities the club was known for. Pamela chose lamb chops, he roast beef. She then turned to him and said, "Richard, you wouldn't go to all this subterfuge if Elspeth were prospering. Tell me what's on your mind."

"Elspeth can't settle. She puts up a good front but I can see she's unhappy. Matters are coming to a head this weekend with the arrival of Charlie Baillie Shaw and the woman in his life, whom he met during the case in Victoria. Elspeth assures me that she will have no difficulty with this but she's burying her feelings about this as well as the whole case in Victoria and its aftermath. Do you think Eric will soften and let her go back to the case?"

Pamela shook her beautifully coiffed hair.

"Not right now," she said without explaining further.

"If she worked on her own?"

"I can't stop her, of course. But the hotels can't offer any assistance. Eric has been quite clear about that. He wants the matter closed. He can be a very stubborn man, Richard. Recently it's been worse."

"So there's no reprieve for Elspeth?"

"He still grumbles about her. He may have hurt her but she hurt him too. Is that difficult to understand? I've known him for over thirty years. I've never seen him this way before."

"What way?"

"So tied to an employee whom he's made redundant. He's let off many people in his career but somehow Elspeth has touched something raw in him."

"Does he still blame her for what happened in Victoria?"

"It's more of a feeling of betrayal."

"Can she do anything? She won't kowtow to him but you know that. Do you think if she solves the case in Victoria that will help?"

"I'm not certain if it will or won't." Pamela looked up as the waiter brought their meals. Once the plates were laid and appropriate words said about the food, Pamela continued. "They're both intractable."

"So in order for Elspeth to get back in his good graces, she would have to eat humble pie?"

Pamela cut into one of her chops slowly. "Not exactly humble pie. I think she would have to come up with a very good reason as to why she acted the way she did in Victoria." She paused. "Solving the case would help too. Can you help her, Richard?"

"I can try. She won't talk to me about the case. Perhaps she'll talk to Henri Gilbert."

"Can you encourage her to do so?"

"I'll think of a way," he said.

Pamela was an old friend and they slipped easily into talking of other things. As Pamela was getting in her taxi, she touched Richard's sleeve. "For both of our sakes, let's do all we can to make things better for the two of them."

During the train trip back to Pitlochry where Elspeth was meeting him, Richard mulled over every way he could think of to approach Elspeth. Finally he decided that a direct approach was the best.

She was waiting on the station platform. At this time of year the nights still descended early on the Scottish landscape. He took the wheel, put on the headlamps and was grateful that the darkness gave them an intimacy in the car that bright sunshine would not.

"I had lunch with Pamela yesterday," he said.

Elspeth seemed distracted and only said, "Oh?"

Not a good beginning. He tried again. "I told her I was concerned about you."

"Concerned about me? Why? I'm quite well. The highland air seems to agree with me and my foot is completely healed."

"About what you must be feeling inside. I feel you aren't happy."

"Happy?" she said.

"My dearest one, I love you more than anything in the world. I couldn't be by your side every day without knowing that this whole thing with Eric is eating away at you. Pamela agrees with me. I want to help and not continually have to skirt the subject of Victoria. Could we talk it through before the Gilberts arrive?"

"What more is to be said?"

He glanced over. She had her chin in the air. He felt her tears more than he saw them.

"If I didn't sense your unhappiness, I wouldn't say anything. Won't just talking about the case, now that three months have elapsed, help relieve some of the bad feelings?"

She didn't respond. They drove on into the darkness.

After a long silence, she said. "I've never been so foolish before. It was I who made a thorough mess of things. Reliving it isn't going to change that or make me feel any better about it."

"We all make mistakes in judgement at times," he said. "I've no intention of being critical. But this case must eat away at you. Do you think the two of us can solve it at this distance? Perhaps Henri can help us when he comes."

"Do you think so? He'll have other things on his mind. Being introduced to the Robertson/Tay/Baillie Shaw family is not going to be easy. Biddy's family, and mine as well, don't quite fit the mould. Surely Charlie will want us to be on our best behaviour and not to bring up uncomfortable situations from the past."

Richard felt exasperated. How could he get Elspeth to relent? But he did not want to give up so easily.

"Why, my dearest, did you continually say you wanted to talk to the Chinese delegate, what was her name?"

"Chin Mei-su," Elspeth said. "I don't want to hash it over again."

Richard took a large risk. "But you do hash it over in your mind all the time. I can feel it."

She laughed and touched her fingers to his cheek. "I can't hide anything from you, can I? Yes, it's continually on my mind. I try to put it away, but it's like a stone in one's shoe. No matter how you twist your foot around, the stone continues to irritate."

"What do you want to know that only this Chin Mei-su can tell you?"

"I want to know what Jason knew about the plans for the Chinese disappearance."

"Their defection has only been alluded to in the press, as far as I know," he said. He followed the daily newspapers from around the world and was continually glad that access to the internet allowed one to do so. "Do you really think that talking to Chin Mei-su is the only way to get the information you want?"

"As you undoubtedly remember," she replied, "I was going to Washington but my plans were pre-empted."

"Wasn't Henri Gilbert going to get answers to your questions from someone in the Canadian Secret Intelligence Service? Perhaps he did but didn't know where to reach you — or thought you had lost interest. This weekend will be the ideal time to ask him."

"Dickie, how can I? He'll want to know why I did a bunk. How can I tell him what really happened?"

He heard the pain in her voice. She had not taken Eric's treatment of her lightly. The situation did require some explanation.

"Let's think of a good way to simplify things. We can tell him you suddenly were called back to London and taken off the case for something more pressing."

"Like what? Retreating into the Highlands. Even a child could smell that fish."

"No, simply say it was something you cannot discuss, but which has required you to lay low for a while. He's a policeman. He'll understand about the need for people to stay out of sight. And I suspect he won't question you further. After all, the case in Victoria was only the last of a long line of your investigations. You might mention some of them, obliquely of course."

"You are becoming as devious as I am, my dear Dickie. Have I led you down that path?"

"Elspeth, do you seriously believe that senior foreign envoys don't use deception as a part of their craft? We just call it diplomacy. If you think the British are bad, think of those involved in foreign affairs all over the world."

"Speaking of foreign affairs, I think often about Oh Seung. I wonder what she is doing and how she is feeling. That's a problem with solving a case quickly. One rushes in, finds a solution and then leaves. Seldom do we see the people left behind again. Somehow Oh Seung struck a chord in me. You see, during the time Alistair and I were married, he had a starlet or two on the side. That wasn't the reason for our divorce, in the end we just lost interest in each other but unfaithful husbands still leave a bad taste in my mouth."

Richard would not be distracted. "I think Henri is our best bet," he said.

"Our?" she countered.

"Yes, my dearest, *our*. I can't have you perpetually down in the dumps without trying to cheer you up. At any rate, we can't go on like this forever."

*

Elspeth could not think why she had not recruited Richard's help before. She had assumed that he would not pick up the *basso continuo* of her life at Tay Farm. She had joined in the designing of the renovated barn with real enthusiasm as well as discussing with her parents their past. She loved her long walks with Richard. Previously they had so little time to be alone and unabsorbed in their jobs. Her ramblings with Biddy and long talks with her parents had given Elspeth time to reconnect with her roots. The intervening years had fallen away. Yet she did not feel young again. The case in Victoria had nettled her and the sting of her last interview with Eric Kennington did not go away despite all her efforts to make it do so. She concluded that she must have a character flaw in her obsessive need to succeed in her investigations. But it was more than that. She had not been given a chance to rectify her ill-conceived choices in Canada.

Richard was right. She could not go like this on forever. Even if she did not go back to the Kennington Organisation, she would not end her time there without solving the murders in Canada.

"I'm sorry," she said and genuinely meant it. "I didn't know I was so transparent. I have no idea what to do next.

But, you're right, I must do something or I shall go mad. Do you have any concrete suggestions?"

"Why don't we explore the stumbling blocks?" he suggested.

"Where I always get flummoxed you mean?"

"Examine what the pieces are there that don't fit together for you. Then find out why."

"The main stumbling block is the motive. If I were sure that Jason was involved in the defection, either in it or against it, then that would constitute some sort of motive. To silence him so that he wouldn't say something. But about what and to whom? I can't think of any other reason for him to be killed. The fact that the defection of the Chinese had not fully surfaced in the press after that last dreadful day in Victoria must mean that the Chinese have had something very important they were bringing over to the Americans. I assume it is the Americans and not the Canadians. If John C. Smith and his crony were doing something illegal, Jason may have been trying to stop it. After all, we all were on Canadian soil."

"If that were the motive," Richard said, "do all the pieces then go together?"

Elspeth shook her head. "Not really."

"Can you think of another motive?"

"What did Henri say at the breakfast we had together about the causes of a crime? Sex, money, jealousy, revenge and now fanaticism. I'd add national security, which would explain why Jason was killed."

Richard drove on steadily. "As an exercise, why don't we explore the other motives?"

"You mean because my thinking has been too focused on the Chinese?"

"No, because you keep reaching a dead end in your thinking. Why don't we reverse and start down a different road?"

"How?"

"Let's consider each type of motive, one by one. Let's start with sex."

"Jason was gay but wanted to rise in the government. He was handsome and witty and used flirtation to hide his sexuality."

"Could he have been murdered by a woman who felt jilted?" Richard asked.

Elspeth was glad for the darkness as she felt herself blushing at the remembrance of her trip up the lift with Jason when he had kissed her. But certainly something like that could not lead to killing someone. That Jason was only flirting was so obvious.

"He married Robert Kahn openly. His flirtations were a cover but they were never serious," she said. She had no intention of letting on to Richard how she had felt in Jason's presence.

"Could someone have taken them as being serious?"

"I can't think who at the conference, except Brittany Rogers. She poured herself over him at the bar but he brought her up short and told her to go finish her report. That hardly constitutes a reason to commit a capital crime. I had the feeling that Brittany was as insincere in her flirtations as Jason was, that it all was an act."

"Was there any other sexual involvement?"

"Oh Seung and her husband fought over his supposed relationship with Chin Mei-su."

"Do you think Chin Mei-su may have murdered Kim Bae?"

"No. Why would she? She certainly must have been concentrating on leaving with John C. Smith. From what I can tell from the tapes, he was with the Chinese all evening after dinner."

"Could Oh Seung have killed Kim Bae?"

"She said that he had strayed before. She didn't kill him those times. Also that wouldn't explain why Jason was murdered. After all Jason was the chief victim and Bae collateral damage."

"Is that true?" Richard said. "Could there have been two separate murders?"

She froze. She never had considered this seriously. "Kim Bae was not even part of the delegation and came only at the last minute. Who would target him separately? He never appeared in the list of attendees, nor was he in any way involved. No, the murders were definitely linked."

"All right, No sex," Richard said. "Let's take motive two: money. Who gained financially from the two murders?"

"I assume Oh Seung and her children in Korea and Robert Kahn, as Jason's next of kin."

"Perhaps the Chinese had accepted a great deal of money to defect and had not wanted anyone know. Or perhaps Jason said he would expose them or have them sent back to China? Would that be an acceptable motive?"

"You're still thinking of a link between the two murderers, aren't you?" she asked.

"I suppose I am."

"I think we can take money off the list," Elspeth said. "Now revenge. Mmm. Revenge for what? That 'what' must have been something deep in the criminal's mind or heart in order to provoke two such violent acts. Other than professionally, the members of the conference didn't know each other as far as I know. Certainly the members of each individual delegation might have been friends as well as colleagues. But the murders involved two different delegations. The only people I know who associated outside the conferences were Katherine Croft and Oh Seung. There were four married couples: the Chinese, the Russians, the Japanese and the Koreans. The Chinese we know defected or we are presuming so. Svetlana Mihailova was more interested in shopping and nightclubs than in her husband. Takanori Sakurai ignored his wife. And then there were the Koreans, who ended their mission sadly."

"And terrorism?" Richard asked.

"State security might be an issue here. I've always suspected this to be the real motive, and that John C. Smith was behind both murders. Jason's was intentional and Kim Bae's by an accident of necessity but I have absolutely no proof other than that the man came from the CIA to check if anything was left behind."

"Considering all your observations, who pops up most often?" he asked.

She thought for a moment. "Oh Seung but that can't be right. She was with Katherine Croft at the time of the murders."

"What time was Kim Bae murdered?"

"I wish I knew for certain. At the preliminary examination, the coroner said between half past seven and eleven o'clock."

"Perhaps Henri Gilbert can find out for you."

"Let's assume that Kim Bae and Jason were killed about the same time. In order for Oh Seung to do this, she would have had to go into Bae's room, kill him, come out again and get into Jason's room, since travelling through the connecting doors would be impossible without a master passkey. She would have to know that Jason was coming back to his room because she had the chloroform and covered the mouth of the first person through the door. Unfortunately that was me, not Jason. Jason's room was terribly torn up, so I assume there was a fierce fight. Oh Seung is a slight woman. Jason could have easily overcome her. But why would she do all that? In any case, we saw her on the tapes leave the room she shared with Bae, take the lift and go up to Katherine Croft's room."

"What if the person who went in Jason's room could have left by the Koreans' room?"

"Again the same problem with the connecting doors," Elspeth said. "I still opt for John C. Smith. If he works for the CIA, he would have a way of breaking the locking system code, which is fairly standard for good hotels. Nowadays, it's all controlled by computer."

"Blaming John C. Smith is too easy," Richard said. "Didn't you say the person who went in one room and came out the other was probably a woman?

Elspeth put her head back on the headrest of her seat. "Probably. Women walk differently from men, even men trained as dancers or actors. So here we are back to square one. Oh, Dickie, I've played every scenario over and over in my head and I still can't find a reasonable solution."

Richard swerved to avoid an animal crossing the road. Terrified eyes caught the headlamps and then disappeared.

"Damn," he said. "I'd better pay attention to my driving but I want to continue to talk."

"What's the use?" she said glumly.

"The use is that we need to get our lives back," he responded.

They did not speak of the murders again that evening.

The next morning, over bowls of porridge with a baked apple, Richard approached Elspeth again.

Elspeth looked at him over her coffee cup as he spoke. He wondered what she was thinking. She seemed a bit more cheerful this morning and he hoped it was because of his talk with her on the way back from the station.

"You should get in touch with Oh Seung," he said.

"Good heavens, why?"

"Sex, money, revenge and who knows things about national security. She came up too often last night."

"But she was so open when I talked to her in Victoria."

"What better cover than feigned innocence," he said. "Do you know how to reach her?"

"I suppose I could go through the Korean embassy in London but I would feel odd doing so."

"Why would she be averse to answering your questions? She has no idea that you have moved on from the case in Victoria. Also, I suspect she of all people would like to know where the police investigation is now."

"But I don't know where it is," Elspeth protested.

"You will once you talk to Henri."

"What are you proposing I ask Oh Seung?"

"About sex, money and revenge?" he said, licking his spoon to get the last bits of porridge. He had performed this act so many times as a boy and was even today still extremely fond of Scottish porridge.

She glowered at him. He wondered if it was because of his boyish act or his proposal about Oh Seung.

"Do you think she did it?" Elspeth asked.

"Perhaps not but she may have some vital bits of evidence that even she doesn't know she has. You're clever, my dearest. I'm certain you can think of the right questions to ask her. It's a fresh start anyway."

Elspeth pursed her lips. He had seen her do this before when undecided about an issue. "Let me think about it."

"Is there a better way to get your life back than by continuing the investigation?"

"Do you seriously think it will work?"

"I think it's worth a try."

Together they cleared their breakfast things and washed up in the small kitchen area that was cleverly disguised behind cupboard doors in their sitting area. The area was the result of Biddy's first husband's planning for guest suites in the main portion of the rambling house at Tay Farm. Elspeth and Richard seldom went down to the big kitchen for breakfast. Biddy was always off early to her farm chores and Max always hurried through his breakfast on weekdays before rushing off to his office in Perth.

Elspeth fetched her laptop and began punching the keys madly.

"In for a dime, in for a dollar," she said in her American voice.

He was always startled when she spoke this way. He often forgot that she had spent twenty years in California, where she had learned Standard American English in order to avoid being asked if she were 'English'. He often had the same question but always replied gently "British" and left it at that. Elspeth was fiercer about Scottish nationalism and more annoyed to have it questioned despite her normal received pronunciation.

"I've got it," she finally said.

"What?" he asked.

"Oh Seung's email address. It's at the Ministry of Foreign Affairs and Trade in Seoul, I presume it isn't a direct line but I'll send something off anyway. Dickie, my love, we can only hope."

Hope did pay off. The next morning a reply came in. The return email address was a personal one.

The message read: Dear Elspeth, Delighted to hear from you. Actually I will be in London next week. Is there any chance we can meet? Best wishes, Seung."

He leaned over Elspeth's shoulder as she typed back. She expressed her pleasure over hearing so quickly from Oh Seung, and suggested they meet at Richard and Elspeth's flat in Kensington. When working for the Kennington Organisation Elspeth would not have invited business contacts to their flat. Had she changed her view now that she owned it? Initially she had been annoyed when the lawyers in Malta, who oversaw her legacy from Magdelena Cassar, had insisted that Elspeth become the sole owner of the flat according to the terms of Magdelena's will that Elspeth could only spend money on herself. Richard did not mind. He said to Elspeth that Magdelena had given him her palace in Valletta and he would go and live there if Elspeth kicked him out of the flat. In any case the sailing was better in Malta than London. He sent her off into giggles when he said this, although he never had been sure why. Magdelena had provided for them both. He also assumed that he and Elspeth would be together to the end of their lives and that the names on legal documents had little relevance.

"I'll call Mrs Brown and have her get a meal sent in. Do you want to come, Dickie?"

"I'll leave it to you."

"Probably a good idea," Elspeth said. "Oh Seung may talk more freely if it's just the two of us."

22

Through all the days before the Gilberts arrived from Canada, Richard watched Elspeth closely and tried to assess her mood. She often lapsed into long moments of silence but he sensed she was thinking rather than brooding. Occasionally she would utter small sounds of comprehension and then nod her head up and down. She took to taking long walks by herself when he was writing. She would come back with a frown on her face but would smile at him once she came in the door to their rooms.

"Any interesting thoughts?" he would ask.

She would shake her head. "Just filtering ideas," she would say. He didn't question her further.

On the Friday when the Gilberts were due to arrive, he found her in bed, her laptop on her legs, pounding the keys furiously. She ran her fingers over the keypad and he could hear his printer regurgitating something in the other room.

"There," she cried. "My list of questions for Henri Gilbert. Let's just hope he's cooperative and Biddy and Charlie don't mind if I sequester him for a half an hour or so. Dickie, may I be so presumptuous to ask that you be with me when I talk to him?"

"Of course. May I see the questions?"

She fetched the paper and handed it to him. He read it down quickly.

"All you seem to be doing is establishing a timeline around the time of Jason Ravensworth's death and getting the forensic evidence on Kim Bae's death. Nothing on Jason's death itself."

"The list includes all the things I don't know already. After our discussion coming back from the railway station, I have a new idea."

"Do you want to let me in on it?"

"Not yet because it is dependent on what both Henri Gilbert and Oh Seung tell me. I've been wrong too many times on this case. This time I want to be right, for the sake of being right if nothing else. I don't care what Eric Kennington thinks," she added defiantly.

*

Charlie held Michelle's hand as they emerged from the security area at Edinburgh airport. He could feel it was damp and shook slightly.

"Do you think they will like me?" she whispered.

"Max will. He likes everyone. You'll see. He's meeting us."

"And your mother?"

"I expect every mother is a bit critical of her son's girlfriend. She will be polite at first and then warm up to you once she sees how terrific you are."

"She won't mind that I'm not English?"

"She will be relieved. She's a true Scotswoman. The Scots are always leery of the English, who have not always treated us well."

Michelle giggled. "Then she won't mind if I am half French Canadian and half Irish?"

"Don't worry. She won't care."

They pushed through the security door. Charlie looked up and saw Max Douglas-Forbes waiting outside. Charlie liked Max, most particularly what he had done for his mother. Charlie had been worried that his mother after his father's death had too often resorted to a glass of whiskey to curb her loneliness. Max had cured her of that. Charlie could see the affection between them in little things, gestures, glances, half-smiles. His mother spoke now of Ivor Baillie Shaw, his father, as being part of her life previously but not with the great longing she had shown after he died and before she had married Max.

Max stepped forward as Charlie, Michelle and her parents came into the main body of the airport.

Max shook Charlie's hand and then took both of Michelle's hands in his in a gesture of welcome. He was more formal with Michelle's parents and bid them welcome to Scotland and gave hope that they had had an uneventful trip. Charlie knew that air travel was no longer pleasant and was glad Max had not asked if they had a nice trip. No transcontinental trip was anywhere near as pleasant as it had been years ago.

Charlie pointed out places along the way to Tay Farm. He had reassured Michelle that all would be well but he wasn't so sure himself. He had never brought a woman to Tay Farm nor had he been so serious before. He wanted to propose to Michelle down by the loch in a place where he used to go to dream about the future and who his lifelong partner might be. He had not bought the ring because he thought they might like to choose one together in New York. In a weak moment, when Michelle said her parents had planned to travel around Britain, he had invited them to the farm as well. His mother had seen through him and asked his intentions. He admitted them but had sworn her to secrecy. But would his mother have that knowing look, an unnamed suggestion that a future mother-in-law had in her face when she met the intended? He hoped his mother would be busy with all her guests and not focus on Michelle.

His mother had told him that Richard and Elspeth would be there as well. They were staying in the large wing of the house. Michelle's parents would stay there in the rooms next to them. Charlie's mother had said she would put Charlie in his old room and Michelle in his sister Mary's room next door and that they could make of this what they would. For this he was grateful.

His mother was standing by the door to the kitchen when they arrived. She was fussing with a large flowerpot filled with lavender. Charlie had never seen his mother fuss this way before. She usually left the pots to Jean Macpherson, who came in to help with the cleaning and cooking.

She stood as the car came down the drive. Charlie noticed that she was dressed in tweeds, good ones, not her usual jeans or corduroys. Her hair was beautifully cut and she wore light makeup, which was not her everyday custom. Charlie suspected Elspeth had something to do with this. Tobey, the Border collie who stayed in the barn, was at his mother's side, as he was much of the day. Tobey's manners were excellent as a result of long training as a sheep dog. Charlie hoped Michelle liked dogs; he had never asked her.

They stepped out of the car and introductions were made. Charlie could see his mother eyeing Michelle but her expression was welcoming and Charlie inwardly let out a sigh of relief. The weekend had begun well.

Elspeth and Richard came in an hour later at the end of what Charlie thought must have been a discreet walk. No introductions were necessary and Henri Gilbert and Fay Fitzhugh expressed delight at seeing them. Charlie could tell that Elspeth was uncomfortable and he could not tell why. Lunch followed and then the obligatory rest for weary travellers.

Charlie drew Michelle into his room and kissed her.

"That wasn't so bad, was it?" he asked.

She hugged him tightly. "I like your mother and Max. I hope they like me. Do you think they find me too young? I don't speak the way you all do. Will that be a problem? You all seem so very British."

"They will love you, the way I do."

Michelle posed the question he had wanted to ask. "Why are your Aunt Elspeth and Uncle Richard here?"

He did not know the answer, it being one of those family things that to date had not been disclosed to the younger generation. He knew Richard and Elspeth had been in Scotland since their abrupt departure from Canada. His mother said they were renovating the barn by the loch as a retirement home. But Charlie knew Richard and Elspeth well enough to sense that something else had happened. They had mentioned nothing in Victoria just months before about retiring to Scotland.

"My family is often filled with mysteries," he said. "As children, my sister, brother and I would make up fanciful stories about the adults, particularly Aunt Elspeth. Her life was filled with strange events that never were fully explained and only whispered about when the children were in the room. Someday I shall corner her and find out the truth. Supposedly there was a murder when she was a student at Cambridge and she was involved in it somehow. My mother always said that it was best it was never talked about."

He kissed her again. "Get some rest and then we will walk down by the loch. I want to show you my favourite place in the world."

*

Richard and Elspeth returned from a walk up the path along the burn that ran from the highlands above through the farm and down to Loch Tay. A shower passed and the sun came out, dappling the bracken along their way.

"I always think of places like this as a fairyland," Elspeth said. "As a child I would come here and dream about all the places my grandfather showed me in a large atlas he had in the library. I know now that the maps were of the world's countries before the Great War, when most of the plates were mainly red and showed the extent of the British Empire. Grandfather and I would get lost in the fantasy of the names of faraway places, Kuala Lumpur, Nairobi, Delhi, Tasmania, Buenos Aires, Singapore. I have been to so many of them now; I never thought I would. When there was still a little money in the Tay bank accounts, Grandfather was sent on the grand tour of Europe. I don't think he left the UK after that."

Richard walked contentedly at her side. He knew she had been talking about family history with her parents. He did not speak because he did not want to break her mood. They walked on in silence.

She stopped. "If we retire here, will we have to give up

travelling?"

"I shouldn't think so," he said. "Only it will be for pleasure not business."

"It's strange," she continued, "that in all the years I worked for Eric, I made few friends. Pamela, of course, and Jean Henderson, whom I knew at Cambridge. I see Sarah Brixton occasionally as well."

"And me," he said, feeling a bit shy.

She turned to him. "And you, my love. You are my friend, my lover and my life. How strange it's been to be so close to you these last three months. Every day has been a gift. I didn't know they would be so precious."

Warmth fled through him. He was a sixty-year-old plus man who suddenly felt like an eighteen year old boy. For more than forty years he had loved Elspeth. For forty years he had hoped for moments like this with her. He took her gently in his arms and they stood softly together; the seconds passed. But he knew Elspeth well enough to know that she would not stay content for long.

"Now I suppose we have to go and face the music," she said. "The Gilberts should be up from their rest."

*

Elspeth did not want the moment with Richard to end. When she wrote out the list of questions the day before, she had felt so confident that her new theory on the case in Victoria would prove to be the correct one. Pieces were missing from the puzzle and she doubted Henri Gilbert could give her all the answers. Her interview with Oh Seung was vital but only after Henri had told her what she wanted to hear.

Elspeth and Richard entered the large kitchen that was the centre of life at Tay Farm. Jeanne Macpherson was at the Aga and waved a greeting, her hand had a large spoon attached. She went back to stirring a pot that let off enticing aromas. Biddy was at the large table working on her accounts and talking to Robbie Macpherson, her farm manager. They were discussing the recent lambing and how many lambs needed to go to the abattoir in August to make a profit for the farm. Biddy ran the farm and was as sharp a stickler for detail as her first husband, Ivor, had been. Together Ivor and Biddy had turned the farm from a decaying vestige of the past to a modern agricultural enterprise. Robbie Macpherson had been a full participant in the whole process and worked closely with Biddy to keep the farm out of the red.

Biddy looked up as Elspeth and Richard entered. "The ewes have given us two hundred lambs. We can save the best twenty ewes for future breeding stock and still turn over a handsome return. Thank you, Robbie. I'll make sure Jean gets home in time for your tea."

Biddy had the common touch, which had always eluded Elspeth. She admired her cousin, who had opted to stay in Perthshire and make her life fulfilling in a small area. Elspeth had chosen the world as her venue and now was looking back at her life with a certain futility. Elspeth wondered what her world would have been if she had come back to Perthshire from Cambridge and settled down as a partner in her father's firm of solicitors. But her grandfather's atlas has left its mark.

"Are Henri and Faith down yet?" she asked.

"We're here," Faith's voice said. "Henri says we

shouldn't sleep for more than an hour or we won't sleep tonight. Something smells delicious."

Faith went over to the Aga to smell Jean Macpherson's concoction. Henri came up to Elspeth and Richard.

"I can see why you have come to this place. It's magic."

Elspeth plunged in, making up her words as she went along. "It's where I spent a great deal of my childhood. When I had to leave London quickly in January, this seemed to be the place to come. I suppose I could be traced here eventually but it would take time. And this is where Richard and I met. We're renovating a barn down by the loch for our retirement. Biddy's brother, who owns the farm, has given us a long-term lease."

Henri looked puzzled. "Can't you buy it?"

Elspeth cleared her throat. She was not sure if Charlie had explained the situation about Tay Farm to the Gilberts.

"The farm is the last remaining bit of the grant given to our ancestors by George II when they gave our ever-so-great grandfather the earldom," she said. "I'm afraid the rest of whatever fortune there once was has now been squandered away."

"Earldom?" Henri said.

"Biddy's father, my uncle, was the Earl of Tay, as is her brother now. It means nothing. Johnnie, that is Biddy's brother, lives happily in Perth with his new wife and their young son, and is a small businessman somehow involved in the computer industry. The earldom is a bit of an embarrassment but there is no way for the family to shed it. One can't simply say that they won't be an earl anymore."

"Elspeth and her mother always hated the title," Biddy

explained. "Both are truly equalitarian, although short of being republicans. The title was given to our family when they sided against the highlanders at the Battle of Culloden."

"And with the Butcher of Brunswick, who slaughtered the clansmen," Elspeth said with some feeling. "It's still a hot topic in Scottish history."

Faith laughed. "I had no idea we were in such distinguished company. My family in Ireland were vilified as English landlords, although in the end we settled in and became as Irish as all our neighbours. I was the first to leave Ireland in four hundred years. I think family histories are intriguing."

Biddy stowed away her accounts and Robbie left with Tobey wagging his tail and following him to the barn. Richard offered drinks and they all settled around the kitchen table. Elspeth wanted to relax but she knew that she would have to approach the subjects of the murders in Victoria soon.

She sipped her sherry and cleared her throat. "Have they concluded the case at the Kennington Victoria yet?" She knew they had not because Pamela would have let her know if they had.

Henri accepted a whisky from Richard. "After our breakfast together, I took more interest in the case. Strangely Inspector Clough has come to a dead end. We all were concerned. He blamed it on not being able to interview all the witnesses because of diplomatic immunity." As he said this, he raised an eyebrow to Elspeth. She blushed inwardly.

Biddy rose and said to Faith, "They seem to want to talk about crime, which doesn't interest me in the least. Would you like to come out to the barn and see my hens? It's time for me to feed them. So far this year I have been able to keep the fox away from the henhouse. It's a constant bother."

Silently Elspeth thanked Biddy for luring Faith away. Richard led them into the morning room and stirred up the fire, which already had been lit.

"I'm afraid that because I was called back to London so suddenly I did not get back to you after I asked you to intervene in the case. Did you ever contact the Canadian Secret Intelligence Service?"

"I did actually. As always they were not forthcoming but they did say that the Canadian government had full knowledge that the Chinese were going to defect to the US. Beyond that they gave no details. They assured me that Jason Ravensworth did know about what was to happen in the hotel that night. They thought his death had nothing to do with it."

"A rather belated thank you for that," Elspeth said. "I've come to the same conclusion but it's nice to have it confirmed." Did they ever do postmortems on Jason Ravensworth or on Kim Bae?"

"Normally I don't follow such things but since you had asked me to be involved, I did keep an eye open as to what went on."

"Did they ever establish what time Mr Kim actually died? Was it before or after Jason?"

"They couldn't tell who died first. Both died between half past eight and nine o'clock. As you know Mr Ravensworth was stabbed; Kim Bae was smothered, probably after being chloroformed. But interestingly enough, there were no signs of any prolonged violence on their persons. Neither had bruises or cuts that one would associate with extreme physical resistance."

This perplexed Elspeth. Jason's room showed every sign of a violent fight. She had always assumed that her foot had been trod upon during this fight whilst she was lying unconscious on the floor.

"Other than the skewer being from the kitchen or dining area, did your detectives pick up any other physical clues when they first examined the rooms," she asked.

"They think the destruction of the furniture in Mr Ravensworth's room was done after he was killed, probably to indicate that there had been a fight."

"I always thought it was a cover-up of sorts," Elspeth said. "I wonder why?"

"I talked with Inspector Clough about a month ago. He still was muttering about the case and about you in particular."

"I wasn't on my best behaviour," Elspeth said with a chuckle, "but I did want to do my work and he was doing everything he could to prevent me. I still want to know who the murderer was."

"Inspector Clough speculated that there might be two murderers."

"That was my theory," Richard said.

"What do you suppose the odds are of two murders being committed within a few feet of each other at almost exactly the same time and not having a connection could be?" Elspeth asked.

"Highly unusual but you cannot rule it out," Henri said.

"I still think that our murderer was a member of the delegation and the reasons for the murders were connected.

I wish I knew who was murdered first but it's useful to know that the murders were about the same time. I'm still mystified as to how the murderer got from one room to the next. If I could work that out, I think a big piece of the puzzle would fall into place. Do either of you have any ideas? You see when the murderer moved from one room to the next, she or he must have gone through the connecting door. The security tapes show that. But how without the master pass key?"

Both Richard and Henri shook their heads and acknowledged that it was indeed a puzzlement.

Elspeth blew out her breath. "If Jason knew about the Chinese, the motive of his trying to be silenced goes away. I was already beginning to suspect that we are looking for someone who had other reasons to have killed both men and that one or the other of them was killed purposefully and the other circumstantially. But I'm still not certain which was which."

Richard cocked his head. "Are you implying that Jason might not be the main target and that Kim Bae was? Who in the hotel would want to kill Kim?"

"Most probably his wife," Henri said. "Most murders are committed by people close to the victim."

"Yes, I know," Elspeth said. "But I'm not convinced it was Oh Seung. I think, however, she may know who the killer was, even if not consciously. I'm going to see her next week when I'm in London. Are you and Faith going to be there as well? Perhaps we could have dinner together?"

"Take care, Elspeth. If Oh Seung, whom I am assuming is Kim Bae's wife, is hiding anything, she may not like you stirring things up. And if she is the murderer . . ." Henri let his last thought drop.

"I have a feeling that she won't rest easily until she knows who killed her husband. I may be wrong. Certainly I have been before but I don't think I'm in any danger. Thank you, Henri, for telling me what you know."

The detective superintendent from the Canadian police looked at her from under lowered eyebrows and then said with an amused glimmer in his eye, "We're practically related, aren't we?"

Elspeth laughed. "That's now entirely up to Charlie and Michelle."

*

Charlie had not thought that proposing would be so nerve wracking. Michelle had skipped down the path to the loch from the farmhouse in a merry mood. Twice she threw her arms in the air.

"I can't believe I'm in Scotland," she said. "Everywhere is so beautiful. Why did you ever want to leave?"

He grinned. "Can't you imagine what life was like here when one was a teenager? We all wanted to get away from the numbing stillness of this place. Nothing ever changes here. Yes, this is one of the most beautiful spots in the world, but no place for the young and ambitious."

"Are you ambitious, Charlie?" she said, suddenly stopping and turning toward him. "Tell me about your ambitions."

She was giving him the perfect lead-in but his stomach still clenched. He froze, when he knew he should come forward and take her in his arms.

He bleated out, "I want to marry you, Michelle. I know we haven't known each other for a long time but I knew from that evening we walked along the breakwater in Victoria that you were the one. Will you marry me, please?"

Her eyes found his. "Of course I will, Charlie, if you'll have me."

He swallowed and said seriously, "I will have you." Then he shouted out with glee, "I will have you, I will have you, I will have you. I'm the happiest man in the world." He twirled around, stumbled on a root, and fell over. She knelt beside him.

"I love you, Charlie. Are you all right?"

"I have never been better in my life but I think I have bashed my knee," he said, grabbing her and pulling her to him. She melted into his touch and filled him with joy. "I do love you," she whispered in her ear. His knee did not really begin to hurt until they got back to the farmhouse much later.

23

Elspeth felt a new sense of ownership when she entered her flat in Kensington. In the past, she had lived there as an employee of the Kennington Organisation and always considered this perk as one among many of her employment. She also had supposed her tenancy would end when she retired. Now that she had bought the lease, she felt a sense of home in being there. "It's mine," she said out loud, as she put the key in the lock. "All mine." She sniggered and wrapped her hands together as she might have in one of the melodramas her mother had directed when Elspeth was a pupil at Blair School for Girls. She did not know what overcame her. She was glad that Richard was not there to hear her silly words. She straightened herself up and then said sotto voce in tribute to Magdelena Cassar, who had left the money that had made Elspeth's purchase of the flat possible, "Thank you, Aunt Mag."

On her arrival in London the day before, she dined with Henri, Faith, Charlie and Michelle. The latter two were in their own world and left directly after dessert. Elspeth settled in to get to know Faith and Henri better. She found them both warm and outgoing and felt Charlie had made a good choice in his future in-laws.

Now she had to face Oh Seung. She had gone round to the corner shop to buy fresh bread and flowers but otherwise had their lunch organised, thanks to the help of her housekeeper, Mrs Brown. The table in the dining area was set and Elspeth had carefully thought through her strategy for questioning Oh Seung.

The Korean woman was on time to the minute. Elspeth wondered if she had been waiting outside until the exact moment of the invitation. The flat was on the first floor, up a flight of stairs. This always gave time for Elspeth to compose herself between the time guests rang the bell and their arrival at the door on the upper level. Elspeth had left this door open and called a welcome down to Oh Seung as she began the climb up the stairs. They shook hands warmly as she arrived.

"We recently bought the flat," Elspeth said, choosing the plural possessive purposely, "although I have lived here for many years. Richard never has never had a permanent home, as he was in the diplomatic corps. Now, on his retirement, we purchased the flat and are renovating a derelict barn on Loch Tay in Scotland. Perhaps one sign of getting on in life is the need to be settled."

"Are you still working for the hotels?" Oh Seung asked.

Elspeth skirted the question. "I'm taking a bit of time off whilst Richard gets used to his retirement. I'm overseeing the construction in Scotland and he is writing his memoirs. But I still am interested in what happened in Victoria."

Elspeth poured sherry for them both and they settled into the sofas in the living area.

"They never found the killer but you probably already know that," Oh Seung said.

Elspeth nodded. "I never was satisfied with the police

investigation. I was hoping you could provide me with some answers. I hope you don't think I've asked you here under false pretences."

"Not at all. I'm as anxious as you are to know the truth."

"Then you will not mind if I ask some probing questions?"

Seung frowned. Elspeth hoped this was not a sign of denial.

"My children are old enough now that they want to know how their father died. I have never used the word murder with them. I simply have said he died by accident."

"Do you believe that?" Elspeth asked.

"No," Seung said drily.

"Do you honestly think he was killed purposefully?"

Oh Seung took a sip of her sherry and looked up at Elspeth. "Yes," she responded simply.

Elspeth let the moment rest. Finally she said, "Why?"

"Didn't I mention in Victoria that he . . . that he had affairs on the side?"

Elspeth nodded. "You did tell me."

"It was more than once. I put up with it for the sake of both our careers. Now I think I shouldn't have. But in Korea divorce in high places is still frowned upon. He had ambitions far beyond his position in the Ministry. Each time he pled with me to take him back. I always capitulated. But each time it became harder. I've never told anyone this before. I hope I can trust your discretion."

"Of course. I would not have been successful in my career with the Kennington Organisation all these years if I told things guests said to me in confidence."

How glibly I am covering over my suspension, Elspeth

thought.

"Was your husband having an affair with Chin Mei-su at the time he died?" Elspeth asked directly.

"I'm not sure. He definitely was pursuing some woman in the hotel. I had no way of knowing if it was Chin Mei-su or not. I thought so from the way he looked at her when they were in the same room together. Year after year I put up with the same thing. We no longer lived as man and wife, although at conferences I shared a room with Bae in order to keep up appearances."

"Why then did he come to Victoria?"

"He said he wanted to, that he had some quiet business he wanted to conduct with Chao Kai."

"Did you believe him?"

"I shouldn't have. Chao Kai once served in the Chinese embassy in Seoul, before he married Chin Mei-su. He was a minor official, at least on the embassy rosters. Bae always said he did more than his job description would indicate. Since I didn't know for sure, I couldn't say no to Bae when he asked to go to Canada."

"Do you think Chao Kai murdered him because of his involvement with Chin Mei-su? If the Chinese were considering their mysterious disappearance from the hotel, he would have a perfect way to escape the police's scrutiny. Or might there be another reason?"

Elspeth had considered this question before asking Oh Seung. Chao Kai was a small man and could have been the figure that went into Jason's room and came out the Koreans'.

"I wish I knew," Seung said.

"Was your husband in intelligence? I'll ask but I realise you may not be allowed to answer."

Oh Seung shook her head. "No, but like any person involved with foreign affairs, he cooperated with our secret services. I think if Chao Kai did kill Bae, it would be out of anger that Bae had seduced or tried to seduce Chin Mei-su, not for reasons of state security."

"Jealousy," Elspeth said under her breath.

"Revenge," Seung countered. "I didn't share this with the police because I didn't like Inspector Clough. Is that a good reason? I guess I was so used to keeping Bae's affairs secret that I was good at it. But it's a relief to get it all out in the open. Do you think you can establish that Chao Kai was Bae's murderer?"

"I don't think he was," Elspeth said.

"Why not?" Seung asked.

"Because I think the murderer was a woman."

"Chin Mei-su?"

"For a long while I thought so but now I think not. Don't ask me why. I'm not sure myself." Elspeth had not expected to say this. She just had a sudden flash that someone other than Chin Mei-su had killed Bae. Suddenly she thought she knew who and why. Now she had to work out how and prove it to the police.

"Did your husband have affairs with any of the other women who were at the conference?"

"He may have tried. That would be like him. But did he succeed? I have no idea. We spent most of our waking hours apart."

"Could he have had an assignation the night he was killed and started his disagreement with you to chase you away?"

"I don't know. We seldom fought in public. That night he wanted to."

"Would he have expected that you would run to Katherine Croft if he argued with you?"

"He knew I was close to Katherine."

"Had you ever discussed his affairs with Katherine?"

"No. You are the first person I've ever told. Somehow I trust you to help."

"I know this may be painful but do you know if he ever was rebuffed when he made advances?"

"He had lots of sex appeal but over the years there probably were women who did not appreciate his attentions to them."

"Any woman who was at the conference?"

"I've no idea. I had stopped trying to find out."

"I'm sorry you have been through so much," Elspeth said and meant it. "Shall we have lunch and talk of more pleasant things?"

"Thank you for letting me get all this out. I hope it's been useful for my children's sake. They loved their father, even if I no longer did."

After Oh Seung left the Kensington flat, Elspeth got on her mobile to Henri Gilbert and asked if she could see him that afternoon. Her new insight could mean that she would have to return to Canada and work with Inspector Clough again. She could not pursue the case in Victoria any further unless she had his cooperation and she felt Henri Gilbert might smooth the way. She invited Henri and Faith round for tea. She could use the leftover cake she had bought for lunch and slice up the remaining bread to make some cucumber sandwiches. A typical British tea. They would enjoy it, she hoped. Had she still been working for Eric Kennington, she would have invited then to the Kennington Mayfair but that was in the past. She would have to get used to the change and make do with her own resources. She should really learn to cook better. Even when she lived in California with her first husband, she had a cook.

Faith preceded Henri up the stairs to the flat, all the way exclaimed about the charm of London and its 'tucked-in architecture' as she dubbed it. Upon entering Elspeth's flat, she took in her breath.

"Why, it's filled with light," she exclaimed.

"The advantage of skylights. They give both privacy and interior light," Elspeth said. "They're the reason I chose the flat in the first place. Only the bathrooms and kitchen area needed serious attention when I moved in. A famous Hollywood interior designer owed me a great favour and paid for it by designing those spaces."

Elspeth gave Faith and Henri a tour of the flat and then they settled in the sitting area around Elspeth's traditional but uninspired tea. They did not seem to notice.

They talked of the Canadians' experience in London that day. Elspeth let them ramble on without interruption. She waited until the second cups of tea were poured before coming to the point of her invitation.

"Henri, how do you think Inspector Clough would react if I went back to Victoria? I'm almost certain I know who murdered the two men in the hotel and why. I'm still working on the 'how' but I'll get there soon. Will Inspector Clough stand in my way?"

"He's a proud man," Henri said, "and a determined one. But he still is smarting from the open case at the Kennington Victoria. I suggest that if you do return, you let me help ease the way. Do you really think returning is necessary? Can't you send an email to him with your suspicions?"

"Would he be convinced or would he be put off by my sticking my nose in again?"

"It's hard to say," Henri said. "He still harbours bad feelings towards you. He thinks it was you who threw the spanner in the works."

"Would an apology at this point help? I could tell him I was under the influence of painkillers and not thinking straight when I was there. I also would like to undo any damage I did by diverting his constables and his sergeant. I hope they didn't get into much trouble."

Henri smiled. "They survived because he put all the blame on you."

"Ouch," Elspeth said. "But isn't solving the case more important than the animosity that my actions stirred up?"

"Can you offer proof?"

"I can offer a theory that I don't think can be disproved. I'm not sure that's the same thing but I think if the murderer is confronted, they will confess." She used the gender neutral term advisedly. "Because I feel some contrition on how I handled Detective Inspector Clough and his team when I was there, I certainly would allow all the credit for the solution to go to the inspector. I also think that when my prime suspect is questioned, Inspector Clough should conduct the interview as a member of the RCMP. I have no authority but he does. If he can break the suspect, he will emerge as the hero in the case. I don't need to."

"Are you sure of your theory?" Henri asked.

"Ninety-five percent sure. Only two pieces are missing, but I think I can work them out before I get to Victoria."

"Will you stay at the Kennington Victoria?" Henri asked.

Before Elspeth had to explain that doing so would be awkward, Faith said, "Stay with us. It will be a good chance for us to get to know you and your family better. Will Richard come with you? Both of you are welcome. And bring Biddy and Max as well."

"What a lovely invitation. I'd love to stay and I might be able to persuade Richard. He served in Ottawa early in his career and he might like to go there to do some research for his memoirs. I'll ask Biddy but the lambs have just been born and she probably will want to stay on the farm to see if they are faring well."

Henri glanced over at his wife and then looked squarely at Elspeth. "I suggest you not try to use diplomatic immunity again. That would be a red flag to Clough."

"Richard's retired now. Neither one of us has a diplomatic passport anymore. We'll come as private citizens."

"Good," said Henri. "May I second Faith's idea. We would love to have you come and stay. Michelle will be finishing her degree at the University of British Columbia in Vancouver. She and Charlie want to be married in Victoria in October so we already feel like empty nesters. Do you have children, Elspeth?"

Their conversation switched to families. As they left, Elspeth once again brought up the issue of Inspector Clough's receiving her.

"Don't worry," Henri said. "I'll pull rank if I have to."

24

Elspeth had to resolve the two most vital clues in her investigation. How did the murderer get from Jason's room to Bae's or possibly the other way around? And how and why had she been hurt in Jason's room because she now knew there had been no fight between Jason and the murderer? She had several ideas but it always came back to the difficulty of needing a master key to open both doors. Now that Henri Gilbert had confirmed that Jason's body had no injuries other than the fatal one, she needed to find out why she had been crippled.

When she arrived back in Scotland, she drove her car from the railway station at Pitlochry, where she had left it, and found Richard busily at work on his computer in their sitting area, with an uneaten sandwich by his side.

"How would you like to go back to Victoria?" she said immediately after her greeting. Then she added, "Henri and Faith have invited us to come."

He raised an eyebrow. "Just out of the blue? Or do I see your hand in this, Elspeth?"

"Perhaps I left the way open for their invitation. I think I know who committed the murders but I need the Canadian police to issue the official arrest warrant."

"Can you convince them you're right?"

"I hope so. I have two more things to work out to present a fool proof case. Now that I know who the murderer is, I should be able to do that with just a bit more thought."

Richard smiled at her. "You can't just let it go, can you?" he said.

She could not. She wondered if she was using pinpointing the murderer to absolve herself in Lord Kennington's eyes or because of her deep belief in justice. Her dismissal from the Kennington Organisation still hurt.

"I don't want the murderer to go free and leave the families of the victims without the consolation that the murder has been brought to justice."

He rose, took her shoulders and looked into her eyes. He repeated Henri's words. "Can't you email your suspicions to the police in Victoria? You sound as if you want to be in on the kill. Or is it proving to Eric Kennington that you were not incompetent?"

She had difficulty denying his last accusation. "Dickie, I don't want to leave the Kennington Organisation with my last case being a failure. Even if I don't go back, I don't want to leave with a black mark on my long career there."

"If you don't go back? Is that a possibility?"

"Let me get this case solved before I decide," she said with inner turmoil.

During the last three months she felt she had changed. Not since her childhood had she taken so much pleasure in living in Scotland. She was now as close to her parents as she had ever been and she knew that their lives would not be infinite. She enjoyed planning a country home with Richard and often thought what it would be like to live there with him, close to Biddy and Max and on Tay Farm. But many days came where she missed the challenge of her career and the heart-pounding moments that sometimes accompanied it. Once the barn renovation was complete, what would she do with her time? Richard seemed content to immerse himself in his past; she had no desire to recreate her own life on paper. Her past had too much pain and she did not want to dredge it up. The frenetic activity of her occupation left little time for mulling over what had gone before. Her children were well established in their lives and she could only tolerate being a grandmother to the two young twins for a few days at a time. Would life stretch out ahead of her with no purpose if she decided not to go back to the Kennington Organisation or if Eric Kennington would not have her back? She may have a solution to the crimes in Victoria but she had no answers as to what to do once the case was over. Perhaps that was the reason she wanted to go back to Canada, to prolong her busyness.

She could not yet forgive Eric Kennington for his last treatment of her. Pamela Crumm had said that he was distressed by the illness of his wife but that did not justify his anger towards Elspeth. She had acted badly but she could not remember another time when she had used unconventional methods that he had been so reactive to them. Was it only because she had been unsuccessful? Or was it really his wife's health? Elspeth thought that she must ask Pamela how Lady Kennington was doing. Pamela would probably brush her off. Pamela had only this once given Elspeth insight into Eric's private life.

"What are you thinking?" Richard asked.

"Would my future life be too unstructured?" she asked.

"I think you need a sherry? Have you had dinner?"

"I had a sandwich at teatime on the train."

"I miss having a small French bistro around the corner," he said, "but I went to M&S in Perth yesterday and bought a few things, just in case you came home hungry. Would you like pasta or curry? I'm the chef tonight."

"Curry will be fine," Elspeth said. She did not tell him that all she really wanted was one of the specially prepared light meals made for her at the Kennington hotels.

As they were washing up, Elspeth approached Richard again.

"Will you come to Canada?"

"No, I think not. You seem to need to go, however. Give my regards to Henri and Faith. I do think Charlie has chosen well, despite the differences in their ages."

25

Elspeth did not leave for Canada until the second week in May. Henri and Faith by then had returned from their holiday to Great Britain and Ireland. Henri had assured Elspeth that Inspector Clough was looking forward to her visit. Elspeth doubted it.

She had made arrangements to have Spike meet her at the Victoria airport but had begged him to have a car waiting that was much smaller than the Cadillac limousine he had driven the winter before.

"It's that or my Thunderbird," Spike had emailed back. After some consideration, Elspeth chose the limousine.

Spike was at the airport waiting for her. This time he did not carry a sign.

"I see you couldn't resist coming back," he said. "How's the hubby?"

Elspeth has never thought of Richard as "the hubby" and laughed. "He's fine and said to say hello to you."

"Nice guy, although verrrry proper." Spike rolled his r's and laughed.

"A career hazard. He's loosening up now that he has retired."

"You love him, don't you?"

Elspeth found Spike cheeky but admitted that she did love Richard.

They pulled up in front of a modest house in the countryside outside Victoria and Elspeth told Spike she would call him when she needed him next. She planned only four days in Victoria but having her own transportation, no matter how large the car and flippant the driver were, would be useful.

Faith opened the door to her and hugged her warmly. "It's not as grand as the farm on Loch Tay or as well-situated as your flat in London but it has been our home since Henri was promoted to Chief Inspector. We love the Vancouver Island countryside, despite noises from the police that a home closer to town would have been more beneficial. Henri put his foot down, using me as an excuse, although he sometimes grumbled when he had to go out in snowstorms, which wasn't often. Has Richard ever used you as an excuse?"

"It's usually the other way around," Elspeth admitted.

"Henri is off on business but you will want a rest after your trip. He'll be home for dinner. Michelle will be back on Saturday. She particularly wants to see you, although she has exams coming up."

"Let me send my driver to fetch her."

"In that limousine?"

"He also has offered a Thunderbird. Michelle probably will appreciate it more than I."

"She would love it. Elspeth, I'm so excited about the wedding . . ."

Henri had set up a lunch between Inspector Clough and Elspeth on Saturday and promised to stay during the meal. The thirty-six-hour gap allowed Elspeth to contact Janet Church and ask her two vital questions. Elspeth regretted that she had left the hotel so abruptly that she could not have answered these questions earlier. She also was loath to discuss her departure. She did not know how much Janet Church knew of her dismissal or if Janet had suffered any consequences because of the murders that had taken place in her hotel.

Elspeth no longer had her office mobile with Janet's home phone on it but she found she did have the number recorded in her address book on her laptop. The morning after she had arrived she dialled Janet's number, expecting to leave a message. Instead she found Janet at home.

"Janet, Elspeth Duff here. Do you remember me?"

A long chuckle filled the line. "Elspeth, you would be hard to forget and the events of last January will never leave my mind. Where are you?"

"Here in BC. You may also recall my cousin, Charlie Baillie Shaw. He has just become engaged to someone he met in Victoria last winter. I'm staying with her parents. I wondered if you would see me while I'm here, to catch up on what's happened since I left."

Janet agreed and avoided the subject of Elspeth's current position with the Kennington Organisation. Elspeth wondered how much Janet knew.

"Come to my house. It's not far from the hotel. If you don't mind soup and sandwiches, let's say twelve thirty." Janet gave directions.

At half past twelve exactly, Spike's limousine rounded the corner and stopped in front of Janet's house, a small ground floor condominium with a minimal patio garden. Janet was waiting outside. Janet showed Elspeth into a large kitchen, with a built-in breakfast area. The table there was set for two and a plate of sandwiches, wrapped in cling film, was waiting for them. Soup was on the hob.

They started the meal with small talk but Elspeth could not keep it up for long.

"How much do you know?" she burst out.

Janet's eyes rested on Elspeth's. "Enough to know that you took most of the blame although I wasn't let off completely. I gave my notice but Ms Crumm called back the next day and begged me to return. I feel it's been touch and go ever since then. I haven't lost the opportunity to keep my options open. I was upset when I heard Lord Kennington had suspended you. What happened wasn't your fault. I tried to explain that to Ms Crumm. She said nothing."

"Pamela always stays solidly behind Eric Kennington, although I'm certain she doesn't always agree with him. She feels that they must always present a united front."

"Will you go back if asked?"

"I don't know if I will be asked," Elspeth said, feeling she was being evasive. "But I can't let the murders in your hotel go unsolved. One reason I have come here is to see if I can't gather a few more facts. Do you mind if I ask you several things?"

"Shoot," Janet said.

"I know the general policies on passkeys in the Kennington hotels but I want to confirm that you used this system. Did all the household staff, particularly the room attendants who did the rooms that night, have a master passkey to the rooms?"

"Only the rooms on the floors where they were assigned. Each floor was keyed differently, mainly for security. The code is changed every morning and the cards were updated for the evening household staff when they came on duty."

"Do these cards open the connecting doors between rooms?"

"Only if the rooms are occupied by the same party. If the rooms are occupied separately, the passkeys won't work between them. We changed our system at the end of last year and recommended the new system to London."

"Therefore, the night of the murders, no one with a passkey could have travelled between Mr Ravensworth's and Mr Kim's room. Is that correct?"

"No one except someone with a master key."

"How many of those existed?"

"Four. Mine, my assistant manager's, the night manager's, and the one I gave to you. If the head of security had been on duty that week he would have had one too but he was off skiing."

"How often was the code changed on the master keys?"

"As with the others when the person came on duty each day. Mine and the assistant manager's in the morning, the night manager at five o'clock when he came in."

"And the one you gave me?" Was it updated the morning before the murders and then updated after the murders?"

"I remember taking it downstairs and updating it when I found it on the table by your bedside when they bought you from Jason's room after his murder. I didn't think it was safe for the code to remain the same after you said you had been knocked out. I changed the keycode the next day as well. I didn't think you would need that evening's code, as you were off to the hospital."

Elspeth bit the corner of her lip. "I see. That, of course, makes sense." She did not explain to Janet just how or that Janet had provided her with one of the essential clues she was looking for.

"If I had had more time after I was released from my police guard, I would have asked you about the room attendant service that night on the first floor. May I ask now? Would you remember?"

"I'll never forget a single thing about that night."

"Were there any new household staff on that night?"

"No. We have a tight staff, particularly in the wintertime. The ski crowd goes north and our occupancy drops radically. We need only a skeleton crew"

"Did the room attendant that serviced Jason Ravensworth's room say if any of the guests asked to get into his room?"

"I didn't ask but the room attendant is still with us. Shall I ask her?"

"Yes, please. It's vitally important."

"I'm due at the hotel at three. May I call you?"

Elspeth gave Janet her new mobile number. Content that she had the information she needed, Elspeth asked Janet more about the hotel but not about the night of the crimes.

Later that afternoon, Janet rang Elspeth's number.

"The room attendant said that someone did ask her to be let into Jason's room." Janet named Elspeth's prime suspect. Now the only question that had to be answered was why

Elspeth had been gassed and injured when there was no fight.

On Saturday morning, her meeting with Inspector Clough was fast approaching and she still had no answer to her last question. She decided to talk to Henri Gilbert to see if he could help her. She suggested a walk.

As the strolled, Elspeth told him about her dilemma. She did not tell him whom she suspected but she did describe how she thought the crime had been committed.

"Very clever," he said after hearing her out.

"But why was I chloroformed and then injured?" she said. "I can't work that out."

"Do you think it might have been intentional? It sounds to me as if you got in the way."

"At first I thought so too but now I'm almost sure that the murderer knew I was coming to the room with Jason and was lying in wait for me."

"How would they know?"

Elspeth assumed Henri was using 'they' rather than the awkward he or she. She had not yet revealed to him the gender of her suspect.

"I think the murderer heard me speak to Jason in the bar."

"From what you describe, however, the murders were premeditated. The whole scheme is too complicated to have occurred on the spur of the moment."

"I agree but every murderer gambles on chance," Elspeth said.

"And you think in this case they were waiting for you in Jason's room and not for Jason?"

Elspeth stopped in her tracks. She stared at Henri. She felt her mouth was agape and closed it. She swallowed.

"That's it," she cried.

"That's what?"

"I was the intended victim all along."

"And Jason got in the way?"

"No, he was meant to die but as a corollary to my being in the room. The murderer was trying to pin Jason's murder on me. Jason's death was just a necessity so that I would be blamed for it."

"And Kim Bae's murder?"

"It all fits together. Let me explain it all when we see Inspector Clough."

Inspector Clough was waiting for them in a quiet corner of the restaurant Henri had chosen. He sat uncomfortably straight in his chair and wore a stony face. Elspeth felt he was there under duress. Henri took her arm, gave it a reassuring squeeze and led her to the table where DI Clough was sitting. Without a smile, he nodded his head in greeting.

Detective Superintendent Henri Gilbert took charge.

"Thank you for coming, Brewster. Ms Duff has a great deal to tell you. I believe she has solved the murders at the Kennington Victoria last January. She has promised that you can take all the credit as she has no interest in being involved in the eventual arrest and punishment. She has told me how the crimes were committed but not by whom."

"I suppose the culprit will get away with it using diplomatic immunity," he said gruffly.

"No, I think not," Elspeth said. "Let me tell you in all likelihood what happened that night at the hotel."

"Let's order our lunch first," Henri said. "Then we won't be interrupted."

Elspeth noted that DI Clough ordered the most expensive thing on the menu and asked for a pricey Canadian ale. He must have been told that Elspeth was paying.

She took a deep breath once the waiter left them.

"There were two murders," she said, "and I assumed from the beginning that Jason Ravensworth was the main victim and Kim Bae was killed because he got in the way. I was wrong. Kim Bae was the murderer's target. His murder had been planned from the moment he arrived at the conference. But the murderer needed a scapegoat. She, for it is a she, must have had a reason to want to kill Mr Kim. My hunch is that he may have seduced her at some time earlier and then tried to blackmail her, not for money necessarily but perhaps for more sexual favours. My hope is that after her arrest, she will admit her exact motive in a plea for clemency."

"Do you think I will be able to arrest her?"

"I'm sure diplomatic immunity won't play a part," Elspeth reiterated, "but let me go on. The murderer needed to find a way to throw suspicion on someone else. Until this morning I didn't realise that she had chosen me. She wanted to divert attention from Mr Kim's murder by setting up a scenario where I would appear to have murdered Mr Ravenscroft. She thought it essential that I be knocked out so that she could use my passkey to enter Mr Kim's room. The room she was staying in was directly above Mr

Ravensworth's and had the same floor plan. She had worked out, I think, that the connecting door could only be opened by a master key."

Elspeth continued. "She gained access to Mr Ravenscroft's room by telling the room attendant that she had papers to collect in his room. The staff at Kennington hotels are always instructed to know the names and relationships between the guests. Yesterday I confirmed with Janet Church, the manager of the hotel, that the room attendant had let the murderer into Mr Ravensworth's room. But from the beginning what puzzled me were the movements of the murderer after she went into the room. The tapes show her going into Mr Ravensworth's room and then, wearing the short-billed cap that room attendants wear in the hotel, coming out of Mr Kim's fifteen minutes later. Even if she had tried to convince the room attendant to give her the room attendant's passkey, she could not have opened the connecting door."

Elspeth knew by now that she had caught Inspector Clough's attention. "Well, how did she get through?" he asked, as if he thought Elspeth would not have an answer.

"Only four master keys would open the connecting doors. One of them was mine. Once she had chloroformed me, she confronted Mr Ravenscroft as he came into the room. She must have stabbed him when he least expected it and dragged his body to the bed. She had a skewer that she had taken before she left the dining room. It may have been the one on my plate or she may have had the barbequed salmon as well and secreted one of her skewers. At first I thought it would have been simple for her to press my fingerprints on the skewer when I was knocked out and after she had stabbed Mr Ravensworth but Superintendent Gilbert told me that the postmortem had shown that Jason was stabbed only once, directly through his nose. Therefore she probably took the skewer from my dirty plate, which would have been on the sideboard just inside the kitchen doors. She must have watched the waiter take my plate away and then acted quickly, dodging through the kitchen area doors, as the delegation was rising from their meal."

"How would she have known it was your plate?" the inspector challenged.

"I never have potatoes or rice put on my plate. The other plates would have some residue of rice, which was served with the salmon."

"If you say so but how did she know you were going upstairs with Mr Ravenscroft?"

"I spoke freely to him in the bar after dinner. Our going to his room was no secret. She was in the bar and could easily have heard."

"But how could she have planned that you would?"

"I think she had another plan initially," Elspeth said, "but Mr Ravenscroft's invitation to me gave her a shortcut."

"What plan?"

"She could have sent a note around to my room asking me to come down to Jason's room. And then once I was on my way, sent a note to Jason to come from the bar to his room. She would dispose of which ever one came first, either skewering Jason and then chloroforming me as I came in the door, or the other way around."

"And then?"

"She had to fake a fight and therefore she threw the furniture around the room. She then disabled my foot." Elspeth said with a wince.

"I puzzled over the passkey issue for a long time," she continued. "I should have seen the solution earlier. In order to kill Kim Bae, she would have to pass between the two rooms or go out in the hallway and knock at his door. If she did the latter, her movements would have been recorded on the security tapes. She had undoubtedly seen me use my passkey card to enter the back rooms of the hotel and suspected rightly that it would open any door in the hotel. She took my master passkey, passed through to Kim Bae's room and chloroformed him as well. Then she dragged him to his bed and smothered him. Her concern, of course, was the disposition of the body. One can leave a hotel room without a key but one can't enter one. After killing Mr Kim, she went out into the hallway wearing a room attendant's hat and uniform, and fetched a laundry cart from the linen room. There's one on every floor and earlier she must have watched the room attendants use it. She wheeled it back into Mr Kim's room and put the body in it. Again using my passkey, she took the cart to the service lift and took the body up to the rooftop. She hoped that everyone would assume Kim had left the hotel. Her mistake was that he had left his wallet in the bedside table drawer. Had he truly left the hotel, he would have taken his wallet and probably his passport as well."

"We found the passport and wallet, as you said, in the bedside table. That's when we began looking for the body," the detective inspector said. "Then what do you speculate happened?"

"The murderer had to find a way to return the passkey to me but she did not want to go back into Mr Ravenscroft's room. She knew that the chloroform would not leave me unconscious forever. Depending on the strength of the dose, I could come to at any moment and raise a hue and cry. She had to act quickly. She took the lift upstairs to the floor where I was staying. She found a way to slip into my room and left the passkey on a table by my bed. Janet Church found it there and assumed, incorrectly, that it had been brought into my room with my other things when the staff had brought me up to my room. You see, inspector, room attendants move freely around the corridors and are seldom noted. I made that mistake when I first viewed the CCTV footage."

Inspector Clough grunted. "And so, if the murderer is female, are you saying that Oh Seung or Katherine Croft committed the murders. Or both of them in collusion."

Elspeth shook her head. "That would involve diplomatic immunity again. I promised you that wouldn't be an issue. No the person you are looking for is Brittany Rogers, Jason Ravenscroft's aide. I think you may find her in Ottawa."

Inspector Clough looked at her. "What took you so long to figure this out?"

Elspeth could not resist the bait. "I couldn't get all the information I needed because I was under constant surveillance. Had you given me a bit more freedom, I would have asked the right questions earlier. Don't think I'm being smug, inspector. My employer was extremely dissatisfied with my performance last January. He always expects immediate results from me. I didn't give him any. I was severely reprimanded when I got back to London for trying to evade police custody. I apologise to you for any trouble I caused for your team. The fault was mine and not theirs."

"I have always assumed that," he said unkindly.

Elspeth thought her apology had been sincere. "Please tell them that my methods were unconventional and I should not have tried to fool them."

"I'll tell them."

"When will you make the arrest?" Elspeth asked.

"I'll have to think about what you said and clear it with my superiors," the inspector said.

Superintendent Gilbert had been silent during Elspeth's recitation. Finally he said, "It all makes sense to me."

"Inspector, I don't ask to be credited with solving the crimes committed in the hotels but I would like to know that happens once you arrest Brittany. I hope she will confess in order to get a lesser sentence. I particularly would like to know what Kim Bae did to arouse such passion in her."

Henri Gilbert responded to her request. "I'll see that Ms Duff is kept in the loop. You needn't be bothered."

*

How could she have figured it out? I know it was she who did and not that piece of lard, Detective Inspector Clough. He told me that he had solved the case but the person who did find me out must have been someone who knew the workings of the hotel, the details it took me such careful observation to find out. She was not at the trial but they did depose her. They showed the tape in the courtroom.

It was she who convinced the police that I had committed the crime. I had no recourse but to confess in the end.

I should have picked someone else to put the blame on. Bae's wife? How could she bear him? The American woman? She was too dowdy to attract him.

If it hadn't been for her, I would have succeeded and I wouldn't be in this cell now. Can I bear the next twenty years, even with good behaviour?

Poor Jason. It's a shame he had to die. I think of him often and wonder if he ever would have been elected Prime Minister.

Epilogue

Elspeth returned to Scotland the day after the lunch with Inspector Clough. Richard met her at Edinburgh airport but as she came out of the security area, she felt she couldn't hide her feeling of dissatisfaction with the outcome of the case. He embraced her and welcomed her home. Once she had collected her luggage, they went out to the car park. After putting her case in the boot and clearing the gate of the car park, he turned to her.

"What's bothering you, my dearest one?"

"This case and all it involved. I've solved it for the police but not for myself. I rang Pamela yesterday and told her my conclusions. She was gruff, which isn't like her. I felt I had done something wrong rather than exonerating the Kennington Victoria from any complacency in the crimes. I would've thought she would be pleased."

He drove steadily and took all the roundabouts out of the airport with a practiced hand. "She may be conflicted in her friendship with you and your current status with the Kennington Organisation," he said. "And we don't know what's going on in Lord Kennington's life, which seems to be affecting the mood in London. I suggest you let things rest. Come back to Loch Tay and let's go on living the life we have carved out for ourselves there. Can't you let the Kennington Organisation go?"

"I'm not certain I can, but, dearest Dickie, I will try."

She threw herself into the construction of the renovation of the barn, working with the architect to choose colours, kitchen fittings, fabrics, and wooden floor and slate patterns. She watched the joiners erect the new inner frame of the barn and admired how they handled the large beams that would shore up the structure. When the windows were installed, she and Richard walked around the building and felt the pleasure of the well thought out natural lighting. The two of them discussed the interior lights.

"It must be bright on cloudy days," Elspeth said, thinking of the success of the skylights in their London flat and the carefully chosen fixtures there.

Even with all this activity, Elspeth's mind was elsewhere. It wandered through her past cases with the Kennington Organisation, particularly the difficult ones in Malta, Italy, Singapore, Cyprus, Bermuda and India. She thought Eric Kennington's continual praise of her cleverness in solving these cases and his concern when she had been injured in Singapore. She reflected on her last few cases. Yes, she had solved them but the endings of the cases had not been personally satisfactory. Had something changed in her or was it the nature of the cases themselves? Was her love of detection diminishing? But what else in life had brought her success? Certainly not her family. Her daughter still was resentful about the case in Bermuda. Her son and his wife were steering an independent path in San Francisco. Her first marriage had fallen apart, although her second one was a surprisingly passionate and loving one. Yet she constantly felt she was a disappointment to Richard. She could often see pain and puzzlement in his face when he looked at her. He had always expressed concern that on many of her cases she was in danger and he constantly feared for her safety.

Where did all this musing send her? She had no idea but it was not a place she liked.

She knew she had to come to terms with what had happened at the Kennington Organisation. Secretly she hoped that Eric Kennington would forgive her, that he would call her back and tell her how brilliantly she had solved the case in Victoria. She waited until middle of June but no call came. Her six-month suspension was almost up but no one in London had told her if she was going to be reinstated. She took long walks by herself and her mind picked at the problem relentlessly. When she would get back from the walks, Richard would look at her with distress in his eyes. It was as if he could feel her uncertainty. Yet they never spoke of it.

Elspeth thought of calling Pamela. They hadn't spoken since Elspeth came back from Canada. Never before in their relationship had they gone so long without communication. Such silence hurt Elspeth but she did not want to appear to be pleading for her job back. When she had been out on her rambles, she had taken her mobile out several times to call Pamela but then she had jammed the device back in her pocket, and was resolved not to break the silence. At these times, unwanted tears came to her eyes. Would she take back the job if offered? She then would mentally stamp on the thought. If the job weren't offered, what would she do with her life? If it were offered, did she really want to return to the Kennington Organisation? She knew Richard's solution to her problem. He loved living on Loch Tay, and gloried about the day they would move into the barn. He cheered about how quickly they could get to London and how quickly they could come back. He seemed contented. Finally, three days short of the end of her suspension, the call came. Eric Kennington, not Pamela Crumm, was on the line.

"Where the hell are you, Elspeth? I need you here," he said, without an apology. "There's a problem in Dublin and you're the only one I can count on to solve it. This time, however, I want no shenanigans."

Author's Notes and Appreciation

Every book I write involves my digging deeply into my imagination and searching the many memories I have from my long life. I have skewed these memories to fit the various plots of the books, although my family and friends may recognise some of them. Often I incorporate a chance encounter with a friend or an experience in my daily life or during my travels.

This book is set near where I live. In January of this year (2023) I ventured on the ferry to Victoria on a cold, blustery day for a short stay at the Fairmont Empress Hotel. As an author I was greeted warmly and treated as an honoured guest. I appreciate all the help I had from the front desk, the concierges, the room attendants and the waiters. I was given an extensive tour of the Empress by Devan Balcombe, Sales Coordinator at the Empress, with thanks to her.

As always, many thanks also go to my brilliant editor, Alice Roberts, and my excellent proof-readers, Beverly Mar and Loree Lee.

These books could not have been written without the constant love and support I get from Ian Crew.

Ann Crew is a former architect and now full-time mystery writer who once again can travel the world with her iPad, camera, and sketchbook gathering material for the Elspeth Duff mysteries. She lives near Vancouver, British Columbia.

Visit *anncrew.com or elspethduffmysteries.com* for more.